BLOOD PRECIOUS

Other titles published by transita
A Lifetime Burning by Linda Gillard
An Old Fashioned Arrangement by Susie Vereker
A Proper Family Christmas by Jane Gordon-Cumming
Coast to Coast by Jan Minshull
Dangerous Sports Euthanasia Society by Christine Coleman
Emotional Geology by Linda Gillard
Felicity Fights Back by Stella Sykes
Gang of Four by Liz Byrski
Pond Lane and Paris by Susie Vereker
Slippery When Wet by Martin Goodman
The Jigsaw Maker by Adrienne Dines
The Scent of Water by Alison Hoblyn
Soft Voices Whispering by Adrienne Dines
The Sorrow of Sisters by Wendy K Harris
Toppling Miss April by Adrienne Dines
Tuesday Night at the Kasbah by Patricia Kitchin
Watershed by Maggie Makepeace
Widow on the World by Pamela Fudge

transita

To find out more about transita, our books and our authors
visit **www.transita.co.uk**

BLOOD PRECIOUS

SARA BANERJI

transita

Published by Transita
Spring Hill House, Spring Hill Road, Begbroke,
Oxford OX5 1RX. United Kingdom.
Tel: (01865) 375794. Fax: (01865) 379162.
email: info@transita.co.uk
http://www.transita.co.uk

All rights reserved. No part of this work may be reproduced
or stored in an information retrieval system (other than for purposes of
review) without the express permission of the publisher in writing.

© **Copyright 2007 Sara Banerji**

British Library Cataloguing in Publication Data
A catalogue record for this book is available from the British Library

ISBN 13: 978 1 905175 32 1

Cover design by Mousemat Design Ltd.
Produced for Transita by Deer Park Productions, Tavistock
Typeset by PDQ Typesetting, Newcastle-under-Lyme
Printed and bound by Bookmarque, Croydon

All characters in this book are fictitious and any resemblance to real persons, living or dead, is entirely coincidental.

The right of Sara Banerji to be identified as the author of this work has been asserted by her in accordance with the Copyright, Designs and Patents Act 1988.

ABOUT THE AUTHOR

During the Second World War Sara Banerji lived with her mother, brother and sister, in Oxfordshire, while her father fought in the war. After the war she emigrated with her parents, two brothers and sister, to what was then Southern Rhodesia where they lived out in the African bush in a single mud rondavel, with no electricity or running water.

Sara met her husband in a coffee bar in Oxford when he was an undergraduate at Christ Church. He was a customer and she a waitress. They spent the child rearing years in the high hills of South India, where he was a tea planter and she painted in oils, rode as a jockey on the flat, and wrote her first novel. They returned to England in 1973, with five pounds each. Sara borrowed money, bought ponies in auctions and taught riding. Later, she started a gardening business in Sussex.

Blood Precious is the ninth of Sara's novels to be published. Her first book was long listed to the Man Booker and her last published novel, *Shining Hero* won an Arts Council of England award.

Sara and her husband now live in Oxford, where she teaches writing for Oxford University's Department for Further Education. She also holds regular exhibitions of her painting and waste material sculptures. She and her husband practise Transcendental Meditation and yogic flying every day. They have three daughters and five grandchildren.

For more information about Sara and her work visit www.transita.co.uk

Also by Sara Banerji

The Waiting Time

Nominated for the 2007 *International IMPAC Dublin Literary Award.*

The key to Julia's identity lies somewhere beneath Kitty's home, but digging it up may cost more than she imagines in this riveting tale of sacrifice, denial and misplaced love.

"There is no-one else who writes like Sara Banerji." – Philip Pullman

1 905175 02 7

CHAPTER 1

I DID NOT REALISE A SUICIDE NOTE – I believe that is what it is called – was so hard to write, till I tried to do it.

I started for the fifteenth time, 'Well, that was that ... ' then once again tore up the paper. The wastepaper basket was starting to overflow with my abandoned letters but, even for me, that start wouldn't do under the circumstances. I didn't have to have the letter composed till Tuesday morning, the day that no one came to see me, so I had time. I could not do it on any other day or I risked being found unconscious and resuscitated. Resuscitation is the bane of those trying to commit suicide.

Jack had died a year ago and I had been planning the suicide ever since.

On the morning of the day he died his mind had seemed to briefly operate again like the sun unexpectedly shining through clouds.

He was sitting by the fire as usual. He was always cold in those days, no matter what the season. We used to have a coal fire then, though this has now been replaced by an ultra safe electric one. He would sit for hours, staring at the glowing embers, not speaking, not moving. Sometimes saliva would dribble from his lips and I would wipe them with his handkerchief. He had stopped doing things like that for himself long before.

'I shall be an ember,' he said.

A pain of joy snatched at my heart because it was his old, clear, coherent voice.

We had evolved a theory how after we were dead we might have a way of becoming united again. After death, we had decided, one's essence glows like a hot coal that cooled over a period of time. If, we told each other, both he and I died while our coals were still smouldering, our hot essences would blend together and become fused for eternity. It had only been a fancy really, a way of thinking round the unthinkable but it had lodged in Jack's muddled mind as a proven theory.

'Yes,' I said now. 'Oh, yes.' I felt that breathless excited feeling that I had had more than sixty years ago when I heard his dear voice for the first time.

His voice went tremulous again. 'You ... ember ... me ... ' Now he was completely quavery.

I caught at the sleeve of his jersey, trying to wake him, to bring back, even for another moment, the Jack of my life, that clever marvellous person who once had known so many peculiar things and now knew almost nothing.

I began my letter again, 'As you can see I have killed myself.' Stupid. Of course they were going to see. I tore up that one too. Something simple maybe. 'Farewell.' No, no. Ridiculously archaic. 'Bye bye, daughters.'; 'Tootleoo, kith and kin.'; 'I set off on a mysterious journey.' Perhaps a long essay was the right thing. The problem was that I had never written a letter like this before and, of course, considering its substance, never would again. I even considered abandoning my principles and employing slop and sentimentality, two things I abhor.

I had long ago abandoned hope of getting the letter right first time and was writing it in rough to copy tidily later, in spite of the risk of being discovered. My daughter, Verity, or even M'buta might see early drafts in my wastepaper basket, but I had no option but to take that chance.

M'buta is my daughter's friend. Well. More than friend really and when, after Jack died I went to pieces Verity, said: 'You need some one to look in on you when I'm working and M'buta is willing to come around regularly and give you a helping hand. She used to be a nurse so she's good at looking after people.'

I had felt numb at the time. Only people who know the feeling of numb can understand this. I did not feel in the mood to do anything, not eat or wash or go to bed or anything. M'buta would appear, do all the things that were needed – that she said were needed – I didn't mind if she came or not. A year later, she's still around. I've allowed her to take too much control. I suppose, if I had the energy, or the time, I could take matters back into my own hands. But what's the point now? I shall be dead by Wednesday. Why annoy Verity and offend M'buta, who in spite of everything is always kind to me?

On with that letter. I sighed and began again, thinking that maybe I need give no explanation for my act. My reasons were fairly obvious, well, on the surface anyway. A poor, old, ill and bereaved woman who had lost the will to live. The truth was a little different, but the people around me were so lacking in imagination that there was no way I could have explained it to them. But it seemed a pity to go out in silence.

This was my last chance of making any mark at all on the world. 'Goodbye' perhaps? Which meant, 'God bide with you.' No, no. I did not even believe in God. There is one thing I do believe in and that's the truth. I refused to allow my final statement to be a lie. Also, even if it had not been for its religious context I felt the word 'goodbye' had become devalued by time and overuse.

'Fare well?' Yes, I definitely wished that those I left behind to fare well. No matter what they thought of me – only quite recently Verity had called me an ungrateful old woman because I said I did not want her nosing around among my things. I did not want M'buta bossing me around either, I said. But I don't want to cause hurt to anyone. I like M'buta in spite of her being intrusive. There are sides to her that are really nice. When I feel lonely, I look forward to her company – I felt well intended towards Verity and M'buta. I mean, look at the way in which I plan to take care not to be a nuisance to them afterwards.

I want to look decent after I'm dead, but don't want to put them to the trouble of doing my corpse up, so I have determined to titivate before I die. I had already planned out carefully what I would be wearing and which jewels to put on.

An idea came to me. Should I just this once, as it was a special occasion, pop a little word of affection in. 'Goodbye, darlings', I even went so far as to put it down, but it looked quite quite wrong. Not me at all. I hastily scratched it out again. Fancy me being remembered by such a trite phrase.

'She was really an old sweetie inside, not matter how much she might pretend otherwise,' I could hear M'buta saying. And people laughing and telling tales of other old people who pretended to be nasty but in truth had hearts of sugar syrup. With a shudder, I scribbled through the sentimental words about ten more times so that they shouldn't even be legible when raised to the light. I did not want them to know that the thought had even occurred to me.

'I expect you will relieved to be free of me.' Ah, that was more like it. 'And I will be at peace as well.' How did I know I would be at peace? I cannot imagine there is much peace while you are being rotted under the ground or cooked in a crematorium, or whatever it was they planned to do with me. Which, of course would not be me, because the true part of me would be with Jack, the glowing clinker, blending with Jack's red hot one.

I began to feel like my granddaughter, Naomi, when she wrote one of her brilliant little 'thank you' letters. She is an unusual child and has abilities beyond other four year olds. For a moment I contemplated inviting Naomi round now, to help me. But dropped the thought in a moment. You can't ask a four year old to help her grandmother write a suicide note and anyway, because of the sweetie packets, I have not been able to have her round lately.

I began again. 'Dearest family ... ' This would include M'buta, who being my daughter's partner, was in the role of my son-in-law.

I had chosen the paper for my letter with great care. It was hand-made, acid free, and very expensive. Because, after I was gone, this letter would be the only thing my family would have to remember me by, I did not want the paper I wrote it on going acid or brittle.

My door handle gave a turn. Verity. When she could not open it, she called, 'Mother, have you locked it? What are you doing in there?' her voice stern and suspicious, the voice I had used to her when she was little and was doing something naughty.

I tried staying still in the hope that she would think I was asleep, even did a few snoring sounds, but she kept rattling on the door handle 'Mother, open up at once.'

'Go away,' I shouted, abandoning my pretence. 'Leave me alone.' I knew it was useless though, and if I did not open up to her, her suspicions would be aroused. Later she would surreptitiously search the room. They did that these days, I'm sure they did. Sometimes, when I opened a drawer I would feel sure someone had been searching among my things. And now I had had so much trouble gathering up enough pills to do the job, I did not want to lose them.

You might as well be a toddling child or a pet dog by the age of eighty, the way in which people take control of every aspect of your life, I thought as, reluctantly I put my pad back in its hiding place, behind the dressing table mirror and dropped a couple of disguising tissues on top of the paper in the basket. Sooner or later they would find everything, unless Tuesday came first. It's because they found me out the first time, when I went with them to the seaside, that they are now watching me so closely. Since that first and failed attempt, I have been getting no privacy or peace.

So as to put them off the scent, lately I had been trying to appear jolly and though Verity kept asking me, 'Are you all right, Mother? Is your mouth hurting? Why are you stretching it in that funny way?' M'buta was quite taken in. She is really a very kind person and I should not complain about her. She even complimented me for looking so well and bearing up so wonderfully. But after a while I heard Verity tell her, in one of those silly whispers that people do when they want you to hear and pretend they don't, 'Don't be taken in by Mother. It's some new trick.' In fact the only one who had seen through my playacting right from the start was my granddaughter, Naomi. She is only four and has special abilities.

'Why are you crying in the middle, Grandma?' she asked.

Well, of course I was. Jack and I had been married for sixty one years. After he died, M'buta said, 'At least you've got a daughter. And me. And a granddaughter. Some people don't have any one. You are luckier than a lot of people.' Well who bloody cares about a lot of people. And it's not just M'buta who goes on like that. It's everyone.

When I went to the eye hospital to tell them that my sight had gone so blurry that I could hardly read any more, they said, 'Your eyes are really good for your age.' Same with my hearing. 'There's no way of improving your hearing any further, dear. For your age it's very good.' What they really mean, of course, is, that I'm lucky to be alive at all, let alone be able to hear or see. And how I wish they wouldn't call me 'dear'. When M'buta first became my daughter's lover and called me 'Arabella,' I told her I had not given her permission to address me thus. After all she is a girl several years younger than my own daughter. She had had the grace to look embarrassed.

'What would you like me to call you?' she asked.

I like, in general to be addressed by my full name by everyone who is more than ten years younger than me, whether I know them well or not, apart of course for child or grandchild. But there was a problem with this as far as M'buta and names are concerned, for due to her relationship with my daughter, I could hardly expect her to call me 'Lady Cunningham-Smythe'. Mother-in-law, or even Mother might have been OK if she had been a male but did not seem to be appropriate in M'buta's case either.

For a while there seemed to be no solution to this problem and she told me that she was worried in case the house caught fire and she was unable to call me to alert me to the danger. Which is a situation that does not worry me at all, because I was planning to die anyway. But to M'buta, me being burnt to death is a bad thing.

Chrissy, the woman who has been doing for me for about twenty years, and is the sort that takes liberties when it suits her, calls me by my full name because she is a snob. Apart from that, though, she behaves in ways that I find unpleasantly familiar. After Jack died, because I could not stand her awful humming and prancing any more, I gave her the sack. I told her I no longer needed her. I said that as from Monday, she must not come. You would have thought she had not heard a word I said. She continued to turn up as usual and did her non-cleaning making-a nuisance-of-herself as merrily as ever.

'I told you to leave,' I shouted on Monday morning.

'Oh, did you, Lady Cunningham-Smythe?' she said vaguely, then continued dancing round with her useless duster whacking which always produces more dirt than it removes.

'Depart, woman,' I roared. Nothing would budge her.

'I couldn't abandon you, Lady Cunningham-Smythe. It's not in my nature to abandon the sick and aged.'

'She does a good job of cleaning, no matter what you say,' said Verity. 'M'buta thinks so too. And we both like to think there is someone keeping an eye on you when we aren't around.' They are all in cahoots. There's nothing I can do with a gang like that.

I mean, look at the problems I had collecting the pills. It would have been perfectly simple if I had not been suspicious that they were prying. Paracetamol is only sold in little packets, so that people will find it difficult to gather enough to commit suicide. Therefore you need to go to several chemist shops to gather enough to do the job. And with my mobility problem, of which all these experts also say, 'You get around very well for your age, dear,' this is not easy. For a while I tried saving up the sleeping pills the doctor had given me, but M'buta found them and threw them away saying, 'My goodness, look what I've found, Ladyma—' that's how we have solved the problem of names in case the house burns '—You might have taken an overdose by mistake. They might have killed you.'

'I can't see that that would have mattered very much,' I retorted.

She looked at me with loving disapproval. 'Imagine how sad Verity and Naomi would be, let alone myself. And Gump. How could you even think of abandoning your poor little dog?'

I love Gump. Once I whispered in his ear, when I was sure no one was listening, 'I love you, Gump.' I admit I felt instantly embarrassed. He may be only a dog, but who knows what dogs understand? But all the same I thought it would be a good thing if I was out of the way and someone younger and more agile looked after him.

As for Naomi, I will be very sad to have to leave her, too. Naomi is my granddaughter, because she is Verity's child.

I will never forget Jack's delight when he was told Verity was having a baby. He loved being a grandfather and even in the later stages of his illness, always recognised her. Sometimes she would gently take his hand and her touch seemed to soothe him as nothing else could.

I had, in fact, tried to persuade my daughter to have a baby ever since she fell in love with M'buta ten years before, when she was twenty five. That was when she told me she was never going to have children.

'You will be sorry when it is too late,' I said. 'Even though you are a lesbian you should swallow your distaste and become pregnant. You are not too bad looking. I'm sure there must be some man somewhere who will oblige, even though you are cohabiting with another woman. You needn't get married or anything and can always have a shower after.'

'You don't know what you're talking about, Mother,' she said crossly.

'If that was the case, how do you think I and your father produced you?' I asked her.

I felt I had scored a point there but instead of taking it up she said, in a self pitying voice, 'I don't know why you even bothered to have a child.'

'What? Are you saying I wasn't a good mother? You can't possible accuse me of neglecting my duty in that area.' I was outraged.

'Well, you weren't cuddly,' she said.

'You were a great joy to me when you were little.'

'Really?' she said. 'I never knew.'

'I did not like the way she spoke at all,' I told M'buta later. 'There was a distinct ring of sarcasm in her tone.'

'You ought to wrap it up a bit, Ladyma.' M'buta said. 'She loves you a lot inside her heart.'

'What do you mean?' I asked her crossly. 'Now what have I done wrong?'

'Couldn't you tell her you love her a bit?' asked M'buta. She sounded quite shy to say the word, love.

'Since you tell her that all the time, I can't see any need for me to do it,' I told her sternly.

I and Jack were married for more than sixty years and in all that time never once did I use sentimental language Even our decision to do away with ourselves when the separation time was approaching was done in a businesslike, practical and unsentimental manner. We collected the sleeping pills without even bothering to hide them, those being the days before I had people poking through everything.

Unfortunately, after Jack died, they found the pills and threw them all away.

Later I heard Verity whispering to M'buta, 'You don't think Mother kept those pills on purpose and was planning to do away with herself, do you?'

I did not catch M'buta's answer, but ever since, they have kept thinking up things 'to cheer me up'.

'I do not need cheering up,' I told them. When you are a bereaved person, you can be as furious as you like and no one likes to say boo to you. 'I do not even want to be cheered up.'

But nothing stopped them. They kept organising silly outings, inviting me to come and do things that I had never had the smallest appetite for, a visit to the zoo, shopping at Harrods, an afternoon at the cinema. They even wanted to take me to see the remake of *Mary Poppins*. You really would think I had become a child again. It when they suggested a picnic by the sea, that an idea came to me. They all seemed gratified and hopeful when I accepted. They did, 'There, she's coming out of it', looks to each other. By this time I had managed to assemble a new small collection of sleeping pills, by pretending to put them in my mouth when Verity gave them to me. Not enough to do the full job, but enough, I thought to be effective when in the sea.

'And I shall go in the sea,' I told them. 'So please go and buy me a bathing suit.'

Verity and M'buta went rushing, as though the sun had come out suddenly, after a lot of rain.

I waited till they were all sitting on the Brighton beach, if you could call that heap of oil stained cobbles a beach, when I said I thought I would have a little paddle in the sea before lunch. 'In memory of Jack. I would like to be alone, please.'

Verity and M'buta nodded, looking moved and unsuspicious. Gump, who follows me everywhere, leapt up and tried to come after me, so I asked Naomi to be a dear little girl and hold onto him while I paddled because I didn't want him to get wet and shake water all over the picnic rug. Gump adores Naomi and when he joyfully snuggled into her arms I felt a brief pang of irritation at his fickleness and lack of intuition. Surely he must know what was about to happen. I thought dogs had instincts about things like that.

'I've never known you to mind about a thing like Gump wetting us, before, Mother,' said Verity in a surprised but pleased voice.

'I am trying to follow your's and M'buta's advice and be less selfish,' I told her and managed to put on a saintly sort of smile which did not, this time, draw from her the question, 'Is your mouth hurting, Mother? Why are you stretching it like that?'

When I reached the sea and looked back, Gump had fallen asleep in Naomi's arms and looked comfortable and happy. I felt shocked at his treachery.

By the time I reached the water, I could just make out Naomi waving.

I woke up in hospital. Apparently lifesavers had pulled me out and saved my life. I was furious. It was after that that I began to think that they were poking around and saw I must be extra careful if I wanted to try again.

It took me four months of surreptitious buying and hiding, to get together enough paracetamol in their silly little packs. I would so much have preferred to do it with sleeping pills, but there was no way now that they were on to me. It was touch and go with my new hoard several times and I had had to have a huge show down, shouting that I was surely entitled to some sort of privacy and Verity and M'buta swearing that they would never dream of going through my drawers.

Through a little bit of play acting, I managed to divert their attention from my growing collection of pain killers by continuing to pretend I was holding back sleeping pills which I then let them find. Unfortunately Naomi nearly found and ate the paracetamol.

You may be wondering how it came about that my lesbian daughter is a mother. It was like this. About five years earlier, Verity told me, 'I am giving you a grandchild, Mother.' My gaze rushed instantly to her stomach, which looked as flat as ever.

'I'm not pregnant yet,' she had said. 'I have decided to become impregnated, though.'

'Oh. So M'buta has had a successful sex change has she?'

'No need to be sarcastic,' said Verity.

'How are you getting this child, then?'

'At a fertility clinic.'

Yes. Of course. I might have known. 'What does M'buta think?'

'She's the one who found the clinic. Daniel told her about it.' M'buta is very keen on this holy man called Daniel. She became his follower even before she met Verity. 'M'buta wants the father to be black,' Verity went on. 'And they've got some black men on their books.'

'How much does it cost, though?'

'A thousand pounds,' she said, a quiver of anguish in her voice.

'A thousand pounds!' I gasped.

Verity is a writer but because her books are 'literature' she does not get very much money for them. M'buta has to send money back to her mother in Zimbabwe so the two of them are always pretty broke.

'When you could get a man to do the job for nothing.' I added, 'What does M'buta say?'

She gave me a withering look, but I persisted, 'Men always find sex enjoyable. All you need to do is dye your hair and put aside your glasses.' I did think to myself that if it had been M'buta, not Verity who was planning pregnancy, there would have been no problem at all in getting a man to create the child. M'buta is seriously beautiful in a way that only a tall slim black girl can be.

'I have persuaded M'buta that we could spend some of the royalties of *The Sunset Kiss* on the procedure.' You make love to create a child in the conventional manner, but if it is done by any other means, it is called 'a procedure'.

The Sunset Kiss, Verity's latest book, had just come out. It was a new venture and had M'buta's photo on the back instead of Verity's and M'buta's name as the author. It was doing considerably better than Verity's previous ones. It is the story of a beautiful lesbian couple, one black, one white, who are being forced to separate forever. They go to the seaside, eat a lot of sleeping pills, kiss each other then wade into the sea and die.

The Sunset Kiss sold like hot cakes, which made me feel scornful of the book buying public who hardly bought Verity's books at all when it was her on the cover and were so enthusiastic when it was M'buta.

I had one more go at persuading my daughter to create her baby in the normal way. 'You did sex once before and it wasn't the end of the world, so why not save all that money and do it just once again?'

'Mother, really.' She always gets angry when the Don situation is mentioned. That had been before she met M'buta. When she produced the young man, Jack had been thrilled. Even I had been pretty impressed and also relieved that at last our daughter was behaving like other girls.

Don had been good looking and well dressed but when the relationship ended, she told me they had had sex only once, and that she had found the experience slobbery, unhygienic and uncomfortable.

When it was clear that Verity was determined to have a child without enduring sex, I agreed to go with her to the Bereton Clinic. I was, in fact, rather curious.

M'buta had got Chrissy a cleaning job at the clinic and Chrissy often talked about the place. Her face would light up with excitement whenever she mentioned it.

'You should see the young men,' she would rave. 'They are absolutely gorgeous.' She behaves very inappropriately for a grandmother.

Verity asked me to come with her on the day of the AI procedure because M'buta could not get away. I had never been to such a place before. It was as grubby and shabby as was to be expected with Chrissy as cleaner. But Chrissy assured my daughter that the Bereton had a fantastic reputation for success, no matter what the age or physical state of the mother.

'I can promise you, Verity, that I don't know a single woman who has not got pregnant eventually and most of them get done the first time. And also,' she added, 'the whole thing is done without any fuss, or forms or interference from the government. Nothing to sign. No questions to answer.'

'I haven't got time to mess about,' said Verity. 'This sounds like the place for me.'

Chrissy came rushing out of some dungeon-like back room still wearing her soiled overall and handed Verity a tattered album.

'It's the photos of the fathers. You go through that, Verity, and choose the one you want. And when you've chosen, we've got some tapes of the fathers' voices.'

I must say I felt somewhat astonished at allowing a feckless creature like Chrissy to handle such a sensitive document, but there you are. She had said this was an unofficial kind of place. Totally illegal, no doubt.

'The whole set up looks most unprofessional,' I told my daughter. 'I think you should go somewhere else.'

But already Verity was going eagerly through the photos.

'Hush, Mother,' she said. Then having gone through the album from start to finish, began to go back to the beginning again.

'I haven't got all day,' I told her.

'I don't know why you came in the first place. We are choosing the father of your first grandchild. I really do think you might be prepared to take a bit of time over it,' she said. 'There. What do you think? Does he look like M'buta?' She held up the album, showing the photo of a handsome young black man. 'I think he's perfect,' she said. 'No white blood in him at all. Hundred percent Zimbabwean.' Apparently this was important. If the father was already of mixed race, then there was a risk of the baby being a white throwback.

So, when nine months later the baby was born and turned out to be perfectly blonde and as white as milk, I felt furious on my daughter's behalf.

Verity was lying in the hospital bed, looking into the baby's face, an expression of perfect doting on her own.

'You get cheated right left and centre these days. I expect you will be sending her back,' I said.

Verity looked up quickly, gave me one of those horrible scowls that turned even me silent and went back to baby adoring again.

'Anyway, I don't expect M'buta will be best pleased,' I said crossly, as I got up to leave.

And it was true. M'buta became quite sulky when she came to see the new baby.

'Well, you have the solution,' I told her. 'Next time, you be the one to get pregnant. That will ensure the baby turning out the right colour and also it's your turn to go through all that suffering and discomfort.'

M'buta instantly lost her temper and began shouting, 'Don't you start, Ladyma. I never wanted a child in the first place.'

For a while, after Naomi was born, Verity and M'buta had frequent quarrels about the baby, Verity accusing M'buta of not loving Naomi and M'buta saying that, even though the baby was nothing to do with her, she did more for it than its birth mother.

These quarrels even went on a bit as Naomi got older.

'I am the one that hugs her, puts her to bed and reads to her, sings lullabies to her on car journeys while you have your mind on your latest book or are hunched over your computer not noticing anything else in the world,' M'buta would say.

Verity would shout, 'You don't have to look after her. No one asked you to.'

And M'buta would scream, 'You're a cold fish and should never have been allowed to have a child. There should be a law against women like you having babies. If I had not been there, that poor little mite would have had a childhood of grim perfection and cautious choosiness.'

'I think it's ridiculous the way you slobber all over her as though she was something to eat.' Verity would shout back. 'And I wouldn't have chosen you if I had been a perfectionist and choosy.'

By the time Naomi was three, M'buta and Verity seemed to forget that she was white. She was their child and they loved her. Rightly so, because Naomi was a very nice person, perceptive, clever and compassionate. After Jack died she asked me, 'Granny, why are your eyes sad all the time? Is it because Grandpa is dead?'

'Of course not,' I told her crossly. 'I will be dead soon, and so what is there to be sad about?'

But, as though she had not absolutely believed me, she said, 'You mustn't get sad, Grandma, in case you hurt your blood precious.'

This sweet expression had arisen some time earlier because of her becoming confused with mention of my high blood pressure on the same day as the teacher at her Catholic nursery school had talked about Jesus' precious blood.

So that Verity would not recognise my pills, I put them into sweet packets and unfortunately Verity saw them when she brought Naomi round to spend the day with me.

'Wait till you see the naughty goodies your grandma has got for you,' she told Naomi.

For the rest of the morning, after her mother had gone, Naomi kept pestering me, 'When are we going to have the naughty goodies, Grandma? When am I going to get them?'

Really, when you start to lie there is no end to it. I had to pretend I couldn't find the sweets and went through a great huge pantomime of pretending to look for them with Naomi telling me, 'They're in that drawer, Grandma. I saw them when my Mummy opened it.' And then when Verity returned and asked Naomi, 'Well darling, how many sweeties did your granny give you today?' she looked suspicious when Naomi said, 'Grandma couldn't find them.' And even more suspicious when I said that I was keeping the sweets for Chrissy's grandchildren.

'I did not realise you even knew them,' she said.

'Well, you don't know everything about me, thank goodness,' I told her sniffily.

I had bought the pills on a Tuesday, the only day I am sure neither Verity not M'buta will be coming round. I had called a taxi and told the Pakistani taxi driver that I was looking for a certain type of medicine and that it was quite rare so I needed to visit a lot of chemists and supermarkets. I told him that it might take all afternoon before I ran the stuff to ground. At first it was not too difficult. I hid my little packets of pills in my bag and got into the taxi telling him, 'No. They didn't have it either.'

After a while, when I could fit no more packets into my bag, I began putting them into my pockets and then when they were full I had to stuff them down my jumper until I think even the taxi driver began to suspect something funny was going on and started questioning me about this very rare medicine that was not even available in the big Boots and at the same time looking suspiciously at my bulging pockets. He probably thought I was shoplifting.

I wondered if he was going to report me to the police, in which case all would be lost. But in the end he left me at my flat with enough pills, I decided, to do the job. He held my arm as I went up the steps, then helped me open the door, me all the time worrying that packets would start falling out of my jumper and give the game away. My last sight of him as I closed my front door, was his expression of doubt. For the rest of the evening I really did half expect a visit from the police, but luckily nothing happened.

Then, after I got in and the taxi had gone, I saw that I had drunk all the whisky that I had bought for washing down the pills. For a moment I contemplated making do with water, a substance I am not at all partial to, instead of whisky, a substance I am particularly partial to. I suppressed the water thought in a moment, not wanting my last minutes to be ruined and rang Verity and asked her to bring me some Scotch the following day.

'Surely you haven't drunk the bottle I brought the day before yesterday,' she said disapprovingly.

'I am thinking of doing a little entertaining,' I told her.

She saw straight through that, but after a few exhortations about the effects of alcohol on blood pressure and arthritis, she did as I asked.

I began to imagine next Tuesday when I would fall into a dreamy drunken sleep, waking up to find Jack at my side. I feared he might disapprove a bit at my being drunk when I arrived, but felt sure he would forgive me.

Verity was pregnant a second time by now. In spite of Naomi being the wrong colour, she had returned to the Bereton Clinic. She wanted the new baby to be the blood sibling of Naomi so had chosen the same father as before. The baby was due in a couple of weeks. I felt that this was a good time to go. Verity, M'buta and Naomi would all have better things to think about than my demise, when the baby was born.

I would have liked to wait to see the new baby, but dared not hang around too long in case I was too late for Jack.

That week seemed to go on forever. People kept talking to me about plans for next week, next month, next year, which I had to pretend to be interested in. And every chance I got when I did not fear being spied upon, I would toil at my farewell letter.

Tuesday at last. The letter was ready. I was not entirely satisfied but thought it good enough. I spent the day getting ready. I had plenty of time. I had the flat to myself till the Wednesday morning because Tuesday is the day Verity and M'buta have to themselves and Naomi goes to a baby minder. In the morning Verity, who has my key, would come round to the flat and find me.

I was anxious to look my best for the episode, or would 'procedure' be the right word? I put on my black cocktail dress and the pearl earrings that Jack had given me for my twenty first birthday. I powdered my nose, carefully applied ruby lipstick and did my nails. At last, feeling that I had done a good job, I looked at myself in the mirror and saw that the outfit would not do at all. The black looked depressing and the lipstick was too bright for death. I took off the cocktail dress and put on my red coat and skirt instead. I sprayed a little perfume behind my ears. Instead of the pearls, I put on the diamond necklace that Jack had given me for our golden wedding anniversary.

I was just spreading my packs of pills on the bed when there came a noisy knocking on the front door. For a moment I thought of ignoring it but then I realised that if it was Verity or M'buta and I did not answer the door, they would not go away, but just use their key, find me, and have me stomach pumped or something.

Resuscitation is very annoying. You go to all the trouble of collecting up the pills, steel your nerve a bit to take them and then find yourself in hospital and you have gone through the whole thing for nothing.

I went down and opened the door. M'buta stood there looking desperate and holding Naomi by the hand.

'You've got to look after her, Ladyma, blood pressure or no, because the baby's on the way and I've got to take Verity to hospital and the babysitter has suddenly rung to say she's not coming.'

'It's not due for a fortnight,' I said, aghast.

'It's early. Here's Naomi, I've got to go.' She was panting.

'I can't possibly look after Naomi,' I told her firmly. 'I have plans.' I tried to shut the door, but she got her fingers round it and clung on.

'It's urgent, Ladyma. There's no one else.' M'buta was gasping as though she had been running. She looked me up and down, took in my smart coat, careful makeup and necklace of diamonds, and said, 'I can see you're going out somewhere, but this is an absolute emergency.'

I still kept on trying to shake my head and shut the door, but it was no use. Sadly and reluctantly I opened the door and let my granddaughter in.

Naomi raced ahead of me into the house, shouting, 'You've got to have me now, even though you don't want to.'

I went crossly after her, trying to project my thoughts to where ever Jack was, 'I'm sorry. There's been a bit of a hitch.'

Naomi stopped suddenly in the middle of the drawing room and stared at me as though seeing me for the first time.

'You look beautiful, Grandma,' she said. 'Where are you going? To a party?'

'Not a party,' I told her. 'I'm going to a different place.'

'I could come with you,' she said.

'That's out of the question,' I told her. Really this was too aggravating for words.

Naomi went prancing round the hall. 'Anyway, I'm here now and I promise I won't hurt your blood precious. I'll be really really careful, I promise.'

'You'd better,' I told her grimly and was briefly tempted to give her a little hug. She rushed past me into the bedroom. 'Oh, look, you found the naughty goodies.' She had seen all the sweetie packets on the bed and was already reaching out to snatch by the time I got there. I grabbed them from her hands, but she clung on. 'I want them. I want them. Why can't I have them?'

'Put them down,' I yelled now. 'You promised you wouldn't hurt my blood precious.' I was even starting to talk like her in my desperation. She dropped the pills at once, and stared at me guiltily.

'I'm sorry, Grandma.'

'It's alright,' I said. 'Let's make some fudge. Homemade fudge is even better than all those sweets from the shop.' I had been trying to use up all the food in the house before dying, because I hate waste, but luckily there was still some sugar, a little bit of butter, and a pint of milk because I had miscalculated when I went shopping.

'Be careful. Don't let it splash on your skin,' I told her as we stirred. 'It's dreadfully hot.'

'How can you tell when it's ready?' she asked.

'When it's brown and wrinkly like me.'

After that she kept looking into my face then back into the saucepan and saying, 'It's getting a bit more like you.' Till at last there came the moment when she shouted, 'It's exactly like you, Grandma. It's ready.'

M'buta had still not come back by the evening. By this time Naomi had started fretting a bit, saying 'When are my mummies coming back? Why is it taking them such a long time to get the new baby?' I was feeling pretty tired too, by this time, I must say.

'Why don't you go and have a little lie down?' I suggested hopefully.

'I'm not tired,' she said stroppily.

'What do you want to do, then?'

'Put lipstick and things on, like you've got,' she said.

So we sat at my dressing table and first tried out lipsticks and then I took out my jewel box and began putting necklaces onto Naomi, while she sat gazing admiringly at her reflection.

'Now nail polish, Grandma,' cried Naomi, bouncing up and down on the dressing table stool. She spread out her baby fingers and I unscrewed the nail polish bottle. I had reached the little piggy went to market I heard a sharp snapping sound.

'What's that?'

Naomi was still staring at her reflection.

'Did you hear something, darling?'

'It might be rats,' said the little girl casually. 'They made a noise like that when Mummy had them.'

'Rats? Your mother had rats?' The idea of my orderly daughter coping with rats was rather pleasing.

The sound came again, not so loud this time and it was followed by a soft thud as though something was being thrown onto the carpet. The sound had seemed to come from upstairs, not from the hall. It wasn't at all the sound a rat might make. My heart began to beat with a little rhythm of fear. I told myself I was being ridiculous, that it was only birds walking on the roof but I still felt worried.

I tried to reassure myself. It couldn't possibly be a burglar. There was a security light that came on automatically when anyone entered the garden. There were neighbours just a stone's throw away. Of course there was no one walking about up there.

Naomi wriggled off the stool and began tramping slowly round the room, her lips pouted as she blew on her newly vanished nails. 'This is how M'buta Mummy does it,' she said.

There came another sound. Definitely from above this time. The creak of a door being opened.

'Stop,' I whispered. 'Stay exactly where you are. Don't make a sound. It's a new game. Called statues in the dark. You're out if you make a sound or move a finger.'

Naomi stopped and waited, her fingers still outspread.

I went over, switched off the bedroom light and softly opened the bedroom door.

Holding my breath, I peeped out. There was no light on downstairs. I held my breath and stood listening, but the house had become silent.

I tiptoed back to where the child stood in her 'statues in the dark' posture.

'Come,' I whispered. I took her hand. The nail polish wasn't dry and gummed to my palm. We tiptoed back to the dressing table, where I sat, pulling her onto my knee. I put my arms round her and strained my ears. There came the sound of creaking floorboards.

'What do you think it is, Naomi?' I whispered. I was eighty and Naomi was four. Her hearing must be sharper than mine.

'Perhaps it's an escaped tiger.' She snuggled against me and pressing her ear to my chest, whispered, 'I can hear your heart ticking. Am I winning statues in the dark?'

'Ssh, ssh. Can you hear that funny noise?'

Naomi straightened and tilted her head, listening. After a while she flopped back against me and whispered casually, 'It's probably only Teddy.'

'What do you mean?'

'I left him in the bathroom. He must have got magicked and is walking about up there.'

A fresh shot of fear pulsed through me. 'Is that what you can hear?' I asked. 'Somebody walking about?'

Naomi nodded solemnly.

There was a telephone on the landing. I wondered if I dared leave her sitting here and rush to it, phone 999. But at the thought there came a new sound, the soft rustling of shoeless feet, the sound of someone tiptoeing down the stairs.

There came another long shivering silence. Then Naomi said, 'I'm tired of statues in the dark. I want to play something else.'

'Ssh. Listen.'

From downstairs Gump, who had been shut up in the kitchen with his dinner, suddenly began barking.

'You said Gump never barks except when burglars come,' said Naomi sternly, as though she had caught me out in a lie.

I put a finger across the child's lips and whispered, 'Ssh, ssh.'

'You're smidging my lipstick, you're smidging my lipstick,' complained Naomi, and began wriggling to escape my clutch.

'Can you still hear it?' I whispered.

'No. Let me go. Put me down, Grandma. You're squashing me.'

For what seemed like ages, but perhaps was only a couple of minutes, Gump went on barking. I could hear no other sounds now. The dog's voice drowned everything. Then Gump's barks suddenly became transformed into a short series of high pitched shrieks. Followed by silence.

'Why did he do that, Granny?' whispered Naomi. I felt her body grow tense as though she was catching my fear. I was feeling sick with horror and sorrow as I whispered back, 'Perhaps a mouse trod on his toe.'

Naomi gave a little giggle and relaxed again. We stayed like that for a long time and after a while Naomi sank softly against me and fell asleep.

I must get to the phone. That was the only hope.

Sooner or later, and probably sooner, the person who was in the house would discover us in the darkened bedroom.

Slithering gently from under the child's sleeping body, I crept across the room, to the door and silently pushed it a little way open. The passage was still dark. There was no light anywhere. No sound either. Perhaps whoever had been in the house had gone out again through the back door. I could see the phone on the landing, now only a few feet away. One soft step and I was there.

I lifted the receiver. And there was no dialling tone. The line was dead.

Until that moment, I suppose, I had managed to reassure myself that in a moment I would find a bird in the kitchen or some stray cat that had got in through an upper window, that Gump had stopped barking because even dogs make mistakes and he had realised there was nothing to bark at. But when I found the line dead, I was filled with a terrible fear. For some reason there seemed no need to keep silent any more.

The dead line made me understand that the person in the house knew perfectly well I was here. I rushed to the kitchen, flung open the door and switched on the light.

The loyal little dog that Jack had loved so much was white no longer but stained with the scarlet of his own blood, with more blood pooling onto the kitchen floor from his cut throat.

Rage and urgency overwhelmed fear. Naomi was alone up there in the bedroom. I took the stairs three at a time and rushed into the dark bedroom. For a moment I couldn't see anything, though I could hear the sound of breathing, then a gulping noise. As my sight adapted to the dark, I saw a shadowy figure, face obscured in something black so that only the eyes were visible. The intruder, Naomi clutched in his or her arms, was making for the open window. A black gloved hand was clasped over the little girl's mouth so that the only sounds she could make were these frantic gulpings.

I did not wait to think. I reached out and seized my powder pot, the great jar of crystal filled with pink perfumed face powder, the sort I have worn ever since I was a girl and which Verity always jeers at for being so old-fashioned, and hurled the contents into the kidnapper's eyes, at the same time screaming 'Help, help, burglars, burglars.'

The intruder dropped Naomi and began to wildly wipe at its eyes as the neighbours' windows began opening and voices started calling back. Still yelling, I grabbed my grandchild, while the intruder, stumbling and gasping, rushed for the window and went leaping out. I held the trembling Naomi tightly and the two of us listened to the sound of the intruder kicking and bumping against the walls and windows as he or she climbed down to the ground.

The security lights came on, people came rushing to our garden, and I caught a brief glimpse of the running intruder, who then vanished into the trees before any of the neighbours could catch up with him or her.

I held my grandchild for a long time and the two of us shivered together.

Neighbours came in and brewed tea, then made cocoa for Naomi. One of the neighbours rang the police. Someone brought whisky and we all had a little swig while everyone gathered round the cocoa-sipping Naomi and asked questions. The police arrived and made her describe what had happened and asked if she had managed to see the face of the person who had so nearly captured her.

His face had been covered, she said. She had only seen his eyes which looked shiny but because it was dark she couldn't see what colour they were.

It did not seem like a failed robbery. There appeared to have been no attempt to steal anything apart from the child. Someone suggested that the intruder was a woman who had lost her own child and was now going madly round trying to steal another as a replacement.

M'buta arrived looking hysterical, Verity had been in labour all day and the baby was still not born. M'buta said that she had nearly had a heart attack when the police told her. 'I haven't told Verity. We'll have to let her know after the baby is born, though. Tell me everything that happened.'

The story had been told so often by now, each new arrival being given a description of the silent intruder, the murder of Gump and the face powder attack, that it had taken on a nice steady rhythm in which little contradictions and queries had all been neatly sorted out.

'But what about your blood pressure and your arthritis?' cried M'buta Everyone of the friends and neighbours had asked this question too.

'Lady Cunningham-Smythe temporarily overcame her disabilities to save her little granddaughter,' would be the headlines in tomorrow's daily paper.

'My granny is the bravest person in the world and she fought with a dog murderer and threw powder at them so that they ran away,' said Naomi. She is a remarkable child. I had never seen another four year old who was so knowing.

She had made this statement several times already and each time it was greeted with a satisfactory burst of compliments both for her and for me.

M'buta said, giving me a complicated kind of look which I could not quite interpret. 'The whole thing seems so unlikely. I have never heard of such a kidnapping done like this, unless the kidnapper was someone who knew the child. A parent for instance.'

'What about that little American film star,' suggested someone. 'She was kidnapped by a stalker.'

'Well, yes, but Naomi is not an American film star.'

'I did Holy Mary in the school nativity play,' said Naomi proudly.

'There you are,' said someone. 'Maybe there was a loony in the audience who got a thing about Naomi.'

'Why should they be a loony?' demanded M'buta hotly. 'Naomi is a very lovely little girl.'

CHAPTER 2

'WHEN SHE HAS RECOVERED A BIT, try gently to get out of her what details you can,' the police told me. It seemed to me that Naomi was more than recovered by now and enjoying the fame of being the child who had nearly been kidnapped.

'Do you think it was a man who grabbed you?' I asked her. We were having breakfast. She stopped eating, spoon loaded with cornflakes in mid air while she considered this. After a long pause she shook her head, spattering milk. Gump would have had the puddle lapped up in a moment. A burning sensation arose at the back of my eyes. Rage, not sorrow, I assure you.

'No,' said Naomi slowly.

'Oh, a woman was it.'

Naomi shook her head again then looked at me closely. 'Don't cry, Grandma,' she said softly.

'Of course I'm not crying,' I told her furiously. 'Why on earth should you think I'm crying?'

She patted me gently on the hand as though she was the adult. 'Grandma, what happens to dogs when they die?'

'I don't know,' I told her. 'I don't even know what happens to people, so we have to invent things.'

'What did you invent for Gump?'

'I haven't started doing that yet.'

'But you did invent something for Grandpa. I know you did.'

Her words gave me a shock. How does this little child know? Can she read minds? Several times lately I had had the feeling that she could.

'It's too complicated to explain,' I told her briskly. I hoped this would work, though it's hard to know where you are with mind reading people. 'Now, come on. Try to think. That person who grabbed you last night obviously wasn't your teddy, because he was still in the bathroom so it must have been either a man or a woman.'

'It might have been Teddy,' she said proudly. 'He's very clever, you know. He's full of tricks. He could have been pretending.' She frowned in further thought then said, 'But really I think it was probably a witch and she had a broomstick out there and that was how she flew away and she was going to eat me, you know, like the one in Hansel and Gretel, but you saved me by throwing your powder at her.'

Verity's son was born that night, so Naomi had to go on staying with me.

'Shall we have a funeral for Gump, like there was one for Grandpa,' she said next morning.

'Don't be silly. Who's going to dig the hole?'

'I expect, now that you've got so good at fighting burglars, you might be able to do anything because I think your blood precious has gone away. I think you've got like Spiderwoman, Grandma.'

'Who on earth is Spiderwoman?'

Naomi was amazed. 'She's the most famous woman in the world,' she said. 'Except for the queen, of course. I can't believe you've never heard of her.'

A robin bounced hopefully around our feet as Naomi and I went into the garden shed and took out two of Jack's spades.

The robin hopped all the way back with us to the kitchen garden, where we had decided to make the grave because the ground was softer. Naomi held my hand, danced excitedly and talked some nonsense about getting a leg up onto the blood precious as though Blood Precious was a horse.

I said, 'Here under the apple tree would be a good place, I think. It's where Gump used to bury his bones.'

As we were standing looking at the spot, the robin hopped onto Naomi's toe, making her laugh. She quickly stopped and asked, 'Will Gump mind?'

'Mind what?'

'Me laughing. Will he think I didn't love him?'

'No,' I said.

'M'buta said I mustn't laugh in the church when it was Grandpa's funeral.'

She began to struggle her spade into the turf.

'I think he would have liked it. I think it was silly of people to tell you not to laugh,' I said and I thought to myself, perhaps Jack can see us now, digging in the autumn sunshine, me, Naomi and the robin.

'Will Gump's soul be able to talk to Grandpa's soul by now, do you think?' asked Naomi.

I paused in my digging and looked into the hole, as though in there would be something that answered her question. When Jack and I were young we had decided that there was no afterlife. We were absolutely sure. We had no doubt at all. It was only when the time seemed to be getting near, that we invented our red-hot clinker theory.

The robin, undeterred by the burst of infant happiness, had remained perched on Naomi's toe and cocked his head from side to side as though ordering us to keep on digging. 'You'd better be careful you don't fall off the blood precious, even if it is better,' said Naomi as I lifted out a little shovel full of earth.

The police came to see us again that afternoon. A police woman was going to stay in the house with us for a day or two 'just till they got things sorted out. Because I don't expect you'll want to go on living on your own, after what's happened.'

So that's what was going on, was it? Verity was getting them to persuade me that I should move in with her. She had been going on like that ever since Jack died. 'How are you going to cope, now, Mother? I do wish you'd see sense.' Now she had found an even better reason.

'I'll cope perfectly well, thank you,' I had said then, though I feared that sooner or later, Verity would find a way of winning. She is a very strong minded woman and used to getting her own way. Look at how she twiddles all those publishers round her little fingers. She's the only author I know who chooses her own book jackets and now I had been burgled, well intruded upon, her argument had been even further strengthened. The fact that I had fought off an intruder and saved my granddaughter from being kidnapped seemed to cut no ice with either the police or my own family.

I went round to the hospital to see her that very day. 'I am definitely not leaving my home. You can all make what plans for me that you like, but here I stay.'

'Do you want to see your new grandson?'

'Of course I do,' I said quickly. 'Show him to me at once.' She rootled in the bed and pulled out, like a conjuror taking a rabbit from a hat, a little black baby with a mop of shiny curly hair.

'My goodness,' I said.

'No need to be nasty,' said Verity.

'I was merely taken by surprise,' I said. And added briskly, 'Your father would be pleased. He longed for a grandson.'

'So you are going to be sensible, aren't you, Mother, and come and live with us? I shall be having my hands full, with the two of them and my deadline is not far away and I could do with some help.'

'So my face powder attack and the way I sent the villain rushing off weeping violet perfumed tears and how I saved the life of your daughter has cut no ice at all,' I told her with dignity.

'Of course it has,' she said. 'But just suppose the fellow comes back. And now you haven't even got Gump to look after you, though I don't suppose that little dog was much good at protecting you. But better than nothing, anyway.'

'I am planning to get a gun,' I told her.

'Oh, don't be so silly, Mother,' she said. 'You have never used a gun in your life.'

That evening after the police woman had settled into the dining room, where, apparently she was going to spend the night, the inspector who had questioned me in the morning rang and asked if I had managed to get any new information out of Naomi.

'Yes,' I told him savagely. 'That the intruder was a witch who flew away on a broomstick and I wish you would leave us alone my because me and my granddaughter had a nasty fright, and we don't want to go on being reminded.'

A detective came the following day. He was a large man with a red face and a mournful expression. 'I wonder if you would fill me in on the background of little Naomi.' He had already been to interview Verity in hospital, and had seen the new baby. He knew about M'buta and the AI.

'Naomi is very fair skinned. It seems unlikely that she is the child of an African donor,' the inspector said. 'Is it possible that your daughter is hiding something from her partner?'

'You mean has she had an affair with a white man and that Naomi is the consequence?' I hate the way people beat around the bush when it comes to subjects like this. Also I do believe in calling a spade a spade. Verity, who is a writer of popular books and is always on the watch, therefore, for examples of bad writing, says I should not use so many clichés. Well, I love clichés and shall use them if I want to. I don't get much freedom in this life, but at least I shan't allow that one to be taken from me.

'Certainly not,' I told the inspector crossly. 'Verity would never do anything to hurt M'buta. Also I went with my daughter to the clinic and was there when she chose the father of the child. I saw the fellow's photo.' I felt extra annoyed at the detective's suggestion because the idea, disloyal as it was to my daughter, had already occurred to me. 'I think the ones you should be investigating are those swindlers at the Bereton Clinic and not my daughter who is an innocent victim in this matter.'

As though I had not spoken, he said, 'Because if this is the child of your daughter's lover, then perhaps it is a case of the father of the child, come back to claim his offspring.'

I let out a fierce growling sound, which shut him up.

The new baby and his mother were deemed well enough to come home and Naomi was returned to her two mothers.

Tuesday came round again which was the day Verity and M'buta usually went dancing. In my day, no pregnant young woman would have done such a thing, but times had changed.

Now was my chance, I thought. There was even a little whisky left. Not much, but enough. Where the goodness does it go?

But somehow I couldn't get myself going. I had geared myself up thoroughly the first time, and it was really difficult to start doing it all over again.

All day I kept telling myself, 'Now. You won't get a better chance,' but a sneaky little whisper inside me kept saying, 'Just one more day. There's always next Tuesday. Just one little peep more at the new grandson this week. After all I haven't even held him, yet.'

Also I was not feeling at all well and in my opinion, speaking as a person of potential experience, you have to be in top form to kill yourself. I felt stiff all over and could hardly find the energy to get out of bed.

Then at last, when I felt sufficiently energetic and was just about to get up and take out the pills, M'buta appeared.

'What are you doing here?' I demanded. 'It's Tuesday.'

'Well, Verity and me aren't going to be able to go out today, are we?' she laughed. 'Come on, Ladyma, you should get up.' She stayed for the rest of the morning. She was extra excited about her holy man, Daniel daSilva, who, she said, had performed a miracle. Apparently he had made a lame man walk again. I did not laugh at her, because she has faith in this man and gets such joy from going to his meetings. After Jack died, M'buta urged me to allow him to visit me.

'No thank you,' I had said firmly. 'The last thing in the whole world I want is some priest holding forth on virgin births, sacred hearts, precious blood, etcetera,'

At midday she said she must get back to Verity and the baby, and I thought I might just have enough time, after she had gone, but then she said that she was going to pick me up in the afternoon, so that I could visit Verity too.

So that was another Tuesday gone.

I must say, the grandson is a dear little creature and in spite of everything, has a look of Jack about him.

'M'buta says you've got depression again. Are you sure you won't change your mind and come and live with me?' Verity asked.

I disdained to answer.

'We're taking Naomi to Brighton for the day,' Verity said. 'You know, so she won't feel left out because of the baby. Also, though she seems OK, she's probably a bit shaken up inside by the intruder and an outing will be good for her.'

I was shocked. In my day a woman who had just had a baby stayed in bed for at least a week. My mother stayed in bed for a month after having me.

'I am perfectly alright and strong as an ox and I'm sick to death of leading the life of an invalid because I have had a baby,' Verity said to me sternly. I knew better than to argue.

She said, 'Will you come? I think it would be nice for you too. You've never been back since – since—' She could not bring herself to say, 'since you tried to die in the sea.'

'Certainly not,' I said. 'Vulgar place.'

'We used to love it.' She spoke a little wistfully. When she was little, Jack and I had taken her to Brighton every summer. We had stayed in a nice hotel on the sea front and spent the day paddling in the sea or roaming among the seafront stalls, buying winkles, sugar dummies, rude balloons. The sun seemed to always shine in those days. Verity told me that I had spoiled all her memories by trying to die there.

'Please, Mother,' she said now. 'It will make things alright again.'

'I've got things to do here.'

Verity began to use her wheedle voice. The childhood one. 'Please, please, Mummy, I beg you and beseech you—' to buy that doll, take me to that film, let me go out to tea with my (totally unsuitable) friend. I had had Jack to hide behind when I needed to refuse her. 'I'd let you go, buy it for you, take you, but your father wouldn't ever allow it.' She was quite big before she found out that Jack would allow anything and by then I had protected her or preserved myself.

'We could go on the pier and have lunch in a pub. Just like the old days when I was little and went with you and Daddy,' she said.

I sighed. 'Which day?' I asked.

'Wednesday.'

Ah. That's all right then. I could say yes or no whichever I pleased and it would make no difference. Tuesday came first.

'Good. It's all fixed.' A cheery laugh from Verity.

As we left, I felt happy that next Wednesday I would be with Jack and the rest of my family would be having a nice day out to take their minds off me. I would be with Jack? The trouble was, I wasn't sure of anything. It seems strange that after centuries of priests and philosophers speculating about what happens after death, still all that we had was guesswork. These are the things that seem unlikely so I dismiss them as not meriting further consideration. Christian Heaven, with God on a cloud and all those singing angels. Or a Muslim one thronged with virgins. Or one of those ancient underground ones. Also unlikely becoming recreated again at some point. I mean do you get your nails back, the ones you have been cutting all your life? Or your hair? How much of you has to be left, for it to still be you to be recreated?

'And for us it will probably be Hell, because suicide is a mortal sin,' said Jack.

In the end Jack and I opted for a sort of outside consciousness which did not require a body. It was a bit of a stitch up, we both agreed, but there did not seem to be any other way of approaching it. There are two ways in which this could be, we decided, though only one would make it possible for us to find each other again. The first, and rejected for that reason, though as Jack pointed out, just because we don't like it does not mean that it is not true, was the ocean theory. In this, all consciousness was like an ocean, with individual consciousness being like drops of water, functioning on their own to a certain extent until mingling again with the main bulk and losing their individuality. The theory we fancied, so therefore chose to believe, was that afterglow one. We were not sure how long this would last, but felt that if you can get there quickly enough after a person dies you can still find their slowly fading glow. I tried to explain this to Verity once.

'Oh, ghosts you mean.'

Well, you would not have expected her to understand, would you? She may be a creative writer, but her mind seems to be a fairly closed book.

Hang onto your glow, Jack. Keep it burning till Tuesday and then the two of us can sink into forever as a single gleam.

On Tuesday morning the phone rang. It was Naomi. 'I'm excited because you're coming to Brighton with us, Grandma.' Verity or M'buta had put her up to it, I felt sure. They suspected something.

'Thank you darling,' I said. No four year old in the world could possibly be made happy by their grandmother coming with them on a day's outing, could they? But then Naomi was not like other four year olds.

'Could you bring that little spade, Grandma and the big one for you, because I want you and me to dig in the sand like we did for making Gump's grave. And we could fill it with water and we could put a castle in the middle ... '

'There's no sand on the Brighton beach,' I told her.

'Oh.' Her tone was bleak.

'But you can hire little cars there. We could go driving together. Would you like that?' What on earth was I saying? I wasn't even going to be there.

Naomi squeaked with excitement. 'Oo, that'd be gorgeous, Grandma,' and then her voice distant, away from the phone. 'Mummy, Grandma and me are going to drive a car together when we get to Brighton.'

I sighed and closed the drawer in which I had been keeping the pills. 'Not this week then, but next I promise you, Jack.'

Verity was not sure of the way, so M'buta sat in front with her and read the map while Naomi sat in her child seat at the back, the baby in its car seat between us. Verity had made a fuss about this, saying that these days babies had to have their car seat on the front seat and secured with a seat belt. I was determined not to be done out of the proximity of my new grandchild for the whole of the long journey, but it was only by staunchly refusing to get into the car till my wish had been granted, and with Verity muttering things like, 'We'll have to go at about five miles an hour in that case' and 'I just hope to God that we don't get stopped by the police,' she gave in.

I and Naomi played 'I went out to dinner'. We had fish, we had fish and custard, we had fish and custard and mulligatawny soup, we had fish and custard and ... The person who remembered the lot without a mistake was the winner.

'It's making me feel queasy to listen to the two of you,' said Verity.

'As a matter of the fact I'm hungry,' said M'buta. She eats a lot for such a slim girl.

Verity stopped at a motorway café. Coloured flashing lights were strung all along its roof. Naomi began leaping with joy and shouting 'It's Christmas here. Christmas has come,' which woke the baby.

It was raining hard and a strong wind was blowing as the car came to a halt in the car park.

'Not a good day for Brighton,' said Verity.

'Don't be sad, darling,' said M'buta. 'There's lots of other things to do there apart from sea.'

Naomi was already going ahead of us into the service station.

'Come back, Naomi. Wait for us.' Since the near kidnap Verity had been nervous about having the child out of her sight. 'Hold my hand.'

'You are being paranoid, Verity,' I told her as I struggled after them, Really, you would think she would be helping her poor disabled old mother, instead of making a silly fuss about a perfectly healthy and sensible little girl.

Inside, out of the wet wind, it was all light and noise and people. Around the brilliant foyer, open shops sold glittering useless goods. People all around us were saying things like, 'Good Lord, we forgot to get Granny a present. Here's a nice ostrich-feather ball point pen.' Or, 'Let's get those golden bath salts for Aunty Flora or she'll feel left out.'

'A person could live on the motorway forever,' sighed Naomi. 'You'd never have to go home at all. You could just buy everything you wanted in the shops here.'

'Where would you sleep, though?' asked Verity.

Naomi looked round carefully, said 'There don't seem to be any bed shops but we could sleep on the grass if it wasn't raining.'

'What would you do then?'

'Then you'd have to sleep in your car. Oh. Look. Fruit machines.' Naomi began dashing towards them.

'Don't you dare,' shouted Verity. 'Don't even think of it.' She tried to grab the child, but she was too late.

'Come back at once,' Verity yelled. 'Here. Hold the baby, M'buta, while I go after her.' Naomi had almost reached the machines. Verity began running. There was real panic in her voice as she called, 'Naomi, Naomi, come back this minute.'

'What's the matter? Why is she in such a state?' I asked M'buta.

'We don't let Naomi get near fruit machines.'

'Leave go. Leave go,' yelled Naomi, as Verity caught up with her and grabbed her by the arm shouting, 'No. I forbid it.'

'Why can't she?' I said. 'Come, Naomi. Grandma will give you a fifty pence to play with.'

'No, Mother, absolutely not,' commanded Verity.

'Why on earth not? What's the harm? Let her have a go. What does it matter if she loses a little bit of money?'

Naomi was still howling. People were turning to stare with disapproval.

'It's not like that,' said Verity, trying to be heard over the roars of her usually obliging child.

'What then?'

'She wins,' whispered M'buta in a tone of horror. She made winning sound like some disgusting and perverted vice.

'Really, you are being too ridiculous.' I opened my purse to take out the money but Verity smacked a furious hand on top of mine. 'I absolutely forbid it,' she said. 'There are some things that you do not know.' She is a very strong willed woman as I have said before.

Still, Naomi was behaving rather badly. She was never like this before the arrival of the baby. Or perhaps it was the result of the horrible shock of being nearly kidnapped.

Naomi was still sulking as we settled down in the cafeteria. To get her mind off it, I asked her, 'How are you enjoying your new little brother?'

'I wish they'd send it back,' she muttered. 'It's not at all what any of us expected. They said it would be a companion for me, but it's much too little and stupid to play anything.' The two mothers by now were bent over the baby with expressions of doting joy.

'He'll grow,' I told her. 'They all do.' Actually I had been a little sad when Verity grew up and stopped being my little girl.

Suddenly Naomi grabbed my hand and whispered, 'Grandma, look.'

I couldn't see anything amazing. 'What? Where?'

'There, Grandma.' She pointed and I just caught sight of someone in a black knitted cap before they went out into the car park. 'Do you think that's the person who tried to steal me?' The hand that held mine began trembling.

She isn't over the shock, I realised. Somewhere down inside her all the horror was still there and perhaps would be for the rest of her life.

'It's just a lady wearing a knitted hat. The nasty person has gone away and won't ever dare to come back again because I threw all that powder at him. You mustn't think about it any more.'

'Grandma,' she said, suddenly changing the conversation in the way children do. 'Could you come with me to the fruit machines to cheer me up, because I've had such a nasty shock? And let me have a pound?'

'Your mother said you mustn't.' I really did think Verity and M'buta were being most unreasonable. They were taking the poor child to the seaside to get over it her fright and the very first thing she wanted to do, they forbid it. The two mothers were now fully concentrated on the baby.

'Here,' I whispered, putting a coin into Naomi's hand. 'Don't let your mother see, though.'

'I love you Grandma,' Naomi whispered. 'You are the best person in the world. Much better than my mummy and M'buta,' and she reached up and gave me a kiss on the cheek.

'Cut the slop,' I said.

Naomi giggled.

M'buta heard and smiled. 'I knew we were right to insist you came, Ladyma. You have a real way with Naomi.' She had clearly not heard what it was that had made the little girl laugh, though.

I gave Naomi a conspiratorial nod and the two of us began to slip quietly off. Verity looked up. 'Where are you going? Not to the fruit machines, I hope.'

'No of course not. Just to the shops. Shall I buy you anything?'

'Yes. Something for the baby. He's been sick again.'

As soon as Naomi and I got outside she began to laugh. 'We outwitted them, didn't we, Grandma?'

'We certainly did,' I said.

We reached the fruit machines. The sight seemed to almost take Naomi's breath away. I wondered if the horror at the fruit machines was something to do with M'buta's holy man. Most religions seem to forbid gambling. Perhaps M'buta had converted Verity. She was always trying to convert me.

But anyway, now that those silly mothers were out of the way, with their priggish prohibitions, there was nothing to stop my grandchild from having her bit of harmless fun.

The machines twittered, clattered, sparkled and throbbed and the hope, disappointment and triumph of the other young gamblers was almost palpable and they bent over their machines with total concentration.

Naomi grabbed the money from my hand and rushed to a free one. There was no one even nearly as small as Naomi but although she was only four she seemed to know exactly what to do. She put her money in and had to stand on tiptoe to reach the handle. She began to turn it, apparently as much an expert as the teenagers around her. I stood by, watching, charmed at her delight and competence. After a couple of turns she was rewarded with a gush of money. The people on either side turned to look, their expressions envious.

'Well done,' I said. 'Stop now. Let's go back to your mummies before they get suspicious.'

She seemed not to hear me. It was as though she was in a trance. She won again. Verity had said that Naomi won but I had not taken it as literally as this.

People began to gather and watch the tiny child operating the machine with such successful efficiency. She seemed unable to lose. No matter what she did, money poured out.

She stuffed the new shower of coins in her pocket and said happily, 'I'll get you a present, Grandma. Would you like some of those sugar false teeth?'

'Thank you very much, dear,' I told her stiffly. 'Now that's enough. Let's go back to the mummies.'

'Just one more, Grandma.' She popped another pound in. Another money gust.

I began to feel tense. The child must have won about fifteen pounds. 'Stop now, Naomi. That's enough.'

But the people around were enjoying it. 'The little girl's on a winning streak. Don't stop her now.'

'Just one more go, please, please, please,' cried Naomi piteously and gave the handle another tug, pulled down another gust of money.

I began to feel flustered. I had never seen anyone win so much money in such a short time. Men that looked like security people had now gathered in a whispering group and were giving us suspicious glances. Then one came up, and asked, 'What's going on here?' There was threat in his expression. I was afraid we were going to be in trouble. But the money shower went on pouring and there seemed no way to stop it. By now Naomi was laden with money. It was falling from her pockets and she had gathered it up in her skirt till she was bent with the weight.

'My granddaughter won it fair and square,' I told the man. More gamblers were leaving their machines and coming to look, their expressions turning from admiration to suspicion.

'I think we had better go and have a word with the management, Madam,' said the man.

'I don't think there's any need for that,' I said quickly. 'My granddaughter will give it back to you, won't you Naomi. There must have been something wrong with the machine.'

'No,' said Naomi, clinging on. A few coins fell from her pockets and rolled over the floor. 'And it's not broken. It's just that I always win.'

'Come along with me,' said the man. And to the others 'What are you lot staring at?'

The gathering crowd shuffled back a bit but went on looking.

'Give that money to the man at once, Naomi,' I demanded. And to him, 'I think it's outrageous to expose a small child to a piece of faulty machinery. She could have been injured. She might have got an electric shock. Give it back at once, Naomi.'

My tone was as commanding as I could manage but Naomi continued to clutch the money. She said defiantly. 'It's mine. I always win and you can't take it away from me.'

'Look, Grandma will buy you a nice ice cream if you give the man his money back.'

'It's not his, it's mine. And I could buy about a thousand ice creams with it myself,' she said.

Someone among the watchers giggled. The security man gave a blazing look which silenced the sound instantly.

Then Verity came running.

'You promised, Mother. You lied. How could you do it?' she screamed and began tearing the money from the child's arms, pulling it from her pockets. 'Throw down what you've got. Go on, do as I say this minute.'

Money was tumbling, pouring, rolling. The watching crowd went racing round the foyer grabbing it. The security man pursued them, threatening, yelling, gathering what he could. Naomi, screaming now, clung to what money remained, but gradually her mother managed to leak it away. When the last of the money was gone, Verity gripped Naomi grimly by one hand and me by the other.

'Come with me,' she said in the grim tone of a person about to perform an execution.

'Leave go of me at once,' I commanded as she dragged the pair of us back to the cafeteria. Naomi was still howling. Verity paid no attention to either of us, though everyone else there turned to stare at the noise.

'I think the two of you are the wickedest people in the world,' Verity growled when she had got us seated back at the table with M'buta and the baby. And to Naomi, 'Shut up, you.' The tone was effective. Naomi stopped screaming and began to sulk instead. 'Grandma and me had such fun and she's much kinder than you are,' she scowled.

'At Madam Tussauds they called the police and we got taken to the police station and questioned,' M'buta told me. 'That's why Verity is so upset.'

We were getting ready to go when my bladder began to act up. It's something to do with my new blood pressure pills.

'Can't you wait till we get there?' Verity said. She had already packed up the baby and got hers and Naomi's coats on.

'No,' I said firmly.

'I want to go too,' said Naomi.

'Don't be so silly,' her mother said. 'You've just been.'

'No I haven't. Nothing came. I want to go with Grandma.' That had been a good move, letting her use the fruit machines. I was really in favour now.

'Come on,' I said.

'No, Mother. I don't trust you any more. You'll take her to the fruit machines, or buy her more chocolate or something.'

'Look, if I stand here arguing any more, 'I'll wet my bloomers. And you wouldn't like that in your car, would you?'

Verity sighed. 'Promise not to go anywhere except the loo.'

'I promise.'

'And hold her hand all the way,' Verity called after us as we set off out of the restaurant.

'All right.' I was in a real hurry now.

'Promise?'

'I promise.'

'And watch her all the time. Don't let her out of your sight.'

Really, that near kidnap had made her too windy for words.

'And take her in the loo with you. Don't leave her standing outside.'

'Don't go on like that, Verity. Anyone would think I knew nothing about children at all. How do you think you survived to become a mother?' I was having to twine my legs by now.

As soon as we got out of the cafeteria, Naomi began to wriggle her hand out of mine.

'Hold my hand. I promised your mother.' I tried to speak strictly but I was in a hurry.

'I'm a big girl now and Mummy is silly.' She went on wriggling. I held tightly and would not let her go. I kept a tight grip on her as we thrust ourselves through the crowd, to reach the ladies. There was a long queue. Would I make it?

It seemed like forever before my turn came. 'There. You go first,' I told my granddaughter. The sacrifices you have to make for children. I stood outside the door like a sentinel, my legs wound. Another came free nearby, but some other woman, quick as a flash, got in first. There is no honour in the ladies room.

'Do hurry up,' I called to Naomi through the closed door. 'How long can you take?'

She emerged at last. Only just in time, too. 'You've got to come in with me,' I told her. 'You mummy said so.'

'I won't. I hate being squashed in there.'

I tried to pull her. She pulled back.

'Do as I say,' I told her.

'No,' she said.

'Look, are you going to go in, or not?' asked the woman behind me. 'Because if you are going to stand there arguing, I shall use it.'

I was defeated. And desperate. 'Stand outside the door and don't move a step till I come out again.'

At intervals, after I got inside and locked the door, as I got things off, I kept saying, 'Are you there, Naomi?' and each time got the answer, 'yes.'

My corset got stuck. Oh, Lord, once you get in there and are so close it always becomes an emergency and a race against time.

'You're taking ages, Grandma,' wailed Naomi outside. 'I want to go back to my mummies.'

'Don't you dare,' I shouted. 'Wait till I'm ready. I won't be long, I promise.' My tights got swivelled round.

'I hate it here.'

'You wait.' The more I hurried, the more problems arose. There are some things you just cannot do quickly.

I kept calling, as I pulled up underclothes and did up buttons 'Are you there? Are you being good?'

'I'm going,' said Naomi. 'I know exactly where my mummies and the baby are, I could go back there in a minute.' She clearly did not like the thought of Verity and M'buta making a fuss of the baby in her absence. 'I'll run like anything, Grandma. I won't stop on the way.'

'No,' I shouted, but I could hear the sound of her running footsteps and the door slamming. She had ignored me. Anyway, what could possibly happen to her? The place was thronged with children. The restaurant was only across the passage.

I was ready at last.

Verity was going to be cross, I thought, as I went back to the cafeteria. But what else could I have done? Anyway, it was my daughter's fault for bringing the child up to be disobedient. Or having another baby and making the child jealous. Though now Verity would never trust me again. Good thing, probably. Then I won't be lumbered with the responsibility and inconvenience of a naughty four year old. I had nearly wet myself because of Naomi.

'I will be so furious with her,' I vowed as I hobbled along the corridor.

In the restaurant, M'buta had the baby on her knee, was looking into its face. The two mothers were humming it a love song. They were like people at a religious ceremony worshipping a god, I thought and felt sure I had never behaved in that silly way when Verity was a baby.

I had made myself so certain that I would find Naomi here, at first my eyes would not allow me to accept that she was not. M'buta looked up smiling, saw the horror in my face and in a moment panic spread over hers as well.

Verity came with me back to the loo. She was too panicky even to be annoyed with me. No Naomi there though. 'Perhaps she went back inside one of the cubicles,' I suggested.

'Naomi! Naomi!' Verity and I were both calling almost at once The room was full and all heads turned to look at us. I thrust my way through the crush of women. Verity went dashing, banging on loo doors, calling, calling, 'Naomi, Naomi.'

'A little girl in a blue coat. Did you see her?' People shook their heads and looked at me with a blank pity.

Verity was now peering under wash basins. Looking seemed hopeless. One did not know what to do. I returned to the loo I had used because that was the last place I had seen her. Someone was in there. Perhaps it was Naomi. Perhaps she'd gone back. I banged on the door a second time. A strange woman's voice answered me. 'Go away. What the hell do you keep banging for?'

I found the attendant inside a store room, sorting towels. 'I've been in here for the last ten minutes,' the woman said. 'I haven't been out there in that time.'

No one had seen Naomi. I saw a look of reproach in one or two of the faces, because I had been careless with a child. By now Verity was shaking from head to toe.

While Verity rang the police, M'buta and I went round and round the service station asking questions. One lady said she thought she had seen a little girl fitting the description some time ago. 'She went out with her Daddy.'

'Blonde child? Blue eyes?'

The woman shrugged. 'I never looked as close as that, love.'

'What was the man like?'

She shrugged again. 'Just a man.'

Surely Naomi wouldn't have gone out with a strange man. But suppose he had told her some story about us having already gone to the car.

'Well, I did see someone going into the car park with a little girl in a blue coat,' someone else told us.

'Was the man forcing her or anything?'

'It didn't look like it.'

Got to keep calm, got to keep calm.

CHAPTER 3

WE STAYED THERE FOR HOURS, searching and shouting till in the end it became obvious that Naomi was gone. She was not anywhere in the service station.

We drove to the police station after that, travelling in silence, M'buta and Verity were so frightened and sorrowful that they did not even say a word of reproach to me. Even the baby was silent and fast asleep.

We were given photos to look at in case we recognised any of the people there. It felt a bit like looking through the catalogue of the Bereton Clinic, except that time we had been full of expectation and now we looked with panic and dismay.

'Can you see anyone who looks like the person who tried to snatch your granddaughter the other night? Because there probably is a connection.'

'The person was completely covered up. You couldn't see anything.'

'All the same, you never know.' I could tell really that they didn't expect anything, that they were just doing their duty. I ploughed through page after page, filled with the horrible awareness that every minute we spent here, Naomi was getting further away from us.

I slammed down the book at last and said, 'This is a ridiculous waste of time. You should be chasing the car that my granddaughter was in otherwise she will probably be on some ship or plane ... '

'We are doing our duty, Madam. Until we know which car to chase, our only hope is for you to recognise one of these people.'

It was when he said that I understood how perfectly hopeless all this was. The police were just doing things for the sake of doing them. They had absolutely no idea what had happened to Naomi or who had taken her.

That night was terrible. I lay there for hour after hour, waiting for the phone to ring, for them to tell me Naomi had been found. I felt so ill with worry that guilt hardly fitted in as well. The only thing that made it bearable was the thought that, when M'buta came in the morning she would tell me that Naomi had been found.

But when she arrived, I could see from one look at her face, that there was still no news of Naomi. M'buta was trying to act as normal, I could see, but her mind was not there at all. Her hands were trembling all the time and her eyes kept filling with tears.

She said things like, 'Come on, now, Ladyma. You must get out of bed. We can't have you staying in there all day.' But she spoke in a mechanical sort of way, as though her mind was not on the words at all.

'I'm seriously ill,' I told her.

She took my pulse and blood pressure very quickly, glanced at the readings and said in a tone that was uncharacteristically snappy,. 'You are all right. You are just working yourself into feeling ill. If you get up you will start to feel better. Come on. Upsy daisy.'

The words were her usual ones, but her voice had lost all its authority and conviction and really you could see that she did not care if I laid in bed for the rest of my life.

As she reached over to pull back the curtains, she suddenly shouted angrily, 'Why the hell did you have to leave her standing outside?'

'Don't open those curtains. I want them shut,' I demanded but as though she had not heard me, she ripped them open, filling the room with a harsh and horrid light.

Why? Why? Why? That's the kind of thing I kept asking myself as well. Sometimes mixed up with, if only.

I would have eaten my hoarded tablets that moment, if it had not been for the presence of M'buta. I think she had come so as to increase my feeling of guilt. But that was so intense that nothing could have made it greater. I considered doing it any way, thinking that M'buta might be so angry, that she would not try to save me. But I dared not take the risk, just in case.

At midday, shortly after M'buta left, Verity came in, threw herself onto my arms and cried and cried and cried. I tried to think of words to comfort her, but none came.

Apart from that, the two of them left me alone for most of that day and I lay listening to my heart gurgling and bumping. I still dared do nothing, for they might come back at any moment. Feeling seemed to be draining from my toes and fingers. The idea even came to me that perhaps Naomi was dead. That that was why the police had found not the smallest trace of her nor had the least idea what had happened to her.

Perhaps not only would Jack be waiting for me and Gump, but Naomi too.

The thought, oddly, made me feel uncomfortable. I had planned for so long that the last glow of Jack's identity should blend with mine. I had imagined Jack and me, alone together in our no time, no place. Would the added glow of a child change things? And then there was Gump as well. Would I, Jack, a granddaughter and a dog all dissolve into forever in the same gracious way Jack and I had visualised when there had only been two of us? Somehow I could not fit the light of the other two into this. I wanted us to be me and Jack. The nasty thought even came to me that there might be limitless others able to combine with us. Where would it end? But on the other hand, who else had the poor little girl got to mingle with? Oh, God, the reeling thoughts were probably pushing up my blood pressure higher than ever

At six Chrissy brought me soup and toast on a tray. She had been treating me in a very impertinent manner ever since I had given her the sack. Now, in addition to her obvious feeling of triumphing over me she was clearly feeling she had the moral high ground. I had lost Naomi. I was in disgrace. Chrissy was enjoying it.

'That poor little Naomi. I can't get my mind off her. What do you think's happened to her, Lady Cunningham-Smythe?' Chrissy's own household was full of her own grandchildren, abandoned to her by her feckless daughter and she had never even seemed particularly interested in them, let alone in my grandchild. Now you would think Naomi was her favourite child in the world.

'And I was only saying to my ex when he came around for a loan, how could a grandmother go into the toilet and leave a little kiddie standing outside with all these paedophiles roaming the countryside?'

I pulled my eiderdown over my head but her voice kept on coming through.

'And the only thing the police seem to care about these days, is giving you a number so you can collect insurance, though I can't imagine what good that would do when it's a child that's been taken..'

'Shut up, Chrissy.'

'And it's happening everywhere. Even in the best of families. There's been some chap poking around after that grandson of Lady Delane, for instance—' Lady Delane is my friend, Janine. How I regretted ever having recommended Chrissy to her. In those days I had not fully appreciated Chrissy's lack of cleaning skills. Her voice went burbling on. She had worked for me for so long that usually I could blot her out, but since the loss of Naomi my nerves were so shriekingly on edge, that I seemed to have lost the knack. '—Anyway, here's your lunch, Lady Cunningham-Smythe. I've done you a nice sausage and some mash à la Chrissy.' False French was one of her pretensions.'

'Take it away. I couldn't eat a thing.'

'Have a look. I know you'll like it.'

I gave the plate a glance, just to shut her up. 'That's disgusting,' I said. She was giggling now. She had arranged the sausage and the two tomatoes on the form of male genitals.

'I thought it might cheer you up,' she said.

She went in for this kind of smut. I never laughed, but it never stopped her either, I suppose because Jack had found this kind of thing funny.

I could hear through the eiderdown the cutlery clatter, the chair creak and Chrissy grunt as she sat on the chair by my bed, tray on her lap. I had a peep and, yes, there she was, and probably would remain for hours. Once she sat you were absolutely lost. Her hair was bright purple today and she wore large imitation gold hoop earrings. She knows perfectly well I don't like it, but she carries on as though we are a couple of friends, though now it was friends engaged in a quarrel..

'And did you know that that little Melanie's been nabbed? Naomi's not the only one.'

I got a shock when she said that. I knew Melanie's mother, Barbara Lovedale. She was an artist, and I had been to several of her exhibitions. I said, 'Please go away, Chrissy. I want to be alone.' I could not bear to hear anymore.

Ignoring this she went on, 'You know. That friend of Lady Delane. She gave me a reference and I cleaned her house for a bit.'

'Please shut up.'

Ignoring me completely, as though I had not spoken, she went blathering on, 'It's the paedophiles. They're everywhere these days.'

Chrissy knows all my friends. She made a point of it long ago and then managed to worm her way into all their households.

'Do stop, Chrissy. You are giving me a headache.'

Chrissy first came to work for me and Jack twenty years ago.

She had arrived to be interviewed dressed so brightly it made my eyes wince.

Although she was probably, even then, well into her fifties, her dress plunged so low that you could almost see her navel. Her crimson lipstick had been applied a little wider than her lips as though she was trying to achieve a pout. The smell of her scent was so strong that it lingered in the room for a week after she had gone.

'My goodness,' I said to Jack, when she had gone.

'I thought she was hilarious,' Jack said and burst out laughing. 'The only reason she wants to work for us is because we are titled. Can you imagine admitting such a thing?' And because I liked his laughter, because in spite of myself I had found Chrissy rather funny too, we let her stay. Her gaudy clothes, violent makeup, the extraordinary colours of her dyed hair and the way she leapt round the house in a parody of a dancer, doing a parody of cleaning made us laugh. We had continued to be amused by her, so she had stayed on. Somehow after Jack died, though, all that changed. I could no longer see the joke. Instead I just began to wish she would go away and stop reminding me of what I had lost.

Now I began to pretend to eat the lunch, making chomping sounds with my teeth and clattering my fork while she went springing round the room doing what she called 'a tidy'.

'No, leave that. Don't go in there,' I shouted, spilling a forkful of mash down the front of my night dress. Chrissy was opening the drawer in which I kept the sweet wrapped pills. She had drawer open now.

'Please shut that. Those are my private things.'

'And as I was telling you, there was this person in a black knitted cap, just staring over the fence at Lady Delane's grandson ... Oh, look at all those sweeties, and the poor little Naomi snatched away by a paedophile and you unable to give them to her.'

'Put them back,' I told her, trying to sound furious, not flustered. Thank goodness her mind was so taken up with the kidnap, that for once she did as I asked, though going on, 'And what could you have been thinking of, Lady Cunningham-Smythe, giving a kiddie so many sweeties. Haven't you heard of the danger of sugar to children's teeth?'

After she had gone from the room, I sat, filled with urgency. I must do something fast, for soon they would find my pills and then I would have no escape but would be trapped here while in some other no time no place, Jack slowly ebbed away. I might live on for years and die of pneumonia, or heart attack, or stroke and by then Jack would be lost forever. I would never find him again. I would never see him any more. Oh, Jack. Oh, Jack. Oh, Naomi. These meddling people would keep me on, alive, pointless and miserable and I would never get away from them. I threw the tray off with a jerk of my knees and felt a small satisfaction as the chops and new potatoes went bouncing onto the floor.

M'buta had fallen to bits completely. A dead look had come into her eyes. She walked with rounded shoulders.

'Why don't you go and talk to that religious friend of yours, David?' I suggested.

'Daniel,' she corrected me.

'You said he performs miracles.' I was going to add, 'Needs must where the devil drives,' but the words seemed inappropriate. Instead I said, 'I think that this is a time when all of us should take what comfort we can. And shut the curtains when you go out. I can't bear all this light.'

'I don't know what even he can do.' She ignored my request for the curtains to be shut.

'The police don't seem to be able to do anything, so why not give him a try.' Fancy me talking to her like this. Until two days ago it had been completely the other way round, her trying to persuade me to see the fellow and be healed and comforted by him and me scornfully dismissing the idea.

'I might,' she said. 'It's worth a try. Thank you, Ladyma.' As she was going out she turned back and said, 'I'm sorry I shouted at you.'

I began to wonder if I could contact Naomi with my mind. After all had I not often suspected of her able to read my mind?

And I knew it was possible for, when Jack was alive, often things happened which made it seem as though we were doing it. Once, while I was shopping, I got the sudden feeling that he was in trouble and, dumping my loaded shopping basket without even going through checkout, I dashed home. I could run then. It was before my blood pressure and arthritis.

Jack was standing in the kitchen, his thumb outstretched and bleeding. He had been trying to open a tin of stewed steak for Gump and cut himself on the tin. And that was not the only time. There was that terrible day when he lost his memory. It started with Jack getting himself locked out. I know that is the sort of thing that people often do, but not Jack. Until then it had been me who was muddly and forgetful. I had found him waiting by the front door in the pouring rain and worked out that he had been there for an hour. A week or so later he began to fumble for perfectly ordinary words like 'butter' or 'garden'.

The day he lost his memory absolutely, I was on the train to London. Verity had employed a nanny and decided to leave the young woman in charge of Naomi so that she and M'buta come too. I needed to do a little shopping. Fortnum and Masons is the only place where you can get a decent smoked oyster and properly prepared marron glace. Jack was not coming because he was not keen on London.

We decided to go by train because of the impossibility of parking. We were only into the journey for ten minutes when the feeling that something was dreadfully wrong with Jack swept over me. 'I'm getting off at the next station,' I told Verity. 'Something has happened to your father.'

'Don't be so silly, Mother. You're always getting those feelings. Of course he's OK and I spent a fortune on the train tickets.'

I would not listen to her. I leapt from the train at the first chance and took a taxi home. Jack was lying on the bathroom floor. His eyes were open but he seemed not to recognise me. He never recognised me again.

After he died, I began to try to communicate with him, hoping that death would have restored his memory. I would attempt to force my mind on his, then pause, keeping my spirit open in case his had a chance to pour his into it. But perhaps the gulf between the living and the dead is too great, for nothing ever happened.

But it might be different with Naomi. There was no reason at all, in spite of Verity's gigantic grief, to suppose that she was dead.

You have to imagine your mind as a long and luminous rod along which to project your thoughts. 'Naomi, Naomi, can you hear me?' One of the last things she had said to me, as we went into the ladies' loo was, 'You are the only person who loves me now that the baby is here.'

I tried it out myself now. In my mind I said something I had never said aloud. 'I love you, Naomi.' I did this over and over and once or twice imagined that a strange little wind like a whisper had murmured, 'I am here, Grandma. I am alive, Grandma. I love you, Grandma.' I knew I was deceiving myself but all the same it gave a small comfort.

In bed I began to lie awake, trying to caress my lost granddaughter with my mind and several more times I would think that I heard her tiny, far away voice calling me. I would fall asleep feeling hopeful and comforted, but when I woke I would tell myself I had probably been dreaming and imagined the voice in the night. All the same, because the little voice seemed to be saying, 'I am here, I am here,' I went on trying with my mind to find out where 'here' was. There must be a 'here' for Naomi. Spike Milligan once said 'Everyone has to be somewhere'.

I began to think up all the possibilities where that place could be. Of all the people she might be with. Of all the men who might have taken her. It did not seem like the kidnap of a pretty child by a prowling paedophile, no matter what Chrissy thought. If the police were right in thinking there was a connection between the intruder who tried to grab her and the person who had taken her from the service station, then this was someone who was hunting Naomi in particular.

Then there was the case of Melanie Lovedale. She was the same age as Naomi and had been kidnapped at around the same time. Was there a connection between the two of them? What connection? Was Melanie the result of AI like Naomi? In the back of my mind, I remembered someone commenting on how Melanie had not taken after her father in the least. The father idea again? The man whose sperm had been used, finding out which were his children, and snatching them back again. But how could he know which they were, for were not the identities of people connected with AI always kept secret? But from what I'd seen of the Bereton Clinic, nothing was secret there. Anyone could have found out anything.

All the same, why grab the children? For all he knew, the mothers might have allowed him access anyway, yet he had never even approached Verity. If a man had turned up saying he was Naomi's father and asked to be allowed to meet his child, Verity would probably have said 'yes'. Unless, of course, there was something wrong with the man. What sort of thing? He was a criminal? A drug addict? Suffering from some disease or deformity which did not show up in the photo? Of course I was not even certain that Melanie had been conceived in the same way as Naomi.

More questions came to mind. Then there was the odd thing about Naomi's colouring. Verity had chosen a black man, yet the child had turned out utterly blonde. And Melanie was blonde too. Perhaps the same thing had happened to Barbara

Lovedale, as had happened to Verity. The wrong sperm had been used on her. And to avoid a scandal, the Bereton was trying to steal back the children so as to hush it up. Very unlikely indeed, I decided.

Or was the father someone known to the two mothers? Someone the mothers had quarrelled with perhaps. There had been that man called Don with whom Verity had had a short affair. Could it be him? Had she been having an affair after all? Had the mother of Melanie had an affair with the same man as Verity?

Chrissy kept going on about my friend, Janine's, grandson, but the man lurking there must be something different altogether. There was no way the little boy could have any connection with the clinic, if my theory was correct, because Jeremy Delane was his father. No, it was just the two little girls.

But then another connection sprang into my mind. Chrissy. She worked for me as well as for Janine. And she had once worked at the Bereton Clinic. I remembered her telling Verity when she was recommending the Bereton, that a lot of other well-to-do and well connected people used it too. I suddenly felt sure she had mentioned Barbara Lovedale, Melanie's mother.

So Chrissy was connected with all three mothers. Was someone in Chrissy's family a child abductor? Using children for sex reasons? To get a ransom? I knew hers was a dysfunctional people and that sons and son-in-laws had all got prison records.

This is silly and far-fetched, I told myself. But all the same, because I could not bear to abandon any idea at all that might lead me to Naomi, I did not drop it.

Then another idea came to me. Chrissy had said something which I had not properly taken in at the time, but I now saw might be a connection. She had said that Lady Delane's grandson was being watched by a man in a black knitted hat. And Naomi had said she had seen someone in a hat like that at the service station. And the person who had broken into my house and tried to grab Naomi had worn something black and woolly that could easily had been such a hat pulled down over his face. Where do you buy hats like that? Perhaps someone should go and ask around the shops. Silly idea, I knew at once. Lots of people wore those hats. The shops were full of them.

All the same, the next time Verity rushed in, weeping, I was about to suggest she went to Chrissy's home and find out if anyone there wore a black knitted hat. I quickly stopped myself. Verity was in such a state that she would probably burst upon the Chrissy household, accusing them right left and centre of child abuse, kidnapping, anything.

'M'buta says you would like to meet Daniel,' she said.

'No, I didn't. I told her she should talk to him if it gave her comfort,' I said indignantly.

Verity sat down heavily on the side of my bed and let out a sigh of despair. 'We must do something,' she said. A sob filled her throat so that she could not go on for a while. At last she said in a choking voice, 'It may help. Daniel may be able to do something. We should try everything. M'buta says he has miraculous talents.' And you are the last person to see Naomi...

I imagined joss sticks, chanting, ludicrous hand holdings. 'Don't pester me,' I said crossly, then felt guilty and reluctantly agreed to see the fellow. Anything that gave her, gave any of us, comfort, should not be rejected.

'She wants to take you on Tuesday,' Verity said. 'I bet we will have found her by then, but just in case..' I could see she was going to weep again.

'But you always keep Tuesday free,' I said trying to keep the panic out of my voice.

Verity burst out crying in earnest.

'Well I can't possibly come on Tuesday,' I said, trying to hide my rising panic. 'I have an appointment on that day.'

'Of course you haven't. I looked up in your diary. There's the doctor on Monday, the chiropodist on Friday and the dentist is going to mend your dentures the same afternoon. There's nothing for Tuesday at all.'

'Look, Verity, I know you are sad, but I won't be pushed around. I am not going on Tuesday and that's that. I'm not at all keen on seeing him anyway.'

She looked at me with sorrowful bitterness. 'M'buta also says he is a medium and can connect the living with the—' She fell silent and hung her head. A tear fell onto my eiderdown. When she was able to speak again she said, 'I know you have done things like that before, after Dad died, and didn't think much of it, but M'buta promises that this man is different.'

The medium I had gone to had been a stout lady wearing ethnic clothes and a lot of necklaces, who, after lighting some candles and burning incense, leant back and showing the whites of her eyes, began muttering in a gruff voice that, I suppose, was meant to be Jack's, saying how he loved me and had only gone ahead but was not lost forever. She had said, suddenly, 'Give the little white dog a hug from me, darling,' and though I wondered briefly why Jack had said, 'the dog' and not call him 'Gump', and wondered at the oddness of Jack calling me darling, I had been quite taken in till I got outside and saw that I had little white dog hairs on the bosom of my jersey.

After Verity had gone I lay feeling restless. I needed something to take my mind off. An idea came to me. Perhaps I would go to Chrissy's home. See for myself if any of her family looked like child molesters. Or if I could see a black knitted hat. I knew it was stupid, that I would find nothing, that if I had any evidence like this I should tell the police. I had nothing but a wild feeling that this was a possibility.

I knew her address.

I got out of bed, pulled on my clothes. I felt very weak and dizzy and every joint was agony with the arthritis, but at least I felt I was doing something, instead of just waiting and worrying.

Though Chrissy had worked for me and Jack for so long, and though she was forever describing her household and her home, I had never been there.

I got out the local map and found the road where she lived. It was the other side of the town on a well known slum estate. Because of my cataracts I am forbidden to drive but normally would have asked either M'buta or Verity to take me. This was not a normal situation, however. And it was not a normal visit. I realised, gloomily, that I would have to go by bus.

It was not a long journey but not a pleasant one either. The bus floor was littered with rubbish. There was a half eaten bun that kept rolling onto my shoe each time the bus did a turn. Someone had written Fuck Tracey, into the glass of the window. They must have used a diamond ring to groove the glass, I thought, and reflected on the oddness of the present culture where a vandal could afford a diamond ring.

As I approached Chrissy's address, the patches in front of the row of houses, you could not call them gardens, were piled with tangled junk out of which sprouted rank weeds. Chrissy's house, when I arrived, was the worst of the lot. Thank goodness it was just by the bus stop so I did not have to walk far.

Her garden was one of the most chaotic too. I squeezed my way through old mattresses, chucked out TV sets and a huge crate of empty gin bottles. Gummy nosed children trundled on trikes up and down the front path. Tattered washing flew from a crooked line. Scrawny hedges had trapped waste paper. Old tins and bags lay tossed over bare earth and worn grass. A burst of burnt food smell surged out of an open window. A man and woman were having an enormous row in some upper room, a row punctuated by the sound of crashes as though china was being hurled, then whacking sounds as though bodies were being struck. A child in a dirty t shirt opened the door after I had knocked and let me in.

In the hall were a couple of lads working on an upturned motor bike. Around them spread pools of black oil and rusty bike bits. They sprang up, saying, 'We bought it, honest we did. We didn't nick it or nothing.'

There seemed to be two TVs both on, full blast, in different parts of the house. More sticky looking children emerged from doorways and stared entranced at the sight of me. They seemed unperturbed by the clamour.

Chrissy emerged looking as glamorous and colourful as ever, like a bright bird on a rubbish heap. A cigarette dangled from her mouth. She looked amazed to see me.

'Ah, God. I thought it was the man from the pub, pestering me to pay him for the TV.'

'Is there somewhere we can talk?' I said.

She looked doubtful. The place rang with a roar of voices and TVs. 'I suppose we could try the kitchen,' she said. She led me in. It looked more like a store room than a kitchen. I wondered how long it was since anyone had cooked in here. Chrissy herself looked around as if the environment was unfamiliar to her. She pulled a heap of anonymous possessions, toys, hair tongs, several pairs of very high heeled shoes, a large blonde wig, several packs of cigarettes and tins of beer from one of the chairs and invited me to sit. 'A gin and lemon, Lady Cunningham-Smythe?' she asked, in the tone of one who is meeting me for the first time. You might have thought the pair of us were at a smart cocktail party, not in a chaotic and non-functional kitchen.

Now I was here, I didn't know what exactly to ask nor, to be honest, knew exactly what I was looking for. 'Are any of your family connected with the sexual trade in children?' seemed hardly possible. In the end I just said lamely, 'I have come for find out a bit more about the man who has been spying on Lady Delane's grandson,' 'Just in case it's the same person who has got Naomi.'

Usually she was over enthusiastic to pour out every bit of information about absolutely every single person she could, especially if they were titled, but this question seemed to silence her. She mumbled something vague about never having seen the person herself and how Lady Delane hadn't told her much either, which was not at all what she had said to me earlier. Ha, I thought, she is clearly hiding something. I was right. She is involved in some way with all this.

All the time my eyes were flicking about, looking for glimpse of a black woolly hat.

A child trundled past the window with something black on its head, but it turned out to be only a bit of dustbin liner. Why on earth would a child wear a dustbin liner on its head to ride a tricycle? Chrissy, following my glance, said, 'He fell off this morning and cut himself but I couldn't find a plaster.'

Stalling for time, I asked, 'Have you got Janine – Lady Delane's – son's phone number?' Janine had sometimes asked Chrissy to go and help out with her son's cleaning. 'I'll ring him and ask how to get there.' A flash of panic crossed Chrissy's face. Subdued in a moment, but I saw it.

'I'll have a look,' she said and began to dive among piles of every kind of paper from newspapers to paper bags, amongst which it seemed unlikely one would find, or there could even be a phone number.

'Chrissy, tell me about the Bereton Clinic,' I said at last.

She stared at me. 'Bereton Clinic?' she said as though she had never heard of the place.

'Yes,' I said fiercely. 'And no good putting on that air of silly innocence.' God, I hated the woman. 'I wish you to tell me, this instant, why you stopped working there.'

'Ah. Uh.' She stared with her mouth open.

'You were sacked, weren't you?'

'No,' she said.

'I know. I have found out.' Sometimes it is necessary, in a situation of emergency, to dispense with truth. 'I have spoken to them.'

'My son said I should have taken a case against them for unfair dismissal. And they never managed to prove that I'd done it ... '

Ah, I thought, and asked her before it was too late. 'A bribe? The fathers tried to bribe you?' I imagined a man winkling out of Chrissy the address of the woman who had been inseminated with his sperm.

She flushed violently. 'Sperm donors,' she said. She added, 'No. Anyway, you never meet them.' She flushed as though was untrue.

I decided to try a change of tack. Put her off the scent, so to speak. 'What sort of people are they? Mostly broke young students, I imagine.'

'Oh it's all very discreet.,' she said swiftly. Too swiftly.

'Really? Why should it matter?'

She shrugged. 'In case they try to bribe you – you know – they don't want any kind of mix up with the sperm. That sort of thing makes the clients sue. I had people threatening to kill me after I was accused. Not that I did it, of course.'

'Threatening to kill you?' I stared at her, amazed. 'What sort of people?'

'Two women. They said if I told any one I would die.'

'Told anyone what?'

'That I'd fiddled the samples. I didn't do it. I swear I didn't. It was absolutely untrue.'

'But someone else paid you to?'

She stared at me with a sudden horror. 'I shouldn't have said nothing, Lady Cunningham-Smythe. If you tell anyone about this they'll come for me. I know they will. They looked very murderous people.'

I was unable to get another word out of her. She had realised, too late, that she had said too much and shut up like a clam.

I left thinking that someone must be paying Chrissy fairly substantial sums of money still, for though it was clear no one in her household was earning much, yet Chrissy's clothes, jewels and hair do, though vulgar, looked expensive. Cleaning houses doesn't let anyone earn like this. Were these murderous women paying her for her silence? What on earth could be? Was it possible they were mothers who did not want it to be known that their babies had been born by AI? But from what Chrissy had told me it sounded as though it was something to do with Chrissy switching sperm that they wanted kept quiet. Why on earth?

As I walked away back down the vile little path, I looked back. Chrissy was watching me from her living room window. She still looked scared.

CHAPTER 4

I REACHED HOME AT LAST FEELING EXHAUSTED, ill and gloomy. I was reluctant to ring Janine and find the phone number for her son, though before all this she and I had loved a good chat on the phone. But I had to brace myself, for I must not let the smallest chance of finding Naomi be missed. It was my fault she was gone and now a great responsibility rested on me to find her.

I needed to recover from that terrible bus journey first so closed my curtains, then took out my bottle of whisky and poured myself a drink. I like it neat. I enjoy the scalding stab as it hits the throat so never dilute it with all those prissy sodas. Jack had always loved malt whisky but it was only after he died that I took to it too. Before that sherry was my tipple. Until he became ill, he and I would sit side by side on the sofa, sipping our respective drinks before our supper.

When we were blended, I wondered, would we burn with a light twice as bright because of all those drinks? What ridiculous nonsense I told myself, but liked the idea all the same. And when you look at it, there's only one truth about a future after death. If you like it, choose to believe in it. If you don't, discard it. There is no one, as far as I know, who can prove you right or wrong.

Once Verity had come with me to my doctor and told him about the whisky. 'I'm sure it's not good for her. Could you please advise her to give it up.'

'Do you yourself feel it's doing you any harm, Lady Cunningham-Smythe?' he had asked. He is a very good doctor. I can never fault him.

'Far from it,' I said. 'I find it very soothing and would recommend it to anyone whose nerves are jangled.' I paused then added, though I knew it was irrelevant, 'also my husband liked it.'

'No ill effects?' he smiled.

'Oh no,' I assured him. 'I never even get a headache next morning, these days.'

'I see,' he said. Later Verity told me that the reason for this is not increased tolerance to whisky but a shrinkage of the brain due to old age.

'Absolute rubbish,' I told her. 'You want to put a stop to anything that gives me pleasure.'

Now I lay on my bed and took the first scalding sip. I rolled it round my lips till they stung. I slithered it slowly down my throat till it burnt. Ah, lovely. Rip, scald, wallop. A couple of glasses of this and I would find the energy to phone Janine.

Before Jack died, Janine and I would phone each other all the time. We would have lunch together about once a fortnight. Once or twice we got quite giggly on champagne. Jack had teased us about our friendship, saying we were too old to behave like a couple of schoolgirls. We didn't mind. Sometimes you need to throw away all dignity, no matter how old you are. But after he died, just when you would think I needed a friend more than anything, I lost all desire to talk to her or anyone.

We had been friends since school. Chuckle St William had been very posh and attended only by girls of the most ancient and glamorous ancestry, though there was only one other girl there who was as aristocratic as Janine and who, like her, was titled in her own right and that person was not me. I had lost touch with the second titled girl years ago. I think she married an Australian. She might even be dead by now or a grandmother like myself. The thought of grandchildren caused me to gulp down a chokingly large swallow of whisky.

Anyway, when I married Jack and got a title for myself, Janine brought out a bottle of champagne to celebrate my having caught up with her. We got awfully drunk that night. Champagne always has a very bad effect on me. I'm better on whisky.

After Jack died, Janine had tried several times to get me to come and have a meal with her. In the end she gave up. You can't go on and on. But now, after all this time, I needed to talk to her.

It took me about an hour, hovering round the phone before I felt strong enough to manage the call.

'Arabellaaa,' she cried when she heard my voice. 'Darling, what a long time. Are we going to meet, then?' She always dragged out my name so that it sounded like the name of an illness or a horticultural specimen.

'I need Jeremy's phone number,' I told her bleakly.

'Jeremy?' She sounded disappointed. 'OK.'

'Please give it to me.'

'And we must get together, dear. Soon, soon.' she said when I had got the number down. 'Let's lunch at Fortnums and you can tell me all about it.' There was pleading in her tone.

CHAPTER 5

I HAD TO GO TO JEREMY'S COTTAGE BY BUS AGAIN. How I wished they would hurry up and get my cataract operation done. I had been on the waiting list for ages, in fact the way things were would probably be on it forever.

'The waiting list is very long, I'm afraid, Arabella,' chit of a girl at the Eye Hospital had told me.

'Since you are a stranger to me,' I had responded with dignified indignation, if such a combination is possible. 'And are considerably younger than myself, I would like to be addressed as Lady Cunningham-Smythe, not Arabella.'

Her apology was unconvincing. She addressed me by my proper name and title from then on, though rather more often that I thought usual or necessary and I detected a hint of mockery in her tone.

'Look, my need is probably a great deal more urgent than a lot of other people on that list,' I told her. 'Unless I can drive I am absolutely stranded.'

'Can't you use public transport?' she asked. Underlying her question I could hear 'like other people'.

'If that was so wonderful then why do you see so many cars?' I asked savagely. 'For instance do you have a car?'

She shut the appointments book and said, without looking up, 'I will see what I can do.'

Afterwards, Verity, who had accompanied me to the hospital, told me I had been silly to antagonise them and that now I would probably be put as low down the bottom of the list as they could get me.

Clearly, because of my age they did not bother at all and probably even had never planned to the operation anyway, but were only stringing me along hoping I'd die soon. Which of course, I suddenly remembered, is exactly what I planned to do anyway. But all the same it would have been pleasant if I could have driven to Jeremy Delane's, instead of going by bus.

I had not realised that he lived quite so far out. The driver told me when to get off and pointed out the post office to me, telling me that they would be able to give me directions to the Delane house.

Horrifyingly, Jeremy's cottage was at the end of a long muddy lane and there was apparently no taxi nor other available transport in the village. According to the post mistress there was only a single taxi and the driver owner was on holiday. I had to walk. Well, hobble. I ploughed through mud, doing my blood pressure and my arthritis enormous damage, I had no doubt. I stopped to take my heart rate before reaching the cottage and found that it was going at double pace.

I arrived at last, half dead as you may imagine. A large hedge surrounded the garden and through it I could see Jeremy and his son Freddy digging at the far end of the garden.

I stopped outside the gate, realising I should have phoned first. I had to gear myself up so hard to do this journey at all, that I realised now that I had forgotten to do it. I stood, wondering, now that I had taken all this trouble to get here, what I had come for. At the time I had had such a clear idea that there might be some connection between the abduction of Naomi and the man who spied on the Delane child. Now the link seemed tenuous and silly.

The pair looked up. The little boy screamed, 'The horrid man's there again, Daddy,' and rushed to cower behind his father's legs.

Jeremy Delane let out a roar and jerking his spade out of the soil, came marching over to the hedge, clumps of earth and worms falling from it. He kept the spade raised threateningly in the air, as though he was going to bash me with it when he reached me.

'It's only me – Lady Cunningham-Smythe,' I cried, my voice coming out very shrill and quavery. Really, at my age and in my state of health I should not be exposed to all these strains and shocks. 'Aunt Arabella,' I corrected as I raised my hands in the air, like someone threatened with shooting in an American thriller movie. Jeremy let out a laugh and, lowering the spade, turned and called to his son, who by now had crouched behind a large calabrese.

'Come on, Freddie. It's not the man. You can come out from there.' He turned to me and said graciously, 'I do beg your pardon, Aunty Arabella. A man has been peeping into the garden and giving Freddie nightmares.'

I crept cautiously into the open.

'Freddie, come out,' Jeremy called. 'It's Aunty Arabella,' and to me he said, 'His mother only died six months ago and he's been very nervous since. And there's a man who keeps spying on him.'

'I know,' I told him. 'Chrissy who cleans for me as well as your mother, told me and that's what I want to talk to you about.'

'But come in, come in,' cried Jeremy, suddenly seeing the state I was in. 'You look exhausted.'

Freddy emerged and the three of us went inside, to a comfy little kitchen in which things hummed and ticked and there was a good smell of baking. 'I try to keep things like they were when my wife was alive,' he said. 'To make Freddy feel more secure.'

'It must be difficult,' I said.

He nodded. 'Sometimes it seems impossible. I'm no cook, for a start, and Sue was a brilliant one. Oh, that reminds me—' He dashed to the oven and snatched out a tray of biscuits that had already begun to burn. 'See what I mean.'

'Dad does a lot of burning,' Freddy said. He and his father began to laugh.

'I'll put on the kettle and make you a cup of tea. I can't go wrong there,' said Jeremy. 'Anyway, thank goodness Freddy is a good cook.' He poured the water into the tea pot. 'He's only four and already knows how to fry an egg. The other day he baked a little cake. It was quite hard, but—' He smiled softly.

Only four and can fry an egg, I thought. He must be more grown-up than most four year olds then. But so was Naomi.

Freddy went off to watch TV and when he was gone, Jeremy said, 'The police were round here, asking for a description of the prying man and told me about your granddaughter, Naomi. They think there may be a connection. I didn't want to say anything in front of Freddy, because he's frightened enough already, but have you heard anything?'

I shook my head. 'Not a thing.'

'I wish I could help, but, as I told the police, I doubt that the fellow is of any importance at all. I mean, you can see how we live. Far from anywhere. And people walking along the lane often stop and look into our garden, because it's the only house in the lane. And, without wishing to be boastful, I think I have created a beautiful garden, so even this man is probably only looking at that. In fact, it's only because Freddy is so terrified of this particular man that I paid any attention. I shouted at the fellow the last time I saw him hanging about and told him to go away because he was frightening my son. But he went on doing it. I thought perhaps he might be a little bit mentally handicapped or something. But you can't stop people from standing on the road. That's what Sue used to say, when people came and peered at us when we were sitting in the garden in the summer ... '

'When did this man first start coming?' I asked.

'Just after Sue died. At first I tried pretend there was nothing alarming about the fellow and when he came, would tell Freddy, 'That's such a silly man. He'll catch a cold standing out there doing nothing. He ought to be planting beans like us, shouldn't he, Freddy? Not just loafing lazily around like that. At first Freddy was not too frightened and once, at the beginning, even called out, 'Man, man, you'll catch a cold,' but the man did not stir. I think that was the thing about him that frightened Freddy. His silence and his stillness.'

'Why didn't you report this man to the police?' I asked.

'I did,' said Jeremy. 'But my description of a tallish man did not go down very well. Even the fact he wore a black woolly hat in the middle of summer did not seem to impress them. Anyway, they said, it's a public road and anyone who wants to can stand there.'

A black woolly hat?' Could this be a coincidence?

'You couldn't see his face properly,' Jeremy was saying, 'because he pulled the hat down over it. That was the other thing about him that frightened Freddy. His face being nearly blacked out.'

'I'm afraid we can't take any action unless a crime is committed,' the sergeant had said. 'We will take down his description, though, and keep it on file in case some crime is committed in the future.'

'Hopeless' I murmured sympathetically. 'Is there anyone you can think of who might be spying on you?'

Jeremy went on, 'Sue's sister. She emigrated to Australia, got married there and now has four children. After Sue died, the sister sent a message saying that she was looking forward to having Freddy coming to live with her. When, in the end, I refused to let him go, she arrived here and said she had a right to him and had come to claim him.'

'To claim Freddy? But on what grounds?'

He answered reluctantly. 'She said Freddy was her sister's child and that he should be brought up by his own family.'

'What did she mean by that, Jeremy? It sounds as though she is implying that you are not his family.'

He looked alarmed and embarrassed for a moment then said, 'Oh, nothing. She was in a temper and saying any hurtful thing she could think of. Probably she had taken my refusing to let her take Freddy as a personal insult. As if I implied she would not be a good enough mother.' The way he said this made me think there was something more he was not telling me. He added, 'Freddy still misses his mother terribly.'

'Tell me about Sue,' I said, remembering how, after Jack died I longed to talk about him and how people seemed to avoid the subject as though if they did not mention Jack I would not think about him.

'Breast cancer had raged through her body faster than the doctors could assure us that they had it under control,' Jeremy told me. Apparently the dice had been thrown against them every step of the way. A lump that the doctors were certain that was benign but had turned out to be malignant. A very slow-growing, non-invasive cancer, they had said, but it had grown fast and invaded. A cancer that responds well to chemo, but it had not responded at all. 'A total mastectomy will almost certainly give her many more years, for the cancer has not spread.' By the time the mastectomy was performed the cancer had spread already.

'I was in the army, but resigned so that I could look after Sue. Freddy became angry and difficult as his mother ebbed painfully out of his life. He took to smashing things, hurling the cup he drank from against the wall, hammering his toys against the window. I missed the army and my soldier friends, particularly Bernard, but there was nothing I could do.'

'Who is Bernard?'

'A fellow soldier. When Bernard and I were serving in Iraq, Bernard was seriously wounded and could not walk. We hid in an abandoned cellar for a week and each night I would creep out and try to find food and water. In the end I managed to get Bernard out and carry him back to where our regiment was stationed. Bernard recovered and we have been close friends ever since.' Jeremy looked sad. I could hear a little envy mixed with longing in his voice as he added, 'Bernard is back with the regiment.'

'It must be difficult for you, bringing up a child on your own,' I said. 'Wouldn't it have been better to let Freddy go and live with Sue's sister?'

Jeremy sighed. 'That's what I thought at first. When she said, "I've got four already so one more will make no difference," I admit I felt worried. I wanted Freddy to make a difference. But all the same I agreed to let Freddy go, for after all Freddy's happiness was the most important thing. But then Bernard came to stay and was shocked at my decision. He said, 'Being the outsider in your sister's family will make Freddy feel more troubled, not less. He will feel he has been abandoned by both parents, not just one.' I told Bernard I couldn't find a job and he suggested I taught shooting. I had been the crack shot of the regiment. So I told Sue's sister I had decided to keep Freddy, found this cottage, near a shooting range and that's where I work now. My hours fit in well with Freddy's schooling. Sue's sister was furious.'

'Aren't you lonely here, with only a small child for company?'

'At first I was but lately I have started to enjoy the peace. Freddy is calming down and is becoming good company. He's very grown-up for his age, sometimes almost like a little adult. He's a lovely little boy.'

'And a beautiful looking child too,' I smiled. 'Where did he get those blue eyes and blonde hair from?' Sue and Jeremy both had brown hair and eyes.

'Odd, isn't it?' said Jeremy. I thought he looked slightly anxious. Then he went on, 'But I am going on and on about me and you are here with your terrible trouble. The poor little girl. You must all be wild with worry. '

Before I could say anything, Freddy came rushing in saying his programme was finished, he wanted to go on with his digging, but was afraid to go into the garden alone because of the man. We went out with the boy. This time Jeremy took his gun.

The child had started digging, when a robin suddenly flew out of a bush and settled on his head. I was about to express my delight when Jeremy reached out his hand and smacked the little bird away. It rushed off in a flutter of panicky feathers, but stopped a short distance away, and seemed about to try to return to Freddy's head. Jeremy raised his spade as if he would smash the bird into the ground if it came any closer. The bird, as though it read his intentions, wisely stayed where it was. Freddy said, 'Lucky it was only one,' and went back to his digging.

I looked at Jeremy questioningly. He said, 'We have a bit of a problem with birds, you see.' He paused. I waited. He went on, 'Uhm ... Freddy ... is ... you see ... ' He seemed to be searching his mind for a suitable lie. 'He's allergic to feathers.' He added, 'They tend to get on him.'

The child suddenly screamed and pointed at the hedge. 'That really is the man,' he whispered.

'Come on, son,' said Jeremy. 'You mustn't get frightened every time anyone looks through our hedge. Remember how it was only Aunty Arabella the last time.'

But Freddy was still staring, quivering. 'It's him. I know it's him.'

Jeremy squatted down and peered too. 'I do believe it is,' he said angrily. He grabbed his gun and went striding towards the hedge.

By the time Jeremy reached the gate, the man had started walking away. Freddy was still trembling, his face ashen.

Jeremy rushed out and went after the man, his footsteps smacking in the mud.

Freddy began to cry.

There came the sound of a shot followed by a short yelp.

Freddy started screaming, 'He's killed my Daddy. My Daddy's dead.'

'Your daddy must have fired the gun,' I tried to reassure the child. 'He will be coming back at any moment, so stop crying.' The child screamed on as though I had not spoken.

Long minutes ticked by, broken only by the sounds of the child's fear and sorrow and the banging of my heart. Suppose Freddy was right and the man had killed Jeremy. Then, at any moment the murderer would come back here and, what? Kill us? Try to grab the child as Naomi had been grabbed? I would have picked up the child, rushed him into the house and hidden him there if it had not been for my arthritis. But as it was, the best I could think of was ordering Freddy to get behind the rhubarb. The child was not very well hidden, but what else could I do?

Verity had bought me a mobile phone. 'One of these days you'll have a fall or something and you need to be able to dial 999 wherever you are.' It was somewhere in the bottom of my bag at this moment and if I could have, I would have taken it out now and rung the police. On the long bus journey here I had, in fact, tried to work out how to turn it on. But had put it back after a short while of tinkering with buttons which did not seem to reveal anything useful. Anyway, I had thought at the time, since I won't be alive much longer, what's the point of training myself in something so complicated and which was there to save my life, whereas I was determined to lose it. I felt in my bag for it now but it was only a token gesture. This was not the moment to learn how to use the machine.

It must have been at least ten minutes since Jeremy went racing off.

An age seemed to pass. Jeremy still did not come back. He was dead. It must be that. I would have to cope alone somehow.

The child went on weeping and gasping behind the rhubarb.

Then came the sound of running footsteps on the road. The fellow was approaching. It seemed as though, for the second time in a couple of weeks I was to be required to tackle a man and this time I did not even have any violet scented face powder. I saw, near by, an open bag of garden lime. A whole sackful, not just a little pot of it like the powder. I plunged my hands in and was about to seize a handful and throw when Jeremy burst upon us, panting, gun in hand.

'Oi, oi,' he shouted, seeing as I raised my arms to hurl. I put the lime back, with relief.

'I think I winged the bastard,' he laughed. 'I've been searching among the bushes in case he's lying there, wounded. Come on, Freddy. I can see you perfectly well.'

Freddy burst out of his hiding place and rushed, sobbing, into his father's arms.

When Jeremy had at last managed to calm the little boy I asked, 'What happened?

'I saw something moving inside one of the big stands of hawthorn. Well, I did something one should absolutely never do. I just shot into it But honestly in that moment nothing came into my mind but having revenge on that bastard who was terrifying a little boy who was already grieving for his mother. And I heard a small cry, as though I had hit someone.'

'I heard it too,' I told him.

He sighed guiltily. 'I felt panic then in case I'd killed him.'

Later as Jeremy drove me back to the bus stop I asked him, 'Do you know anything about the Bereton Clinic?

'Bereton Clinic,' he murmured thoughtfully. 'Oh, yes. How odd you should ask because I think I saw Mr Bereton's car the other day.'

'Really? Where?'

'Soon after the spying man had been here I heard a car on the farm track the other side of the field. Thinking it might be the man making a getaway and that I might catch him, I raced to the cross roads just as a very expensive-looking Merc drove away. We don't often get traffic round here and I know all the local cars. This was not one of them. Did you get the number?'

'Yes. And it belonged to a Mr Philip Bereton.'

A huge whisk of excitement rushed through me. Perhaps Mr Bereton knew that Freddy's mother was dead and the child had been having behaviour problems so he was checking up on the father in case he couldn't cope. It did seem a little odd that someone in Mr Bereton's position would resort of sneaking around the houses of his ex-clients in this way, but then the centre had been an odd place from the start. Very unprofessional, I had thought when I went there with Verity.

'He must be the owner of the Fertility Clinic,' I blurted out.

Jeremy stared at me blankly.

CHAPTER 6

Next morning I was woken by the ringing of the phone. It was Janine Delane.

'Arabella, daaarling. You simply must tell me all about your meeting with Jeremy. Let's meet. What about lunch at Fortnums, just like old times?'

'I am absolutely exhausted, Janine. It was a terrible journey,' I tried feebly. I knew, even at this stage that I would give in, though. Just hearing her voice always comforted me. She's fun. She's funny. And she's always bubbling with gossip. She has that glorious talent of winkling secrets out of people and telling it to other people, 'in perfect confidence'.

She was saying soothingly, 'If only you'd let me know when you were going I'd have sent my Rolls. So when shall we meet then? Tomorrow?"

I said, 'Fortnums at one.' It came out before I could stop it.

'That's my girl,' she cooed.

In spite of all my worry, I felt a little touch of excitement as I got dressed next day. If only I could have got my corset and tights on at this pace that time I was inside the loo and Naomi out, she would still be with us.

M'buta was coming in as I was leaving. 'What is happening, Ladyma? Where are you going?' These days her voice always seemed to come out in a sad little wail.

'To London,' I said. 'Lunching with Janine.'

M'buta was so sorrowful these days that nothing interested her much. 'That means you must be feeling well,' she said tonelessly. A week ago she would have been delighted and said, 'I'm glad that you're coming out of the doldrums.' Now she only said, 'Be careful.'

I gave her arm a little comforting pat.

I felt quite hopeful as I travelled to London on the coach. I felt I was on the right track about Naomi's kidnapper. She and Freddy definitely had something in common, the way in which neither had inherited their father's characteristics. The more I thought about it, the more it seemed to me that Freddy was not Jeremy's son. I looked over the fleeing countryside and thought, Sue had an affair and the same man gave sperm to the Bereton Clinic. Another shocked thought sprang into my mind. Freddy and Naomi had the same coloured eyes. Those blazing blue eyes with the little purple prickle in the middle were common to both of them. And their noses. They had the same shaped noses, small and pretty with a little turn up at the end. They looked as similar as brother and sister.

Janine was already at the table when I arrived at the restaurant. She is one of those great soft flubsy people, like an overblown rose, and she always smells delicious because of the expensive scent she wears. Her solitary jewel was a large uncut diamond with nestled against her throat. She gave me a whacking kiss that I felt sure had left lipstick on my face. Catching both my hands in her own perfectly manicured ones, she said, 'You can't imagine how much I've missed you, Arabella.' And still holding my hand, she added, 'I heard. Jeremy told me. I'm so sorry, so very very sorry … ' The compassion and warmth in her voice made something hot rise up behind my eyes. For the first time since Jack died I nearly cried and had to quickly poke at my eyes with a thrust of my rigid napkin. Too embarrassing for words.

The waiter, who had just arrived to perform the laying napkin on the knee ceremony, looked shocked to see it already in my hand, eased it from my grasp and opened it with a ripping sound. The process gave me a few moments in which to compose myself.

'Thank you, darling,' I said.

Usually I feel eased when in a calm and gracious environment. Like Janine this place has style. Our cutlery was heavy, our glasses shone and a purple orchid in a vase was set in the table's centre. The large plush room sparkled and hummed with gracious happiness. Under any other circumstances I would have found it good to be back in the world of sophistication and opulence. But now thoughts of Naomi and worry about what was happening to her drained away all enjoyment. The only thing that kept my anguish from being total was my determination to find her.

Because Janine was one of those people in whom I could confide, I found myself saying suddenly, 'I heard Naomi's voice last night. You know, in my mind.' Janine would not tell me that I was imagining things out of stress. I knew her too well for that, and she knew me too well.

She said, 'Tell me.'

'I'm sure it was Naomi, though the things she said were not very helpful or clear. She just babbled things like, "hope is cross today", or "faith says mell's got to eat it."'

Janine squeezed my hand. 'Sounds like too much listening to those nuns. It will be charity tonight, no doubt. Did you try to talk to her in your mind?'

At school Janine and I had tried thought transference on each other and once it had worked during an exam. Janine had transferred the answer to a maths question into my mind. I agree the answer had turned out to be wrong, but all the same ...

I nodded, 'But I don't think she could hear me.' Then, trying to brisk things up, I said, 'We'd better have a look at the menu.' I got out my glasses, put them on and raised the weighty ornate menu card, but these days, since Naomi was lost, I seem to have lost my appetite as well. I put it down again, sighed, and Janine sighed in sympathy.

We managed to order something at last, settled back in our velvet chairs and for a short while I tried to pretend that life was good again.

'Now, darling, tell me why you went to see Jeremy,' Janine commanded at last.

I explained that I thought the man who had been spying on Freddy might be the same person who had taken Naomi.

'Oh, my god,' said Janine and pressed her hand against her breast.

'While I was with Jeremy the man came,' I told her. 'Have you any idea who he might be?'

Janine sighed and shook her head. 'After Sue died, even without all this I did not think Jeremy would be able to manage a little boy all on his own. Much as I love Freddy and would have missed him greatly, I thought it would be sensible for Freddy to live with Sue's sister. Better for Jeremy and for Freddy. I mean, after all ... ' Her voice trailed away and she did not finish the sentence.

'Janine,' I said gently. 'Freddy is not Jeremy's own child. That's the truth isn't it?'

Janine stared away across the room and did not answer.

Oh Lord, I thought. Sue had an affair with another man, Freddy is the result, and Jeremy does not know. I wished I had not brought the subject up. After a long silence, Janine turned. 'Arabella, we are old friends, so I trust you. I just couldn't tell Jeremy. When Sue came and told me what she wanted to do, I asked her not to tell him either.'

I frowned, feeling a bit muddled. 'What she was going to do?' Surely you would not go and confide in your mother-in-law that you were just about to have an affair with another man.

'They had been married for three years and though they longed for children, she did not become pregnant. She went and got herself tested and found that there was nothing wrong with her fertility. Jeremy was away, on an army posting at the time. She told me that they thought the problem must be with Jeremy.' Janine sighed and pressed her hands together. 'Swear you will never say a word about this, Arabella. Swear.'

I promised her.

Janine went on, 'I don't know, it was stupid perhaps, but I thought the best thing for everyone, including the baby, would be to go ahead and when Jeremy got back – not tell him.'

'Not tell Jeremy what?'

'That she was to have a baby by artificial insemination.'

'At the Bereton Clinic?'

Janine nodded. 'Chrissy said it was an informal sort of place where you wouldn't have to inform the husband at any stage. And now, with Sue dead, and Jeremy thinking Freddy is his own child, it seems too late to say anything. Looking back I can see the whole thing was a mistake from the start. But there it is. What's happened has happened.' She paused, looked mournful, then said, 'You can see how impossible it is for me to tell Jeremy now. I can't bear the thought of Jeremy finding out I had lied to him all these years. He would think that Sue had lied to him. And how would he react to Freddy if he knew? Freddy is Jeremy's only comfort now that he has lost Sue. You see my point, don't you darling?'

I nodded. Sue dying had clearly changed everything. To Jeremy, Freddy was all he had left of her, thought he had left of her.

'But all the same,' Janine murmured. 'I think Jeremy guesses. I think he knows really that Freddy is not his and does not want to talk about it for Freddy's sake. Freddy has already lost his mother and if he knew the truth, might feel he was losing a father too.'

'He seemed a dear little boy and he and Jeremy really love each other,' I said.

Janine nodded, then burst out suddenly, 'There are things about Freddy which make me a bit scared.'

'Scared?'

'He's got this weird animal thing. They seem sort of attracted to him. Birds getting onto him. Cats following him all the time. Frogs, rats, everything. He plays the flute too. Did you know that? Yuk.'

'It sounds rather charming,' I said.

Janine shook her head. 'There's something spooky about it. You know, Pan and all that. It makes you wonder who Freddy's father really is.'

I felt shuddery about that father, too.

She interrupted my thoughts by saying suddenly, 'If it hadn't meant bringing the whole thing out into the open I'd have sued Philip Bereton because Freddy is obviously not the offspring of the donor chosen by Sue. That man, in his photo, looked very like Jeremy, you know, dark haired, dark eyed. Freddy does not look like him at all. I think they used the sperm from someone else.'

'Philip himself?' I asked. 'Do you think he is really the father?'

She shook her head. 'No, definitely not. Freddy doesn't look the least bit like him.'

I told her about Jeremy seeing Philip's car.

'Well, I can't understand that,' said Janine.

'Unless it was Chrissy.'

'Chrissy? I doubt if she even knows how to drive.'

'I know, but she's in all this up to her ears. Apparently when she was working at the Bereton someone paid her to switch sperm.'

Janine sighed. 'All can say is, it's typical of the place. At the time I worried. The place looked chaos. But Sue said she wanted to get it over and done with, and she didn't want to muck up the timing with all kinds of official interference. Also, apparently, the place has a great reputation for success. Well, I can see why now.'

Back home, the following day, I rang the Bereton Clinic and asked to speak to Mr Bereton. He was quite clearly involved in some sort of illegal procedure, though at present I could not exactly work out what it was.

'I think Mr Philip Bereton is still away,' said the girl. 'May I ask who's calling?'

'No. It's all right,' I told her. Thought briefly. Then asked, 'Do you know where Mr Bereton's car is?'

'His car?'

'Did he take it?'

'Oh no, of course not. He's in New York.'

Things were not quite working out. I decided to come a bit boldly out into the open. 'I have just reported a hit and run accident to the police and the car, apparently, was Mr Bereton's.'

There was a brief silence then the voice at the other end, said, shocked, 'I think you must have the wrong Mr Bereton. This is quite impossible because Mr Philip Bereton is not in the country.' There came a sudden silence.

'Hello, hello?' I cried.

I heard a voice say to someone else in the background, 'The fellow Philip lent the car to had an accident apparently.' Another person said something I could not hear. I switched my hearing aid onto full power – it really is a wonderful gadget – and heard the first voice say, 'You know. That chap Philip got so furious about because he thought they were going to have a relationship, but the boy turned out to be straight … ' There came a burst of scoffing laughter, then back into the phone, 'I'm afraid we can't tell you anything. You will have to speak to Mr Bereton himself when he gets back.' The receiver went down.

I was too exhausted to try anything more at present. I took off my shoes and lay on the sofa, keeping my feet tucked back a little to leave room for Gump. Then remembered that he was dead.

It is terrible how long it takes to move into the space of those who are dead. Perhaps one never can. To this day I can't bring myself to allow anyone to sit in Jack's special chair. People would go over to it and I would stop them before remembering he was gone. There was still a dented crease in the cushion from when he had last sat. One of his hairs was lying on the back for a month after he died. I cherished it and I was angrier with Chrissy, the day I found her brushing the chair cover, than I have ever been. I managed to save the crease but the hair was gone. I would dream about Jack's hair after they buried him. He never went the least bit bald. It was not even thin, though when I met him it had been brown, and by the time he died had turned pure white. I cut his hair myself. He did not like the barber's because once Jack had once smelled shit on a barber's fingers.

When the coffin went into the ground, the thing that came most vividly into my mind was that beautiful thick white hair being closed up into the darkness of the grave. I have heard that hair goes on growing for a while after a person is dead and in the grave. I could not get out of my mind, for weeks after, the picture of this happening. It would reach his shoulders, a thing he could not endure and I would not be there to cut it.

I cautiously stretched out my toes, until they took up Gump's place. It felt like sacrilege but I knew I must get myself to do it. I was exhausted and ached all over. If things went on like this I would get seriously ill and then I wouldn't be able to go on with my hunt for Naomi. I switched on the TV with the zapper and the room became filled with the squeaky sound of a young woman crying. 'Wa wa, uhu uhu.' My God, the youth of today are wimpish. There was this female, young, beautiful, with tight skin, bouncy flesh and lubricated joints, blubbing because some male had abandoned her. 'You've got fifty more years of super duper life,' I yelled aloud at the screen 'Don't squander them in blubbing over some idiotic man. Play tennis, run a marathon, climb Mount Everest. Use your lovely body to its full extent while you can.' I hurled a cushion at the TV then began to zap from channel to channel.

On every one there were healthy young people complaining because they had failed to get some job, done badly in some exam, moaning and about how little money they had, how annoying their children were, one sobbing because she had burnt supper, one sobbing because she was too young to get married. 'Fuck as many men as you can, because the day will come soon enough when they won't want you any more. Enjoy what you've got, you stupid fools,' I yelled. 'Make the most of your youth, health and time because it doesn't last long.' By this time the TV set was nearly lost in the heap of hurled things. They've got all that time, I thought. God, what Jack and I could have done with time like that. 'If you don't like what you've got you should have swapped with us,' I yelled, and hurled one last slipper at the screen. 'You should see what my life's like,' I screamed. 'Then you would appreciate what you have got.'

Tuesday. Still no Naomi. Oh well, I must hang on till she's found. After all it was my fault she'd gone and I couldn't leave M'buta and Verity in the lurch at such a time.

I now felt perfectly sure that she wasn't dead, because I had been hearing her inside my mind. That must be because she was still alive, for I never heard from Jack even though we had promised to communicate with each other.

Sometimes I would be worried in case our theory was wrong and there was no hot clinker either. We would never be together again. I had already heard him for the last time and he was not even talking to me. That there was nothing after. Was there any sort of afterlife at all, for instance?

It was extremely frustrating, not knowing the answer to this question with any certainty or precision. I mean, if you are going to travel to another country you go to a travel agent, who tells you what the climate will be like and what you need to be inoculated against. And here was I, off to another life or everlasting death, whichever, I who had been to church every Christmas and paid into the collection plate to support the heaven experts and their information about the next stage was either hazy, contradictory, or absent altogether.

Until Jack died I had felt fairly confident that we were on the right path. It was the complete lack of him, the no feeling of Jack being there at all, though I felt so strongly that Naomi was, that had started making me doubtful. At first I had not been too discouraged, merely thinking I must have been looking in the wrong place, that vicars and Catholic priests were just not up to it, or had been brainwashed or misinformed. Or even were teaching things they did not believe themselves.

I therefore began to shop around, so to speak. And this is what I have found. That many African religions do not believe in an afterlife at all. Since there must be a lot of clever, thoughtful, or dead people in these religions, could they be right? I pressed on to discover that for the people of Ancient

Mesopotamia, the afterlife was a world of darkness and immobility, the apsu, where the diet was dust. In Ancient Egypt the Kings went to a Heaven in the sky and the ordinary people went to a field of reeds that seemed very similar to the Nile valley.

I read that it was Zoroaster, from Northern Iran, who first put forth the theory that behaviour in life could affect one's fate after death. The prophet taught that the soul's fate was decided on a bridge over an abyss. Someone's every thought or action from the age of fifteen, determined which afterlife, bliss or underworld, had been earned. For Zoroaster, at the end of a limited time the world would melt and the liquid metals and rocks would feel like warm milk to the righteous, but would kill the wicked and from then on the earth, itself, would become Paradise.

It was the ancient Greeks who invented the word Paradise. It derives from the Persian, 'pari' meaning 'around,' and 'daeza' meaning 'wall' which was the word for a vineyard or date orchard. Later the meaning must have shifted a bit, because Greeks were buried with a coin to pay the ferry man who took the dead across the River Styx. In the Koran, Paradise is 'a fair garden' and on the day of Doom the righteous shall go there and the wicked get sent into the Pit, which is underneath Paradise. When I was seven, and about to take my first holy communion, I asked a priest what Paradise was like. He said that it was a place up in the sky filled with singing angels who sat upon clouds and played harps.

'I'm a bit worried about it because I can't sing in tune, Father Murphy. And also I think I might get bored,' I said.

The old priest had smiled and said, 'If I was you, Arabella, I would not worry about that until you get there. Which is a long time off.' That was then. It's a short time off now.

'If you get there,' the Reverend Mother had said later. She was angry because I had displayed my ignorance and treated sacred concepts with disrespect.

You really need someone like Mahommed, who had looked on the face of God and actually been there, to describe Paradise.

I was thinking like this when M'buta came in. 'Does Daniel claim to have seen Paradise?' I asked her.

She flushed and look of joy came over her face. 'Oh, Ladyma, he is constantly in conversation with God. He meets Him all the time.' She sighed in ecstasy. 'You just can't imagine how marvellous Daniel is. Sometimes when I'm near him I feel not that he has seen God, but that he is God.'

'You didn't answer my question,' I said.

'Daniel says that not only has he experienced Paradise,' said M'buta. 'But that anyone else can do it too.'

'How?' I asked snappily.

'Through sacrifice. Through the mortification of the self. Through suffering.'

'You'd think I'd be there, then,' I said. 'Considering my suffering and mortification.'

'Oh, come on, Ladyma. You've got lots left to live for. Once we have found Naomi, you will begin to feel happy again. And Daniel has given up much more than you ever will be asked to do.'

'You don't know anything,' I stormed. 'From what you have told me, he's a perfectly healthy young man, with his whole life ahead of him.'

'Sometimes he eats no food for days. Sometimes he drinks no water. Once he did not sleep for a month,' M'buta said.

This is another thing about formal religion that I have never been able to understand and one of the big reasons why both Jack and I rejected it. The God creator of most religions reminds one of a car manufacturer who delights in seeing the vehicles He has created becoming damaged from lack of oil or water. Or even gets delight from seeing his creations being purposely crashed.

'I have seen Daniel do some amazing things. You would never believe. He can levitate, Ladyma.' She gave me a quick suspicious look and said. 'You're laughing.'

'No, no,' I hastily assured her and tried to pinch up my lips.

'Well it's true,' she said fiercely. 'He rises in the air. Just a few inches. Like one of those dreams when you think you're flying.' She paused and surveyed me closely. 'Do come with me to see him. Do. Because I just keep thinking that he will be able to find Naomi for us. I've begged Verity to come and she could bring the baby. There's other children there, but she says she's got to be available in case the police make contact. But you could. You're so sad these days and Daniel can bring happiness to everyone. Even people who are suffering dreadfully feel better when they are with him.' She talked dreamily, as though she had forgotten I was there. 'I would like to go and spend a few days in his presence, but I couldn't really go unless you came too.'

'Don't be ridiculous,' I said hotly. 'What have I got to do with it?'

'Verity is so worried about you being left alone. She wants to concentrate on finding Naomi and she'd only have peace of mind if I am around to look in on you now and again.'

'Poo. Go away. The last thing I want is you or anyone else 'looking in on me', M'buta. You go and stay with your holy man as long as you like. I shall be perfectly all right. Better in fact than when I have you lot nosing around all the time.' I knew what they were all thinking. That if I was left alone, I would commit suicide. Which was indeed the case.

When I think of Naomi, I want to cry,' whispered M'buta. 'But I do really believe that Daniel will bring her back.' As though it was actually happening, her sorrow started lifting. She went on, 'Daniel says that if you are a perfect creature, all your wishes will be fulfilled. And if you offer the perfection you have created as a sacrifice, in exchange you will not only become totally powerful, but you will also become immortal. Then all things will be possible for you and all futures available. That's what he says.'

'What tosh,' I said, though in fact because the need was so great, I felt a little bit interested.

She gave me a glare and went on, 'Because the sacrifice must come from your body, it must be protected from all corruption. Clothes should be made of the cleanest and softest materials. The substances put inside the body or massaged on the outside must never be made of chemicals. The application of make up on the faces of women and the sinful reasons for applying it, must be avoided if purity is to be maintained.'

So that is why M'buta never wears make-up, I thought and decided the man must be a real crackpot.

'He says that when your offering is complete and pure, you will be able to perform miracles.'

'I have always thought the idea of miracles is rubbish,' I told her. 'Why should a creator take the trouble to make a whole lot of laws and then want to see them broken? It doesn't make sense.'

'That is because you cannot see who the creator is.'

'Who is it then?'

'Meet Daniel and you will discover,' said M'buta.

'Couldn't I just give up whisky as a sacrifice? I would do anything to find Naomi. That would work as sacrifice and purification at once and spare me the expense and nuisance of actually meeting the fellow,' I said.

'There is nothing to joke about,' said M'buta stiffly.

Actually, I wasn't quite joking though I doubted if I was able to do it. I mean, it would be an enormous sacrifice to give whisky up, for there was nothing much else for me in life these days. I couldn't read books any more and could hardly see the telly because of my cataracts. Even the blubbing young people were blurry. Hearing the radio was difficult unless I had it turned on so loud that the neighbours banged on the walls.

'Daniel knows everything. People can question him on any subject,' M'buta was saying.

'Perhaps he knows, then, how I can avoid being sent to hell.' Hell was something that had been worrying me lately. If Jack and I had both committed suicide together, as we planned, we would have been together in hell, if that was the punishment, but things were different now. Jack had died without a mortal sin on his soul and I, by killing myself, might go to hell while he went to heaven, in which case we would be separated for eternity unless I could find a way to avoid it.

'Sent to hell? You don't go to hell for drinking whisky.' She looked totally astonished, then burst out laughing. 'Ladyma, that is one of the things you definitely need not worry about.'

'Ah, you don't know, M'buta. Please just ask him.'

'You could ask him yourself, if you came with me,' she said wistfully. 'Anyway, I don't think Hell comes into it as far as Daniel is concerned.' She went away looking doubtful. I hoped I had not aroused her suspicions.

This is the thought that had come to me while she'd been talking. If I could make myself pure and provide a suitable sacrifice, my dead spirit might become so acceptable to God, or the creator, or the Absolute or whatever it likes to call itself, that it would allow me to join Jack. Perhaps there was some way of dying that would achieve this. Dying for a good cause, perhaps? Working among lepers in a third world country and dying of it myself, or helping children to escape from the front line of a war zone. I feared, however, that one had to be young and agile for that sort of thing. Would I be able to pull off a bombing for a worthy cause, even though I risked dying myself? I thought not. I was not a gun or bomb handling kind of person. But also some faiths might consider that a mortal sin as well and perhaps worse than killing yourself because others would die too.

I shook my thoughts out of all these complications. For the moment the problem did not arise. I must hang on till I had found Naomi. The police said that they thought she was still alive. How do they know these things?

If she was not alive, after I died I might be able to find her and send her back. I mean, how can one be perfectly sure that such a thing is impossible? One hears of ghosts, doesn't one? Though I did not think that M'buta and Verity would be satisfied with a ghost child. Perhaps this Daniel of M'buta's knew the answer to these questions and also the one about hell.

That Friday I said to Chrissy, 'There's something I want to ask you. It may help in finding Naomi.'

'Ask away, Lady C,' she said cheerily. 'Anything that helps, I'm for it.' She was prancing around humming and whacking her duster vaguely as usual.

'It's about the Bereton Clinic,' I said.

She came to an abrupt halt, feather duster in the air. 'You said you wouldn't talk about that any more. I explained to you. I'd be in danger if I spoke out.'

I pulled a ten pound note from my bag and flourished it.

'Ah.' Her eyes fixed on the note for a long moment. Then she shrugged, turned away and began humming and dusting again.

'Chrissy, Chrissy.' When she turned to look I added another note.

Chrissy gave a deep sigh. The two notes were irresistible to her. 'Go ahead, Lady C.' It's a new this, this Lady C business. It started after she lost respect because of the Naomi kidnap and my involvement in it.

'What do you know about Philip Bereton?'

'He's a homosexual.'

'But I thought he was married and with children.'

'That too,' said Chrissy. 'His wife is the rich one. She is the one who financed the clinic.'

'You said there were switched sperm samples.'

'I didn't do it. Honest. I was scapegoated.'

'Would you mind telling me what happened.' I felt worried for a moment that she was going to get angry, or become silent so gave the notes in my hand a little rattle.

'There's no understanding young men,' she said reluctantly. 'They get whims and if they're prepared to pay for them, why not.' She gave a whack of the duster. 'When Mr Bereton found some phials had got the wrong labels, he got the correct labels, stuck them on, said it was my fault and sacked me.'

'Why would someone want labels to be switched, do you think?' I asked.

'I've said too much, Lady Cunningham-Smythe. Forget what I just said.'

I pinched the two notes tightly and gave them another shake.

'I mean why shouldn't a young man want to know where his kiddies were and even go and have a peep at them sometimes.' There was a slightly hysterical screech in her voice by now. She could not stop looking at the notes in my fingers.

'So you did meet him then?'

'Only the once.' She hastily changed tack. 'No, not ever, honest to God.'

'So Mr Philip Bereton asked you to do it?'

She shook her head. 'Not him. His gay friend.' She turned back to some vigorous polishing. 'But then it turned out he wasn't gay after all. And that made Mr Bereton hit the roof.'

'Do you know the friend's name?' I asked.

She shook her head without turning. 'It seemed like a small thing and he paid well. I didn't think there could be anything wrong, with him being Philip's friend, and, well, like I said, every father wants to know, doesn't he?'

'So this man knew where the mothers of these children lived, then?'

'Well, he had to, didn't he? Because he wanted the right kind of person, so to speak.'

'And Verity was one of the right kind of people?'

Panic came over Chrissy's face again. 'I didn't say that, Lady C.'

'And he asked you to describe people you worked for, to find him the right ones?'

'He said it was an honour, Lady C. That's the thing of it.'

'And Mr Bereton didn't ever find out that it was his friend who had changed the – er – donations?'

'He just saw that someone had been messing around with the stuff and he hit the roof. I told him it was nothing to do with me, which it wasn't really. I mean I couldn't do a donation if you threatened to kill me. But he wouldn't believe me and I dared not tell him about the man, you know, because of these women making these threats.' She paused and repeated tetchily. 'How was I to know that the fellow would cause any trouble later?'

'And the Lovedales. Did he ask you to check out Barbara Lovedale?'

'Well, yes. That's right. But the rest of it isn't my fault. I mean I wouldn't have a kiddie hurt or kidnapped for anything.'

So this friend of Philip Bereton's was the father of Naomi. And he had kidnapped her? Also Melanie? And he was also the father of Freddy Delane and planned to kidnap him?

'How old would you say the man was?' I asked.

She stopped in her polishing while she had a think. Then she said, 'Young. Philip wouldn't go out with an old man, would he? Good looking too.'

So not an old man, then. Someone young enough and good looking enough to find themselves a girl friend or a wife. Also, someone who had not taken any payment for his donation, so money was not a factor.

CHAPTER 7

THAT NIGHT I TRIED TO CONTACT NAOMI, and when I still got nothing back became filled with fear in case she was dead now. I lay awake for hours after that, reflecting on all that I had lost. When Jack and I were nearly seventy, we thought we would only have, at most, another twenty years. Well, twenty five at very very most. It made us feel sad that there was so little time left. Then when he became ill we hoped to be given another month. Two months would be a miracle. Twenty five years had seemed wonderful.

Then he became too ill for wondering and I wondered alone.

Now I stared into a future which held only disease, death, loneliness and despair, and felt so much in need of comfort, that without thinking I put out my foot across the bed and tried to reach Jack's rough heels with my toes.

And remembered there was no one there.

Even Gump was gone.

I started weeping.

After that I lay, jaw tense, staring into the beastly hopeless darkness and thinking that all over the world, there were people suffering like this. That if Naomi was still alive, she might be lying afraid and lonely too.

Thinking a prayer might help I loudly recited, 'From ghosties and ghoulies, and long leggity beasties and things that go bump in the night, Oh Lord deliver us.'

But I had been off God's list of petitioners for too long and had been struck off. I was no longer listened to. The prayer did not help. Instead I saw hell. I tried to shut mind off it, to think of happy things like sitting on the beach with Jack, but the hell was too strong and took over entirely. Giving in, I forced myself to see down the endless hole filled with misery. It was perfectly dark inside, though the religions would have you believe that there was a permanent fire in hell. And as I peered, I began to realise that it wasn't a hole at all, but an opening up to horror and dismay.

Then a white light suddenly appeared in the hole, so bright that I thought for a moment I must have switched on the bedside light by mistake. And a peculiar feeling came over me that I was not at all alone, because I was not me but everything. As if I had expanded utterly, and was now part of everywhere. That my identity was not lost, but joined up with all other things that existed. It was a feeling that was at once thrilling, but also frightening. Fear took over and I managed to jerk myself back into my former identity. It was pitch dark. The heavy curtains even blocked out the smallest light of stars.

I have explored hell, I told myself and felt excited. I might be the only person in the world who has actually been to hell. I wondered if I could ever managed to get back there.

When I was young I wanted to be an explorer but it had never happened. Jack and I had had some good holidays, but we had never gone anywhere extraordinary. I suppose we were just content with what was on offer and with each other's company. In all the years of our marriage, I don't really remember asking anything more of our holidays, than a nice hotel, some pleasant weather and Jack. Oh, the lovely times we had, sipping ouzo as the moon rose on some Greek island beach, sitting out on the pavement under an awning, drinking espressos on the Champs Elysees, roaming round Scotland with rucksacks on our backs. I lost my ambition to be an explorer during my years with Jack because I was contented, and the desire only returned after he died when I was eighty and sad and it was too late. But I had been somewhere unusual at last. I had been in hell.

It was dawn when I dropped off and I was asleep when Verity came in.

'I don't know how you can be so calm,' she said accusingly. Then she paced around the room, clenching and opening her fingers, till the joints made cracking noises, and at intervals gasping out, 'I can't bear it. I can't bear it a moment longer.'

I did not tell her of my meeting with Jeremy Delane nor the information I had got from Chrissy or Janine. In her present state, anything I told Verity would result in disaster. 'Oh, my baby, my poor little girl, where are you? Where are you?' she wept as she strode round and round my bedroom carpet. 'And the police don't seem to be getting anywhere. They haven't even found Melanie Lovedale. I don't think they are even looking.'

I decided to go and visit Melanie's mother that day. It was something I had often considered doing before, but each time felt reluctant to intrude on her at a time when she must be overwhelmed with worry and grief. Also I feared she might be annoyed with me for having recommended Chrissy. I had done that in the hope that Chrissy would give me up for Barbara's expensive and superior home. To persuade her to take Chrissy, I had exaggerated Chrissy's virtues and omitted to mention her many vices in my letter. Unfortunately Barbara

Lovedale, though rich, was not titled. Chrissy told Barbara she could only do one afternoon a week, because she did not want to lose her job with me.

In spite of the expense, I took a taxi to the Lovedale home and began to seriously worry as the fare crept up. 'I'm an OAP, disabled, and can't drive my car because of cataracts,' I told the driver, a young Asian man, in the hopes that he might reduce the fare, but he just said, 'I'm sorry to hear that, love. But luckily you've got me to take you to your friend's house, so you don't have to worry.' He put on a tape and a moment later the taxi was filled with the roar of some hideous Bollywood music. I leant forward and shouted, 'You will ruin your hearing, young man.'

'Can't hear what you said, love,' he roared back.

With a sigh of resignation I leant back in my seat and tried to enjoy looking at the countryside at least, since I was clearly not going to be allowed to hear it.

And as we drove, a tasselled religious symbol swung alarmingly between the driver's vision and the windscreen. Also alarming was the way in which he swayed wildly back and forth in time with his music. My anxiety which became total when we reached a notice at the head of Barbara's rutted muddy track, proclaiming *The Cloisters. Private. Trespassers will be prosecuted*. The driver stopped so abruptly that his holy hanging hit him on the forehead. He said something which I did not hear over the din of the music. I mean, really, my deafness is bad enough already without being further damaged by the taxi driver's music. I presumed he was refusing to go any further. Well, in that case, I decided, I shall just sit here. And I certainly shan't pay him. I had ploughed my way down one muddy lane already this week and had to take a whole day in bed to recover. I certainly was not going to increase my arthritis even further by doing something like that again.

He turned off the music and asked, 'What do you think, love? Is this the place? You said we were going to the house of some rich people but this doesn't seem like a rich person's road.'

'Oh, what a relief,' I gasped. 'I thought you were about to abandon me.'

'I would never do something like that, love.' He sounded shocked. 'I've got a grandmother back in Pakistan so I know about old people. I'll look after you. You don't have to worry.'

People think that women of my age are past being attracted to young men. Well, I can tell you, that's not true at all and this young man, with his thick black hair, smooth skin and strong young body was very nice indeed. He even smelled pleasantly of spice and fresh laundry. Of course I did not for a single second expect him to see me as anything more than a poor old lady but that, in a way, made my pleasure in him even greater. It was as though I was peeping at something beautiful from behind a curtain and remaining unseen myself. I could take a delight in him without having to do or be anything, unlike when I was young and had to always keep looking pretty and being desirable, however great the struggle.

'It's the right place. This is what rich English people like,' I told him.

We turned into the track, and went bumping along it, mud splashing out under the tyres.

'Why would a rich person have such a bad road?' he asked.

'The person we are going to see has her drive ploughed to justify the use of a four wheel drive vehicle, I expect,' I told him smoothly.

The drive seemed to go on and on. Nothing on either side but more fields. The taxi splashed through muddy puddles and was scoured by dangling bushes.

We reached the house at last, a perfect Elizabethan mansion, symmetrical, beautifully proportioned and set in a secret pocket of wilderness in a countryside that had forgotten its existence. The house itself was flanked by a formal garden of yews carefully clipped into geometrical shapes, balls and pyramids, cubes and cones.

I imagined aristocrats in ruffs and trailing skirts wandering among the sculpted bushes. I could almost hear the sound of mandolins and harpsichords. The roses that flowered voluptuously from orderly beds were the spicy smelling rosa de la hay, the favourite of Henry the Eighth.

The taxi came to a halt in front of the vast front door and the lovely young taxi driver got out, gently took my arm and helped me. I did a little more groaning and leaning against his nice young body than my physical condition actually merited, but all the same I did feel pretty battered from the bumpy drive.

'Don't you worry, my love,' he kept saying as I hobbled up the steps. 'You just put your weight on me as much as you like.' Well, what woman is going to refuse an offer like that from a good looking and sweet smelling young man? I took full advantage, I can tell you.

Although I had met Barbara before, I had never been to her home. It was impressive with a giant front door of faded oak and heavily knobbed pewter. I rang a copper bell that hung beside it. The bell looked as authentic as everything else about this house. As the melodic chimes rang though the house like the throbbing of a heart, I thought it might be the very bell that was installed when the house was built.

After a long time, when I began to think there was no one at home, there came the sounds of footsteps and bolts being drawn back.

I had taken myself so far back into the past that when the door was finally opened and a young Chinese girl in jeans stood there instead of a white-haired serving man in breeches, I was momentarily take aback. The taxi driver, who was still holding onto my arm, said, 'Are you all right, then, luv? I'll wait for you in the taxi.' My goodness, this was going to cost me, I could see. But there was no way out now. Perhaps Verity would refund the fare later. But just let me find Naomi and after that there would be nothing to worry about at all.

'Is Mrs Lovedale in?' I asked the girl.

The girl nodded in affirmation, said, 'I will see,' then looked flustered. She had remembered, too late, I thought, that she should not have nodded before saying 'I will see.' She went back inside, leaving the front door open and me standing on the step.

Somewhere quite near, I heard a woman asking excitedly, 'Is it the police? Are they here with some news?'

'An old lady, Mrs Lovedale.'

'Tell her I'm out. I can't possible see anyone. How could I be expected to?'

I decided my only chance of talking to Barbara Lovedale was to walk in before they shut the door on me. I went quickly in and stood in the hall. I could hear slow footsteps upstairs.

'Mrs Lovedale,' I called. 'My granddaughter has been stolen too.' The hall was wide and marble, my words echoed through it like a sigh of sorrow. I could hear the footsteps pause, then start again. Barbara Lovedale appeared the top of the awe inspiring staircase and gazed down at me blankly. She is a tall stately woman and even now was perfectly groomed as though about to attend a business meeting. Only the slight shaking of her hands gave away what she was suffering. And the dark misery in her expression that I recognised, because that was what was always in the eyes of M'buta, Verity and probably my own these days.

She came slowly down the stairs, holding the banister tightly as though otherwise she would have fallen.

'Ah, I did not know you were there,' she lied. She added, 'So you know what I am going through.' Her voice was hollow with despair. There were rings under her eyes as though she had not slept for days. Weeks, maybe. It was nearly two weeks since her child had been taken.

'You lie awake at night longing for the phone to ring. Dreading it ringing. Wanting to know, before you lift the receiver, if the caller is going to tell you that your child is all right, or to say that she will never be all right again. Afraid to lift it in case it is the latter.' She paused, took a quick breath and said. 'So if you know something, tell me quickly.'

'I think there may be a connection your daughter and my granddaughter's kidnapping,' I told her. 'And I am trying to find it.'

'I am afraid I have forgotten your name,' she said. Perhaps tragedy is bad for the memory.

'Lady Cunningham-Smythe,' I told her.

She did not react but only said, 'Come and sit down. Would you care for a coffee?' and without waiting for my answer, called out, 'Mai Lee, bring coffee and biscuits to the garden room, please.'

I did not feel this was a right moment to tell her that, because of the problems with my heart, I only drank decaf. I followed her through the white hall where light flowed wavily through diamond panes of ancient glass set into deep alcoves.

We passed a great abstract work of art in stone which I had seen at the launch of her London Exhibition the previous year. I was impressed again, as I had been then. Marble and granite, malachite and sandstone, so smoothly put together you could not see the joins.

'You have some beautiful pieces of sculpture, Mrs Lovedale,' I told her, addressing her thus so that she would take note of the contrast in our names. The ploy was ineffective for she only said, 'Please call me Barbara,' which meant that I would have to ask her to call me 'Arabella' and thus lose my single advantage.

I followed her past a strange writhing piece that looked like a charging bull or a swooping bird. The daylight filtered, glittered, twinkled through its writhing feathers. The last statue was a large male figure. Well, at least one of its features was large. The erect penis dwarfed the rest of the figure. Taken aback by this priapic vision, I paused to look.

Barbara, seeing what I was gazing at, said, 'My most recent work. I suppose it was wrong of me to keep it where a little child could see it.' Then her eyes went red and welled with tears.

We reached the garden room and she ushered me into a white sofa that was as big and smooth and soft as a snowdrift.

'We never got a ransom note, but I would give away all this and everything else in the world to get her back,' she said. 'I would never sculpt again if it got her back.'

The carpet was so entirely white that it made me blink. Pale and even white paintings hung on the white walls. And standing out in the Eskimo interior was one tall statue in dull dark slate.

'Tell me what happened,' I said.

She shrugged. What is there to say? I have told the police everything. And more. Thank you, Mai Lee,' as the Chinese girl carefully put down the white tray on a white table. The crockery was white as well.

'You like white, I notice,' I told her.

'I would change everything to black, if I could get her back again.' And when I waited, went on, 'The first thing was, my housekeeper said a man was hanging about watching the house. Well, even though the house is equipped with every kind of burglar alarm and special lock, one does not like that sort of thing, does one?'

'No,' I agreed.

'She said it probably was some young man trying to flirt with one of the domestic staff, but all the same ... ' Her voice trailed away and she looked in the distance, hopelessly.

'Go on,' I pressed. 'Could you describe him?'

'I never saw him, but my housekeeper said he was dressed in black and wore a knitted hat pulled down so it was hard to see his face even though the weather was not very cold.'

'And then?'

'I reported him to the police, just in case he was a burglar, though it seemed unlikely. What burglar is going to stand out in the road, in full view, hanging around like that? Even if you couldn't see his face, it would be a bit silly. I felt sure he was someone after one of the maids, like cook said. All the same a constable came round to investigate but didn't find him. And then Melanie was abducted and the man never came again.'

'And how did that happen?' I had read about it in the papers, but I wanted the story again in her words.

'I was out. Ulrika was in charge. The nanny. She is Ukrainian, very well qualified, but had only been with us for less than a week. Anyway, apparently a person came to the door saying he was Melanie's uncle.'

'The same man who had been hanging around?'

'That's the trouble. It was the housekeeper's day off and Ulrika didn't know about the man. It just never occurred to me to mention it to her. I mean, we had told the police. What more could be needed? I never for one moment suspected a kidnapper.' Barbara swallowed a sob.

'And Ulrika saw his face? How odd that he should have hidden his face from you then let the nanny get a good look at him.'

'I think he had been watching us for so long, that he had discovered our habits, knew it was the housekeeper's day off and that Ulrika was new and I was out.'

'Would it be possible for me to talk to Ulrika?'

Barbara nodded, and rang the bell.

When the young nanny came at last, she was red-eyed and trembling. She kept wringing her hands and could not stop saying, 'It's all my fault.'

'Could you tell me exactly what the uncle looked like?'

Ulrika looked miserably at Barbara Lovedale.

'Tell the lady what you told the police, Ulrika.'

'He had a beard. Not like Father Christmas though. It was only a little one and it was brown. A bit funny looking so that I thought it might have been a wig.' Then she paused, wept a little, then went on, 'Anyway he said he was Mrs Lovedale's brother and could he come in and play with Melanie till Mrs Lovedale came home.' She burst out weeping again. Barbara patted her hand. 'It's all right, Ulrika. Go on.'

'I told him that Mrs Lovedale was not due back till evening and he said he didn't mind. So I took him to the nursery and let him play with Melanie. He seemed to love her. He knew exactly how to play with her.'

'Then?'

'He asked me if I could bring him a cup of tea, so I went down to get it. I was only out of the room for about fifteen minutes ... ' She could not talk for a while. 'And when I came back they were gone. Gone.' She pressed her hands to her eyes for a while, too overcome to go on, then said, 'I would never have let him in if I had had the least suspicion. He even looked a bit like Melanie. I did not have the smallest doubt that he was her uncle.'

After the woman had gone I asked Barbara, 'Have you heard of the Bereton Clinic?'

She stared at me. 'Yes. The fertility clinic. How did you know? That is how I got Melanie.'

'Why did you choose that place? From the look of your home, I would have thought you could have afforded something rather better.'

She sighed heavily. 'I agree it's tatty but they do seem to get results. And they cut out all that official stuff. People say that the clinic takes short cuts, but my God, if you want a baby you don't mind what you do. Several of my friends have used it, and it has worked every time.'

CHAPTER 8

BACK HOME, I TRIED TO GET MY MIND OFF NAOMI, stop worrying about her and this other little girl and think of better things, but the only nice thing that came to mind was the young taxi driver, something I would have mentioned to no one. It is considered undignified for a woman of my age to be susceptible to the sexuality of youthful males and I knew that Verity would be shocked if she knew. Even more than most daughters, I supposed, because of her being a lesbian.

'Don't you find young men attractive at all?' I asked her when she came that day. She had said no, she never had.

'Well, M'buta does,' I had said.

'Of course she doesn't. How do you mean?' Verity sounded alarmed.

'Look at the way she goes on about that Daniel daSilva. Anyone would think she was in love with him.'

'Mother, that is religious fervour, not sexual attraction,' Verity said. But I could tell by the way she snapped it so crossly, that M'buta's enthusiasm for Daniel annoyed her.

Hardly a day went by without M'buta urging me to go to one of Daniel daSilva's weekend retreats. 'It's only a hundred and forty pounds. He will help you to be happier.' I knew what she was really saying. That after a weekend with her guru, I would become once more reconciled to life and she could be less worried about me committing suicide. What she was saying was that she was troubled enough already because of what had happened to Naomi and could not bear any more disasters.

'A hundred and forty pounds,' I said, outraged. 'I've got better things to do with my money, thank you.'

'Like taking crazy taxi journeys all over the countryside without telling me and Verity, so that we had a terrible day ringing every hospital and police station in the area.' The two of them had been furious when I eventually got back from Barbara Lovedale's. And even worse, for me, the ride had cost seventy-two pounds.

'I am not a child,' I told her. 'Nor your responsibility. I am a grown-up person and shall do as I like.'

'Ladyma, think about Verity a little,' said M'buta gently. 'Here she is so worried about Naomi, and with a new little baby and I am trying to take some of the worry off her by looking in on you now and again. Just for the moment let me take care of you so that Verity can get on with other things.' She was nearly crying. She added shyly, 'Did you find out anything from Mrs Lovedale, then?'

'I think so.' I didn't want to get her and Verity's hopes up, but I really did feel I was finding connections. 'Melanie was also conceived through AI at the Beresford Clinic.'

'Well, I knew that,' said M'buta crossly. 'The police have found out that already and they think that the kidnapper of both girls is the donor father.'

I felt a bit deflated. 'You really might have told me sooner. Seventy-two quid down the drain. For the taxi.' I hoped she would pass the message on to Verity, who might be disposed to refund me.

'Now you can see how important it is to tell us where you are going,' she said smugly.

'But how do you think he has kept the children hidden so secretly that even the police have not the least idea where they are?' I said.

'They will know soon. I know they will,' cried M'buta. 'Daniel will find out where they are.'

'How can he?'

'Ladyma, I have seen Daniel do amazing things. People he has never seen before have come to him to tell him that they have lost something – never a child I admit – but a valuable jewel or their dog, and Daniel goes into a trance, and tells them where it is. He can read people's minds, too. He looks at the person for a little while, shuts his eyes and keeps silent for a while, and tells the other person what they were thinking. He might be able to read the minds of the kidnappers, don't you think?'

I would have laughed at M'buta's credulity not long ago, but these days I had so often heard Naomi talking into my mind, that I was starting to think anything was possible. The problem is that she does not hear me. Perhaps I am too old to transfer my thoughts. Several times I have asked her, 'Is the man being kind to you?' Your mind does not like to think of the things a man who was not kind, might be doing to a little girl in his power. But from the way she rambled on I got the impression that though she was looking forward to coming home, took it for granted that that would happen soon and that she was not particularly unhappy where she was. Her language had become very grown-up up though, and she often talked about faith and hope, but in a way which made it clear that she had no real idea what these two words meant.

I began to build up the picture in my mind of the kidnapping father. A man who was loving towards his little daughters. Of course Naomi would be longing for her mummies. She might even be longing for her granny. I once heard her darling voice say, 'Is your blood precious getting better, Grandma?' But now she was with her father and maybe he had a motherly wife. I had a vision of Naomi and Melanie being taken to the zoo, or going on roundabouts at a fun fair with the father and his wife. Naomi and Melanie laughing together as they whirled round and round on the swooping horses. The wind whistling through their blonde curls. Naomi had often said she had wanted a sister, had been disappointed when the new baby had turned out to be a boy and had been too small to play with. Melanie was exactly Naomi's age. She was everything Naomi had ever wished for.

Or perhaps the father had taken Naomi because he did not want his daughter to be brought up by lesbians. It had been hard for me, at first, to accept that my daughter would never have a normal marriage and that she was having sex with another woman. I had grown to accept it by now, but maybe, for the father, this was still a distasteful idea. I mean, I knew that some men find lesbian relationships disgusting, or even sinful. Sinful? Could the man's religion, maybe, forbid such relationships, making him remove his child from an environment that he thought was sinful? Perhaps he was a Muslim, but other religions had the same prejudices, I knew. I decided to do a little research into this. At the library I might be able to get a list of religions that were against homosexuality.

But then a problem came to me. I thought, how could the man and his wife take the girls out at all. The police were hunting for them. Everyone in the country must know what the children looked like by now, their faces had been seen so often on TV and in the papers. Films M'buta and Verity had made of Naomi romping at the beach, jumping up and down in her paddling pool, throwing balls for Gump – oh, Gump, how I miss you – had been played over and over. It was horrible to imagine my little Naomi, who so loved to run and play in the sun, now kept shut up somewhere and never allowed out, in case someone recognised her and returned her to her mothers. Perhaps the man had already taken her out of the country and that was why she could not be found. The police had said they were watching at airports and ferry stations. But he could have taken her on Eurostar.

After Jack died, Verity and M'buta took me to Paris on the train and I saw a notice saying you did not even need a passport. An identity card would do. I did not think it would be difficult for someone to take a little girl with him on the train and no one question it.

That evening the phone rang. It was Barbara Lovedale. She was sobbing so loudly that at first I could not understand her. Then I began make out that she was telling me that a little girl's body had been found and the police thought it was Melanie.

I sat staring into the receiver, feeling as though I had become paralysed.

'Are you there? Are you there?'

I could not answer because my tongue seemed to have gone numb too. A strange and terrible feeling began to crash through my brain. The pain in my head was terrible. Shots of agony squirted into my eyes. I stopped being able to see.

I still had the phone in my hand. Barbara was still sobbing into it when M'buta found me.

I have vague recollections of being taken, bumpety-bump, down the stairs on a stretcher, a strange man's face looking up at me from the bottom of it as he went down backwards, carrying it. I could not see who it was that carried the top part.

My hidden pills. I thought and tried to shout out to M'buta, 'Please don't look through my things. Please leave everything as it is till I get back,' but no sound would come. She would not have listened anyway. People of my age are deprived of privacy. Once you pass the age of eighty it is thought that you no longer have any right to it. If you are dying, as I felt sure I was now, you have no right to anything.

'Treat my things with respect,' I wanted to shout, but could not. 'Treat me with respect.' But no words would come.

And, as they carried me out of the house and into the waiting ambulance, I reflected, guiltily, that I had not treated Jack's possessions with respect after he died.

His handmade leather shoes, for instance, that he had valued so highly and had cost two hundred and seventy pounds. He had died because of worrying about those shoes. I'm sure he did. After his stroke he became perfectly obsessed about them and I saw now that I should have gone on polishing them on Sundays as he had always done. It was like an act of worship to him, first carefully taking off any dust and dirt with the rough brush, going over the whole thing with the duster before applying the Dubbin with a careful cloth. Then he would rub in the Mansion polish and hold the shoe up to the light. He would ask, 'What do you think? Can you see any bits I haven't covered?' I would lean against his cheek pretending to check.

But in the end it was because of the shoes that he died.

After he died, because I was angry with his Dukker shoes for killing him, I dumped them on top of the armfuls of his suits and shirts and handed them over, with all his other things, to the charity shop. Anyone might be wearing them by now. I would never know what had happened to them. Maybe they were thrown away or made into rags. Can you do that with leather shoes? As soon as I got back from the funeral, I wished that I had asked them to bury him in those shoes and thought of the Pharaohs, who were put into their tombs wearing all their best things and even their golden jewellery and of civilisations that furnished their dead with food, drink, horses and even slaves and women, for who knows where or what Jack is now, or what he needed or could made use of.

'I think we can make use of these,' said the lady in the charity shop. 'Our problem is that much of the stuff people bring us is soiled and useless to sell on, and we have to pay the council to take it away. But these things look in good order.' She said, 'Thank you,' then asked me to take the stuff to an inner room, where two old ladies were already sorting a mountain of garments. The place smelled of sweat and moth balls.

'Jack will not like it in here,' I thought, as though his spirit was in the shoes.

One of the old ladies took the Dukker shoes from me, holding them by their laces, as people pick up rabbits by their ears, which always worries me. Since rabbits can't cry, and do not have voices, it is possible, I thought, that they were in agony as they dangled.

I never went back to retrieve Jack's things, though I was tempted several times. But there seemed to no point since I was going to join him soon, after which, all our stuff, his and mine, would go to charity anyway. Now I wanted to shout, 'I don't want my things to go to charity,' as they carried me into a startle of sharp sunshine, but no sound would come.

Well, I thought, I'm not blind. That's something. Or maybe this is the kind of blindness that makes you think you see bright light when really it is dark. And that's the thing about where Jack is. He doesn't have physical equipment for seeing light, so what is his experience now? Together we had imagined this glow. It had seemed reasonable to me at the time that even then Jack had had doubts.

I have always wanted to know if the siren goes on sounding after the patient is inside the ambulance. I have thought how terrifying that must be to the patient, and how if someone had just had a heart attack, the noise might finish them off entirely. Yet the funny thing it, I can't tell you if the siren was sounding or not as they drove me to the hospital. I was not unconscious. I can remember the nice young ambulance man saying soothingly, 'You'll be alright, my love. We'll soon be there.' He reminded me of Jack, though his voice was different. Jack's voice was soft and deep and that of the young ambulance man rather high pitched. I did not mind, though.

Did I feel fear? Horror? Dismay? I don't remember anything else except the thought going round and round my head, 'I am paralysed and soon I will probably be demented too.' Several times I tested myself on the journey, trying to see if my brain still worked, trying to remember things. What did I have for breakfast? Oh, God, I can't remember. Not at all. Perhaps I didn't have any. What did I do yesterday? I was in the middle of hunting for Naomi, I remembered. I had made some headway.

'Stop the car – I mean the ambulance,' I yelled with sudden resolution. 'I can't possibly come with you. I have something very important to do.'

'There, you see, you are able to talk after all,' said the young man. He came, squatted at my side and took my hand. His skin was very soft for a young man's.

There was a young woman lurking somewhere in the depths of the vehicle, though I was unable to turn my head to see her and I think that she and the young man must have exchanged significant glances. I don't know what she was doing back there. Rolling bandages, most like. That's what medical people seem to do in their spare time.

For the following days, hours, weeks, I don't even know which for I lost track of time, I had small blips of memory interspersed with gaps. This is something that has always frightened me, losing the bits of my brain that housed my memory. Even before I planned to find Jack again, I had felt that fear. Both my mother and my grandmother had lost their memories because of dementia. Even when quite young, long before such damage is usually done to a brain, I would be chilled with the fear of this. Those times when I went upstairs to get something, then could not remember what it was when I got there, terrified me. I was only a little reassured when a doctor told me that a sign that it is not dementia is if, when you get downstairs again, you suddenly remember. And that if you have dementia you cannot balance on one leg.

I would have liked to do that in the ambulance, but doubted if I could even waggle my little finger. I tried it. It did not waggle. Oh, yes it did. My finger obeyed. I felt a little flush of gratitude and relief and struggled to rise and try the one leg test. The young ambulance man put a hand on my shoulder and gently pushed me down again.

'It's all right. We are looking after you,' he said. 'You don't have to worry about anything, dear.' I heard the crackle of paper. He is looking up my name. He is going to call me Arabella, I realised, and tried to instruct my tongue, which had gone heavy and reluctant again, to say 'Lady Cunningham-Smythe.'

'A glass of water, Arabella? Is that what you're asking for, dear.' It was the woman, this time. I managed to get out half my name as the sound of water being poured came.

'I'm sorry dear, you can't have a cup of tea just yet. Here, take a sip of water. Then just lie still, like a good girl. We'll soon be at the hospital.'

If my fist could have done it I'd have chucked the water in her face but a heavy weariness began to overwhelm me that left me without the strength for conflict. Meekly I sucked at the water, as though I was a baby.

The next memory was being inside the hospital, clattering sounds, sharp lights, clacking footsteps, shrill voices. A person crying somewhere. Enormous groans like belches coming from the person in the next bed. Mine was narrow and so high that I lay level with the nurse's waist. I felt like a dead cod, laid out for sale in a fish shop. People wandered clattering and chatting behind me but I could not turn my head to look. Among the voices were chokey ones of Verity and M'buta. It sounded as though they were crying, or at least about to. I wanted to tell them that the moment I was out of here I would go on with my hunt for Naomi but I could not even shout. Perhaps they had injected something into me to make this happen.

After that I left the hospital quite often, suddenly finding myself walking along the Champs Elysees or swimming off a beach in Greece. Once I was surprised to find myself among icebergs and even more surprised when I looked down at my clothes and saw that I was wearing my bathing suit, though I did not feel at all cold. All around me I heard the wail of gulls, the hollow grunts of sea lions and the crunch of icebergs coming together.

Then, in an instant, it was the noises from the hospital I had been hearing and the glowing blue light of the polar sun was a neon bar above my head. At my back they were still talking. I wondered if the conversation had gone on for hours. It might have even been years. All sense of time had left me. Resuscitation, someone was saying. And then the word, suicide. I could not remember what these two words meant, though I felt sure I had heard them before. Then Verity's face diving, huge and colourful out of the brilliance and calling me, 'Mother, Mother, can you hear me? Wake up. Wake up. You have to tell us what you want,' and M'buta saying 'We know her wishes. Let her be in peace, Verity.' Now they seemed to be sobbing, both of them.

'You wouldn't say that if it was your mother,' Verity said.

'It's because I think of her as mine as well as yours that I am saying it,' said M'buta. 'Her instructions are implied in her frequent attempts at suicide.'

I drifted off then. The place was not at all pleasant this time. There was a nasty smell, a lot of litter lay around, and I wanted to get back to the beach, the Champs Elysees, or even the icebergs, but was unable to.

I was lifted from the bed onto something else. I began to be wheeled away. We seemed to be going down, down. It felt as though we were descending into Hades. Ice, bikinis, suicide, peace, began to float around my brain like midges in summer. Something was worrying me, but my mind would not make enough sense to do anything about it. Sea lions, suicide, polar sun, beach, resuscitation. Sea lions can be quite dangerous. The Titanic was sunk by an iceberg. Janine Delane told me when we lunched together that she had been pickpocketed the last time she went to Paris.

But that was not it.

There is something written behind me. That's where the danger is. I tried to turn and see. Why is everything behind my back now? Is that what happens when you get struck down in the night? Life continues just the same, but behind your back? Murmuring sounds of soothing of the trolley pushers as I made a tiny futile wriggle.

I was in the operating theatre. Masked surgeon looking down at me. Those behind my back saying something I could not understand. Then suddenly I realised what they had written behind my head. 'DNR – Do not resuscitate.'

'I want to be resuscitated. I demand it, no matter what is written there.'

'She's trying to say something,' someone said.

'There, there, Arabella, it will soon be over.'

I will soon be dead. This was not how it must happen. I don't know how to get to Jack from here. I tried frantically, even with moving an index finger, to signal my message but no one understood it. And probably if they had, it was too late to do anything about it. The decision had been made, behind my back and without my permission, to do away with me. I was too old to be worth wasting money on. I had signed my death warrant in a way that might be going to separate me from Jack for eternity. Jack and I had invented a scenario that did not include me dying under the influence of general anaesthetic.

'No, no,' I tried to beg. But it was useless. All I got was pets and pats and strangers saying soothing things in insincere voices.

Another gap here and then the realisation that all my worries had been for nothing. I was back with Jack again. There had been absolutely no hitches. It had been like a journey during which nothing had gone wrong at all, during which we had made every connection in perfect time and on which we would reach our destination without problems.

'What is our destination, Jack?' I asked.

'Do we have to have one?' he asked and his tone was so strong and sure that I knew that he had got the whole of his mind back. That nothing was missing at all. That even the long wait had not damaged his consciousness. 'We will be like this forever,' he said.

'Where will we be?' I asked him. I could feel him smiling in the darkness, you know how you can. The night became rosy with smiling.

'In a place where time doesn't exist,' he told me. And I leant against his chest, and felt his heart beating against mine and it did not matter that we had both died and our hearts were no longer with us, because the memory of them was still there. I put my hands round his face and settled back to a forever of peace in which nothing would happen, bad or good, and in which the only sensation would be Jack. Soon my body would start blending into his and we would become the same substance. After that we would be a single organism till the end of time. Or may be the two of us would come back again, be remade, given a second chance with new bodies. I sniffed deeply, trying to get the smell of him firmly embedded in my mind, so that if that did happen, I would be able to recognise him. But then a piece of me that was still connected to time began remembering. I was the grandmother who had lost Naomi. I was the grandmother who had to find her again. And she might be in the hands of a murderer. Or a child rapist.

'Don't go, don't go,' begged Jack in his gentle whisper. 'I have only just found you again. Don't leave me so soon.'

I wanted to explain to him, but in that place, the kind of words I needed do not exist and when I started tearing my soul from his, the pain was dreadful. 'I will come again soon,' I promised him. 'I am very old and whatever happens, won't be able to stay here much longer. But there is this thing I have to do.'

What's her name?' I heard a woman's voice say. Footsteps, paper being moved. Then the woman's voice calling, 'Arabella, Arabella,' in the strict voice the nuns had used to me at school.

Without opening my eyes, I said, 'The name is Lady Cunningham-Smythe, if you don't mind.'

There came a mutter of laughter, as though several people were standing round me.

'Nothing wrong with her, then,' came a man's voice.

I opened my eyes because I wanted to glare and found myself looking into the bespectacled face and masked mouth of the surgeon.

'Good. So you're feeling better, then.'

I struggled to sit up so that I could glare better but it did not work. 'I am not feeling better at all,' I told him sternly. 'I am feeling awful from head to foot.'

'Well, the operation went pretty well. As well as could be expected under the circumstances. We managed to get the whole of the clot out, but it will be some time before we know how much movement will be restored to you.'

I stared at him, trying to properly understand what this meant but he was turning away, without offering further explanation. 'A nurse will be talking to you, telling you about after-care, that sort of thing.' Then he was gone.

I fell back onto the bed, knowing. My God, I should have stayed with Jack. What the hell made me come back here again?

Someone went by, pushed in a wheelchair. The woman in it wore bedroom slippers and a dressing gown. The younger woman pushing her was saying, 'You are coming home with us, Mother. There's no way you can live alone, now, no matter what you say.' That would be me, quite soon, I realised. Tears begin to leak out onto my pillow.

Over the next days, meals fed to me by Verity, just as once all those years ago, I had fed her. 'One for Mummy. One for Teddy. Here comes a train to go down the red lane.' I tried to clench my teeth, but didn't even have the strength for that. Sponge baths given by nurses and sometimes M'buta. A physiotherapist, a brutal young woman who ignored my cries of pain and sorrow and forced me, using a zimmer frame, to walk on legs that had lost the knack and wave arms that did not remember how to do it.

'I can't. I can't.'

'Of course you can, Arabella. You just aren't trying.'

'Kindly address me by my—' Oh, what the hell. I did not even have the strength for that battle any more. I was beaten. They had won.

Home, where the house was remade inside so that I could manage, though in addition a team was needed, young women coming and going till it made you dizzy. Chrissy gloating. 'Oh, it's terrible to see you like this, Lady C.' She was enjoying it. I would like to see her creeping around on a zimmer frame or pushed in a wheelchair. I would not be the least bit sympathetic, but would laugh at her, as she was secretly doing at me. I found a way, for a day or two, of whacking her with my aluminium crutch and shouting, 'Get out of my way, woman. Why do you always have to get in my way?' till she learnt how to keep out of reach. My only pleasure was going round the flat, well, you could hardly call it going, creeping and hopping more like, and finding fault. I would run my fingers over surfaces hoping for dust, peer into cupboards in case she had left a mess there, then when I found what I was looking for, which was nearly always because you can always find filth if you are seeking it, would give vent to my absolute fury and frustration. I overheard Verity telling Chrissy, when they thought I could not hear, 'I am sorry about the way Mother is behaving, Chrissy. The doctor says that the condition makes people irritable.'

'I am not irritable, I am bloody livid,' I roared from the other room. 'And I don't like people to talk about me behind my back.' From the moment I had been found, ill, this had been happening. It was as if the people of the world could find nowhere else for conversation than just behind me. That was the one decent thing about the devil, I reflected, the way he was so reluctant to get behind people.

Because I got out of bed in the night and nearly fell down the stairs, they put a child's stair gate up which they locked at night. I was let out next morning as though I was a cow. I wrote a note and threw it from the window. 'Help me. I am being held against my will.' After a time I heard a ring on the front door, the murmur of a strange man's voice and Verity's voice saying, 'It's my poor mother. She is a bit – you know … ' Then footsteps on the stairs and a strange man at the door.

'Mother, Mother, this nice man found your note. Now give him a smile and tell him how alright you are.' I once had talked to her like that.

I had scowled so much since coming back from the hospital that I found it almost impossible to provide my failed rescuer with a more ferocious one. Thank God my lips had not been paralysed. Then I really would have been frustrated.

'She's not too well,' whispered Verity.

The phone rang. At first I could not recognise the voice at the other end as Jeremy Delane's and then I realised he was crying. I was amazed. That stern faced square jawed soldier was blubbing. 'He's gone, he's gone, he's gone, he's gone,' sobbed Jeremy.

'Who?' I asked.

'Freddy. My son.'

When he had finished telling me what had happened, I put down the receiver with my heart racing. Freddy had been taken by a man who not only murdered little dogs, but children as well. A third child taken and one perhaps already murdered.

This was a kidnapper who was too fearless, clever and too ruthless even for a soldier and a marksman like Jeremy Delane.

'Lady Delane has come to see you,' said M'buta. 'She's just coming up.'

'Why the hell did you let her in?' I raged at M'buta. 'You know how I hate anyone to see me like this. How dare you. I am a prisoner here.'

'I expect you'll be throwing another note out of the window, asking passers-by to save you from unwanted guests, Ladyma,' she said. There was no time for my hot reply because that was the moment Janine rushed in.

'Arabella, Arabella. Oh you poor darling. You poor darling. I've just heard.' Then she burst into tears. 'He has Freddy. Oh, I know so exactly what you are feeling. We are on the same boat we row ... sharing the same disaster ... sisters under the ... well you know what I mean.'

I refused to help her. Once you start muddling metaphors, it's the beginning of the end, if you see what I mean.

'My son winged the villain,' she wept. 'But he got Freddy all the same. Jeremy says he thinks he shot the man the last time he lurked around as well, but that seems not to have scared the fellow away.'

'Oh, that must have been the time I was there,' I said. 'Tell me everything that happened.' When you are absolutely miserable, or dreadfully worried, you want to talk about it to someone.

'It was all my fault. Freddy wanted to ride his trike on the lane while Jeremy made tea, and I said I'd take him,' Janine said. 'Me and Jeremy had had a bit of an argument then and Jeremy said the lane was dangerous. I wish I'd listened to him. You can't imagine how much I wish it.'

'I can,' I told her sadly and thought to myself, we should start a club of negligent grandmothers.

'The moment Jeremy went in, Freddy started begging to go out in the lane. He kept saying, 'I want to show you how brave I am, Granny. I'm not scared of that man any more, you know, because my Daddy knows how to shoot him now.'

'Oh dear,' I said. And added, 'But before he had been so afraid of that man.'

Janine sighed. 'Jeremy had persuaded Freddy that the man had run away for ever after being shot the first time. So I thought, how much harm can it do? Who can possible kidnap him when I'm standing there?'

I shook my head sadly.

'Freddy went ahead of me into the lane on his little trike. I kept calling to him to wait for me. But I was too late. A car suddenly seemed to appear from nowhere. As I rushed onto the lane shouting, the car stopped, someone leant out and began pulling Freddy off his trike. Jeremy came out with the tea at that moment, saw what had happened, and dropping the tea tray, grabbed his gun that had been lying on the grass. The man in the car had the child in a good grip by now and had almost got him in when Jeremy pulled the trigger.'

'The child might have been killed,' I said, shocked.

She bowed her head. 'My son is a crack shot. He can hit a pigeon in the eye from a hundred yards.' She went on, 'The man let out a yelp, managed to close the car door, and sped off.'

'Dreadful,' I said, and shuddered.

'Now my son refuses to even talk to me till we have got Freddy back,' sobbed Janine.

'If,' I thought, but did not tell her. Even I could not be so cruel. She clearly had not heard about Melanie.

I couldn't help. I couldn't comfort. But I suppose Janine and I were some support to each other.

For the next few days M'buta started up again on me going to Daniel daSilva's course. 'He is a healer, Ladyma. He might be able to get you walking properly again. And it is certain that nothing else will.' She stared at me, with distant eyes for a moment, then added, 'And he really can find lost children.'

Apparently quite recently he had united a mother with her child. 'It was a truly miracle moment,' said M'buta. 'It was just at the end of the meeting, and he asked if anyone had a special request and this woman began weeping and said that her little boy was missing and Daniel told her, 'Go home and tomorrow you will find him.'

'And?'

'What do you mean? And?'

'Well, did she find him?'

'Yes. Yes. It was in the papers and I heard it on the news. A boy had been found lost in the woods near his home and the police found him. He was only ten and had been out all night.

I felt doubtful. 'How do you know it's the same boy?'

'Look, Ladyma, if you are so full of doubts, then go on this course and you will see for yourself. It's only a two day course and if you are over seventy you get a discount. I am going. Come with me.'

Well, we had reached a stage where anything that might help should be done. Also I had become curious about this Daniel.

CHAPTER 9

'OH, DARLING LADYMA, I'M SO HAPPY. I just absolutely know that you won't feel so sad once you meet Daniel.' M'buta and I were heading for her car. I had capitulated. I was going to stay in the commune with her for one weekend.

'It's the first time I've seen you the least bit happy for ages,' I told her. 'That, at least is one thing to be glad about.' Then added, 'I hope you have remembered to pack my bottle of whisky.'

Ignoring this she went on, 'I wouldn't have been able to go if you hadn't come too.' She stowed my case into the boot. 'It wouldn't have been fair to Verity to leave you alone while she is going through such a terrible time herself.' On top of her grief and worry, not only was Verity wrestling with the baby, who still cried in the night, but also trying to meet the deadline for her next book. The publishers, apparently, were indifferent to her troubles and had threatened to sue if she broke the contract.

'Didn't she mind you abandoning her at such a time?' I asked.

'Even she has begun to think that Daniel might be able to find Naomi. Anyway it's only for a couple of days,' she added a little defensively. 'Are you OK, Ladyma? Have you got enough leg room there?'

'I can't see why you've packed me such an enormous suitcase,' I said a little crossly. 'Anyone would think we were going for a month, not a weekend. Well, me anyway.' I eyed M'buta's tiny little rucksack.

'Darling Ladyma, I want you to be comfy. The commune is a bit basic, so I've brought some blankets and hot waterbottles and things.'

We were now driving deeper and deeper into a rather unpleasant type of countryside, lumps of teasel and twisted black trees. Some nasty little brown hills in the distance.

'If I don't like it I shall expect you to turn right round and drive me home again,' I told her. 'And, from what I am seeing now, I feel pretty sure I shall hate it.'

'We must at least stay for the weekend,' she said. 'He holds healing sessions tomorrow and answers prayers on Sunday. By Monday you might be not only walking properly again, but have found out where Naomi is. You wouldn't want to miss a chance like that, now, would you?' She smiled and reached out to squeeze my hand.

'Keep your eyes on the road, M'buta,' I commanded sternly.

'And consider how much you have paid,' she went on. 'You wouldn't want to waste all that money, would you? You know it's not refundable.'

I sighed and saw that, no matter what, I should have to brace myself, though I was determined to do as much complaining as possible and in fact started straight away with, 'I have never known such a ghastly road. Are you sure this is the right way?' Barbara Lovedale and Jeremy lived in the centre of a metropolis in comparison.

'There!' said M'buta joyfully. We must have been driving for about two hours by this time. Through the mist you could see some dim lights. Very dim. 'That is it.'

'You have made a mistake, M'buta,' I told her. 'This must be a local tourist attraction.'

'Don't be silly. What do you mean?'

'A crumbling ruin, dear.' The vast building before us was barely visible through the rain and in the dim light and was in a state of jaded disrepair. There were gaps where walls had fallen, roofs collapsed and windows broken with, here and there, a jumble of standing walls out of the windows of which peaked a blurry glow. Where once there must have been neat beds of vegetables, there were now only dark rank weeds. Scraggy trees and bushes grew from through the walls and sprouted from the undulation of the many roofs. The place was clearly inhabited with tramps and the light came from their rubbish fed fires. You could see at a glance that this could not be the premises of a religious commune nor could there be a group of thirty people, including children, living here.

'Now have a good look at the map, then turn around and find the real place. I am completely exhausted and need my bed,' I told her sternly.

'It's it,' insisted M'buta. 'It's one of the oldest monasteries in the district. Don't you find it at all beautiful?' She was already getting the luggage out. 'Inside it's quite, well, liveable.' I did not like the way she stumbled over the word, liveable. In fact I did not like the word itself. Comfortable was what I needed now. Warm, Cosy. Home in fact.

I waited in the car while she carried the luggage to a lopsided front door. Though I had no option but to go in with her now, the first thing I would do in the morning would be to ring for a taxi to take me home again. Perhaps that charming young Asian man would come for me. I waited in the car for her to come back for me. I was not going to stand out there, exposing myself to the rain for a minute longer than I needed to. God, how I wished I hadn't let her persuade me to come on this crazy trip. As if a filthy, disorganised place like this was going to provide help in finding Naomi. As if there could be anyone in there who would be able to get me walking again. M'buta was out of her mind if she thought such things possible.

She had to knock on the door several times before anyone came. The door frame, which seemed to be stuck on with sellotape, wobbled at her knock, so that I feared that if she rapped too hard, the gigantic oak door, with its ancient iron studs, might fall on her and squash her. Then I would be in a real pickle, I thought, stranded here alone with M'buta slain or stunned. For already I had begun to feel that, no matter how much she knocked, no one was going to come. The whole place could fall down and no one come, I thought. In fact there was surely no one inside but ghosts. And the tramps, who would ignore our pleas entirely.

As these gloomy thoughts were rampaging through my mind, the door began to slowly open and there stood a thin young woman in what looked like a white calico nightie. Entirely unsuitably clad for the weather. She must have been freezing. After a few words with M'buta she came out to where I sat in the car, opened the door and bent in, smiling.

'I am Margaret,' she said, showing a lot of large and rather yellow teeth. 'I am going to be looking after you.'

'Looking after me?' I cried, aghast. 'I do not need any looking after, my dear, I assure you.' I would have liked to tell her about the intruders and violet scented face powder, but it seemed too complicated and she was getting wet and had started shivering.

'I'll show you round, I mean, Lady Cunningham-Smythe. Come. Do you like to be helped out of the car? Would you like a hand?'

With a sigh I accepted her hand and holding onto her arm, we plonked through a stretch of shoe sucking mud. By the time we had reached the front door. M'buta had already gone inside with the luggage.

I hobbled after her on my zimmer frame and found myself in a large, icy cold and comfortless hall. M'buta had vanished. I suppose she had feared a fuss and, my goodness, if she had been there she would have got one.

'Come,' said Margaret.

'How do you get hold of a taxi, here?' I asked her, as I struggled along the uneven stone floor, my zimmer frame skidding at every step.

'A taxi?' Margaret stared at me as though the term was unfamiliar to her. 'I don't think we have any of those anywhere near.'

'Where is your phone, then, for I can see, from a single glance, that I shall not be here long and may have to go home under my own steam.'

'We don't have a phone,' said Margaret.

God, how I wished I had learnt how to use that mobile phone that Verity had foisted on me. She had insisted I bring it here, 'in case of emergencies,' but I still had no idea how to work it. With a heavy sigh I was forced to follow Margaret, vowing that when I caught up with M'buta, she would get it in the neck.

'It's a complicated place,' Margaret said as she helped me up some broken steps. 'Everyone needs someone to show them the way, because otherwise you get completely lost.' She gave a laugh and said, 'It wouldn't even help to have a compass to find your way around the commune, because Daniel daSilva distorts the readings by generating so much magnetic energy from his body.'

'It would be helpful if he generated a bit of electricity for your electric lighting,' I said, eyeing with dismay the single unshaded light bulb that was the only illumination in a vast and echoing hall.

'Daniel daSilva is our light,' she said.

'Well, I sincerely hope so, because I like to read a little before falling asleep.'

She looked alarmed but only said, 'You must be tired. I'll show you your room.'

Where on earth had M'buta got to?

As I followed Margaret, I said, 'I hope my letter arrived, regarding my bed. I explained that cannot abide those new fangled duvet things and expect a properly made bed with tuck in sheets and blankets. Oh, and I hope they took in, not a taffeta eiderdown. I can't stand the feel of that. It has to be silk, or at least cotton. And I hope they managed to find me the correct orthopaedic pillow.'

Margaret continued on ahead of me and said nothing.

Well, I don't even want to talk about the bed they gave me. I don't even ever want to have to think about it again. The bed would have been very interesting in a museum. Anyone wanting to know what monks slept on in the middle ages would have been fascinated. And even a taffeta eiderdown would have been luxury, compared to the harsh hard single blanket.

'I am not sleeping there,' I told her furiously.

'Don't make a fuss, please Ladyma,' M'buta, who had reappeared from wherever she had been, said pleadingly. 'Everyone sleeps like this here.'

'Everybody is not eighty, with high blood pressure and on a zimmer frame,' I told her with what dignity I could muster. 'And it's freezing cold in here.'

'I've tried to fill your hot water bottle,' she said mournfully. 'But there's no hot water. I should have remembered that.' In the end Margaret fetched a second of those dreadful blankets and brought a brick which she said she had heated in the kitchen, to keep my feet warm.

'Please try and bear it, Ladyma,' M'buta whispered. 'Daniel says our wishes are fulfilled through suffering and if you don't make a fuss but bear the suffering, maybe this time on Sunday we will know where Naomi is. Goodnight.' She bent over, and gave me a kiss. It made me feel a little bit warm inside, in spite of my discomfort.

Amazingly I did fall asleep and dreamt of finding Naomi. All this time she had been hiding in a cupboard. 'What were you doing in there?' I asked.

'I was looking for your blood precious,' she said. Then she handed me a little parcel, and said, 'There Grandma. I found it and now you won't have to be sad anymore.'

There was a tiny plastic horse in the parcel.

Next morning Margaret appeared, bringing me a mug of tea. I took one sip, burst out coughing, and chokingly asked her, 'What on earth is it? I have never drunk anything so bitter in my life.'

She took the cup from me as I went on spluttering and looking rather sad, said, 'Dandelion tea. It's really good for the urinary system, Ladyma. May I call you that? M'buta says that that is how she addresses you.'

'What on earth are you feeding me with dandelions for?' I asked her, outraged, after I had got my breath back.

She sat down on the edge of the rock solid shelf that had gone, all night, by the name of bed. 'We try to make do with the things we have round us,' she said in a small voice. 'Real tea is expensive.'

I looked out of the window, into the plethora of weeds and said, 'Yes. I see you have plenty of free dandelions.'

'We do our best, Ladyma. The trouble is that Daniel does not allow us to use money.'

'I like that!' I cried crossly. 'And here am I having spent a hundred and thirty pounds for the weekend. I tell you, Margaret, I expected something better than this.'

'He says the money is needed for more important things,' she whispered. 'None of us in this commune own any money. Everything we have has been signed over to Daniel for we have utter trust that he will spend it worthily.'

'I call that silly and feckless,' I said strictly. 'But, look here, my dear girl. I am not a gullible groupie like all of you must be but a customer who has paid for a commodity and it is cheating to fob me off with rubbish like this.' I smacked the side of the mug she held, sending some of its contents splashing over her knees. 'I'm sorry,' I told her in an unsorry voice. I took out my hankie and gave her knees a wipe. 'But you must admit that I am being shortchanged, if this is the amount of comfort and care I am getting for my money.'

'He is going to give you something much more precious than tea,' said Margaret. 'Today he will heal. Daniel can cure everything.' She added quickly, 'Though you have to be worthy.' She stopped talking here, and looked down.

'What does that mean?' I asked.

'Pure. Nothing will work for you until you have made yourself pure.'

'There's no hope for me, then,' I said with a mock laugh.

'There is hope for everyone, Ladyma,' she said and looked up with a smile. 'I thought that nothing good would ever happen to me again after my husband ran out on me till I met Daniel. Now I and my children have a home.'

'You have children here?' I had not seen any sign of any but then I had arrived late in the evening and so they must have all gone to bed.

'Four,' she smiled. 'Three little boys and a daughter. Daniel likes to be surrounded with children. You will see them all at breakfast.'

'They are very quiet,' I said.

'They are very good,' she said. Was there something sad in her tone? For a moment I thought there might have been, but then she smiled brightly and I realized I must have been mistaken.

'I was among the first people to join the commune,' said Margaret. 'There were twelve of us so he called us Daniel's apostles. Others have joined since. You will meet them when we go down to breakfast.'

'Will Daniel be there too?'

She shook her head. 'He used to sit with us, but gradually as his spirit became purer, he began to stay separate. Now he usually addresses us with his spirit and from afar, though when he is feeling protected, he does sometimes come in and allow one or two of us to sit near him. Never children, though.'

'Doesn't he like children?'

'Only when they have become pure.'

I felt annoyed. 'How can you have anyone more pure than a child?'

There was a slight pause then she said, 'Daniel has the power to instil perfection of the spirit into them but so far none of our children have reached such a stage.' There was, again, a touch of sadness in her tone. When I waited for an explanation she went on, 'My children were quite naughty when we first came here, you know, laughing and romping and kicking footballs. Daniel put a stop to behaviour like that.'

'That doesn't sound naughty. It sounds like the behaviour of normal children,' I said, a little outraged.

Margaret shook her head. 'We who live here want something greater than mere normality. We want our children to know Paradise.'

'Poor little things,' I cried. 'Surely that is a knowledge for the sick and old, not healthy young children.'

Margaret went on, 'The wonderful young man, Daniel daSilva, takes the children for two hours each day and instructs them himself. No other adults, apart from two trusted women, are allowed in the room during this period and sometimes we parents hang around outside and feel amazed at the quiet from within. Eight children, sitting silently listening to every word the saint says to them.'

'What is he teaching them?' The whole thing sounded unnatural. Two hours of pious instruction to young children sounded overdoing things.

'The walls here are so thick that no one outside can hear what he is saying,' Margaret went on. 'We can hear only the murmur of his voice, uninterrupted by children.'

The very fact that the parents hung about in this way showed that they were a little anxious, I thought and asked, 'But what on earth could he be saying, to engross them so?'

Margaret hung her head, as though touched with a small shame. 'Daniel is a saint so would never teach children anything that is wrong.'

'What about their happiness? Is he making sure that the children have happy lives?'

'We are not put in this world for happiness,' said Margaret.

'Don't the children mind going to these sessions when they could be out, playing?'

'Daniel insists they go.'

I thought of the time when Verity was little and made a fuss about going to school. 'It's not easy to force children to do things they don't want to,' I said.

She did not answer this but went on, 'When Daniel was little, he encountered bad children in India.'

'In India?'

'His mother joined a Hindu commune there, in Kerala, when she was nineteen. She had run away from home and went backpacking through India. Daniel never talks about these things, but there are other people here who know the story.'

'So Daniel was brought up in a Kerala commune, was he?'

Margaret nodded. 'His mother became pregnant there. It is said that the guru, who was an old man, was his father. Then, when Daniel was three, his mother caught cholera and died. For the next seven years or so, Daniel was brought up in the commune. He was the son of the leader and it was assumed, therefore, that he in due course would inherit his father's role.'

'And when he was ten what happened?'

'The father doted on Daniel, who was his only child. He was immensely proud of him and I think this must have aroused the envy of the other members of the commune. But when the father became old, he began to suffer from dementia and he became unable to lead the commune any longer. The others in the commune, who were by this time mostly South Indians, did not want a ten year old foreign boy as their leader and began to rebel.'

I thought of Jack and how the wonderful person he had been had begun slipping away. Day by day a little less Jack there. It must have been like that for Daniel's father. 'Then?'

'They began to bully Daniel. He was punished and beaten for minor offences. I think some of the men sexually abused him, though there is no proof of this. The other children were taught to laugh at him and despise him for him because he did not look like them. He was, after all, the only foreign child in the commune. His father tried to defend him, but was too weak and ill.' She sighed. 'Any other child would have been psychologically damaged and otherwise traumatized by all this. Daniel never showed any resentment or hatred for the people who had deprived him of a childhood. He said, instead, that harshness had purged his soul and strengthened his spirit so therefore, he was grateful to them.'

'How very wonderful,' I said, managing to keep the sarcasm from my voice. After all, the woman seemed sincere. And I had not seen this Daniel daSilva yet so was prepared to give him the benefit of the doubt.

'The terrible things that happened to him as a child have given him the ability to perform miracles,' Margaret said,

'Perhaps, today, he will perform a miracle and improve my sight, thus sparing me the annoyance and discomfort of a cataract operation,' I told her.

'People do not always get miracles but at least you will hear his beautiful teaching.' She added quickly, 'Of course you will have to sit at the far end of the room from him for he does not have contact with impure people.'

'Impure people?' I cried indignantly. 'I would have you know, my dear, that I am an extremely clean person and have also paid a lot of money to be here. How could a little Indian upstart possibly complain about a person of my breeding and nationality being too impure to sit close to him?'

Margaret looked pained and shocked. 'Daniel daSilva is no little Indian upstart, Lady Cunningham-Smythe. I can assure you of that. And if you wish to encounter him today and avail yourself of his spiritual help and healing, you will have to clean yourself inside and out.' She had become quite sniffy and stroppy sounding, but I was determined not to be pushed around.

'You can assure your beloved Daniel that I am perfectly pure. I have had a good bath before leaving home and washed my hair last Friday. And if this sordid place had any sort of hygienic facilities, I should also have bathed this morning. As it was,' I continued stiffly, 'I have managed to do a flannel wipe in freezing water and that is the most I would imagine anyone else in this benighted place can do.'

'That is not really it, Ladyma,' said Margaret softly. 'I am sorry I talked crossly. But before the meeting we must be prepared not only physically, but spiritually too. It is a mighty privilege to be in the presence of Daniel but if you wish to be with him, you must follow the proper procedure.'

'Tell me what that is and I shall consider it,' I told her.

'For one hour before coming into his presence, you must stay in silent prayer till your metabolism slows and your mind settles.'

'That's ridiculous. I have not come here to pray. If I had wanted something like that I would have gone to church.'

Ignoring this she said, 'At first he had been unable to tolerate the presence of people from outside at all. He said that they had come out of the world bringing all their stresses with them and its smell had sickened him.'

'The smell of stresses?'

'He said that though the stink of cigarettes and newspaper, food and petrol, stale cloth and fresh sweat repelled him, it was the stink of their minds, whirling with thoughts of money, transport, food, sex, time, that he found most unendurable.'

'Well, he certainly needn't worry about me,' I told her proudly. 'I haven't smoked for thirty years. ' Ah, how I remembered those cigarettes Jack and I had smoked after making love. Sitting up in bed, smiling inside, holding each other's hands with the cigarette in the other. 'I do not read newspapers. My cataracts have made that impossible. I do not smell of petrol, because I do not drive. Cataracts again. And I certainly do not smell of stale cloth or fresh sweat. Never have. I am a perfectly non-perspiring person.'

'All the same, Ladyma,' said Margaret. 'If you want to be with him you have to go through the process. Oh, and then there is the breathing.'

'What?' I cried. 'Is this man even going to dictate how I breathe?'

'His hearing is intense. He does not like to hear the sound of breathing. You must take in the air through the nostrils and let it out quietly from the mouth, or he will be troubled.'

'This is totally ridiculous,' I cried. 'I refuse to subject myself to such tyranny from a—'

'No, please don't say it again, Ladyma.' She put her hands over her ears, as though she would not be able to bear it.

'So what happened to him after he was ten?' I asked hastily, to change the conversation. I admit I felt a little guilty, for she was clearly very smitten with this young man.

'He ran away from the commune and lived the life of a beggar, or vagrant child in the streets of Cochin, where he contracted polio and became too crippled to walk. He was found, very ill and half starved, by a monk from the Syrian Christian church in Ernakulum. On a whim Father daSilva carried the crippled child back to his monastery. At first, apparently, the other monks objected, saying that there were plenty of beggar boys in Cochin and why bother with this one, why not find a healthy mobile one who could be helpful around the monastery.

"Because, from his colouring you can see he is a European, like us," Father daSilva had explained. "And because Europeans are Christians, not Hindus."

'When the boy had recovered enough to talk, they asked him his name and he told them he was called Ganupati.'

'Good Lord,' I said. 'What kind of a name is that?'

'It is the South Indian name for the elephant headed god, Ganesh,' said Margaret stiffly. She went on, 'Of course he could not be called that in a Christian community, so his name had to be changed. After some discussion, it was decided to call him daSilva after the Goan priest who had found him. And that his first name should be 'Daniel' because a monk was reading aloud from the Book of Daniel when the child was carried in.

'There had followed years during which the monks tried to train the boy out of his Hindu ways and turn him into a Christian. They hoped that the day would come when he would become their brother monk. Their community was ageing and not getting replacements. At first, apparently, in spite of his weakness and disability, he was stubborn and determined to hang onto the things he had been taught in the Hindu ashram. But with whippings and punishments the monks managed to train him into Christian ways. And of course, he could not run away this time, because he had lost the use of his legs.

'As he grew older, at first they felt very satisfied at the excellent job they had made of the child, but after a while they began to grow anxious and feel that things were going wrong, and that he was becoming too devout. He took to refusing food and in this poverty stricken monastery, such behaviour was an unheard of thing. The monks never seemed to get quite enough to eat at the best of times.

'The main meal of the day, served at eleven am, on plain plank tables, usually consisted of boiled rice with either a lentil or vegetable gruel, sometimes served with a spoonful of curds or chutney. The water from the boiling rice was conserved and taken in the evening, spiced up with limejuice, salt and chillies. In the morning they ate dry bread and sweet tea.

'The refectory monk, growing alarmed at Daniel's increasing emaciation and fearing he might die of starvation before reaching maturity, in which case all their efforts would have been for nothing, went to the abbot and told him of his worry.

'The abbot called Daniel in. The boy came into the room, crawling on his hands and knees and was asked for an explanation.

"Are you ill? Should you see a doctor? You look like a skeleton."

"I am very well, thank you, Father," said Daniel politely.

"How old are you?"

"Twelve. I think."

"A boy of your age should have a huge appetite. Why don't you eat?"

The boy would not answer.

"Weren't you hungry?" demanded the Abbot. Perhaps it was not only the boy's legs that had been damaged by the polio, he thought. Perhaps he had digestive problems too.

"It is different for me," said Daniel.

"In what way?" asked the Abbot.

"I am chosen by God," said Daniel.

'The abbot became angry. "You are trying to become a greater saint than the brothers who care for you, I suppose? If you do not eat, you will die."

"I will not mind," said Daniel. "I am purifying myself of my sins. You said we must sacrifice the most precious and perfect thing we own and I do not own anything except my body."

"I will not have you giving away your food. Do you understand me? The amount I manage to give you all is barely enough anyway. Do you realise that even the grown monks have too little? When you are old enough and join us, you will see that merely living our proscribed life style is penance enough. That's all."

'Next day Daniel ate two spoonfuls of his food as usual then, crawling from the table, dragged his tin plate of rice and dhall into the monks' refectory.

"Please eat this," he said.

'The abbot, at the table's head, let out a roar. "You have disobeyed me," he bellowed.

'Daniel was given the most ferocious beating of them all.'

'How do you know all this?' I asked.

'Daniel told us. During a talk he gave us, warning us against the sin of spiritual pride.'

'What a childhood,' I said. "No wonder he is such an odd person.'

'But that was not the end of it,' Margaret went on. "He stayed with the monks for another two years. And then two things happened. He regained the use of his legs.'

'Come on, Margaret. The boy has been stricken with polio for all those years, then suddenly recovers. Such a thing doesn't happen.'

She looked at me intently for a while, then said, 'It did to Daniel. The first of his miracles was performed on himself. So you see what a person he is, Ladyma. It is worth following our rules for the sake of coming near him. And who knows, today he may cure you and enable you to walk freely.'

'I would have to be extremely gullible to believe a thing like that,' I told her sternly, though in fact all the way here I had hoped for this. 'And when he was fourteen?'

'One morning men from the UK High Commission turned up at the monastery, saying that they had been sent to bring the boy back to England by Daniel's uncle, his mother's brother. Apparently Isaac Goldberg had been looking for the boy ever since he discovered that his sister had died. In spite of the protests of the monks and of the boy himself, Daniel was flown to the UK. The uncle had no children and at first was delighted to have found his nephew but then shocked to discover that the boy had been brought up, first as a Hindu and then as a Syrian Christian, but had absolutely no knowledge of his own faith, which was Judaism. The boy had not even been circumcised, the uncle discovered and also, although Daniel was a biblical name, the uncle was not quite happy with it. Not happy at all with Daniel's second name which was the wrong one altogether. Daniel was renamed Isaac Goldberg, two. Hastily the uncle began to have the boy instructed into the Jewish faith and Daniel, who had become used to taking in new religions by now, eagerly availed himself of all the knowledge he was given. However, all this chopping and changing had given Daniel an appetite for new beliefs, and after a year with Mr Goldberg, the boy announced that he was about to become a Buddhist. The uncle raged, wept, and threatened, but nothing would make Daniel change his mind.

"I will throw you out of my home if you go on with this," roared the uncle.

"I will leave then," said Daniel. "I have been Jewish for a whole year and have grown tired of it."

'By the time the uncle had finished roaring and shouting and saying, "tired" over and over in a sarcastic voice, Daniel had gone from the house, never to come back. He took nothing with him. Daniel is a person who has no need of possessions. He had left like the Lord Buddha.

"What are you going to do now, you little fool?" shrieked the uncle out of a top floor window as Daniel began to vanish down the road.

"I am going to create the most perfect sacrifice for all the gods of all the religions."

"Why?"

"To be rewarded by all the gods in heaven and all the religions of the earth."

"What reward are you asking for?" demanded the uncle. "I am a rich man and can give you as much money as you want."

"I want more than money. I want everything," said Daniel daSilva.

'He did not remain a Buddhist for very long, however. Passing a mosque, he was inspired by the teaching of the imam and he offered to lay down his life, for Allah. That did not last long, either, though. He met a priest who inspired him and he turned to the Catholic church and arrived here, asking the abbot to baptise him. Come. We have talked here long enough. I will help you down to breakfast.' She gave me her arm and because I had become so stiff from sleeping on that rock hard bed, I was forced to cling to her all the way.

That journey from my cell to the refectory was the longest I have ever known inside a building. We seemed to go along corridors, down winding steps, through archways, up steps again, down, up, round, along, through, so that I knew if I had been alone I would have become completely lost.

'How many rooms are there?' I asked.

'No one really knows,' said Margaret. 'Once a thousand monks used to live here, and travellers would have rooms to stay in, though now, as you can see, many of the rooms are unliveable or too dangerous to enter. But there are three more wings as well as this one and there are also the cellars. Because the monks once brewed liquor here, they had huge cellars. There are almost as many rooms under the ground as there are above it.'

'The underground ones must be in a terrible state if these upper rooms are anything to do by.'

'Sometimes they are used,' she said. She looked flustered. Thinking I had interpreted the panicky look on her face I said, 'So you lot are brewing naughty bootleg down there, are you?' That was a comforting thought.

She flushed. 'Something like that.'

We passed ancient windows, so cracked and blistered, so dusty and cobwebby, that the weak winter sunlight could hardly percolate through them. We passed wrecked rooms with missing floors, we went under places where the roof had fallen so that you could see the sky. We passed closed doors through which one could hear voices, some of them children's. Behind one such door, according to Margaret, there lived the abbot who was now the last monk and the proprietor of the monastery. 'He is a hundred years old, so soon there will be no monks at all living here,' she said.

'Come on, Margaret! A hundred?' Even she could not be so gullible.

She shrugged. 'That's what people say.'

'What will happen when the last monk is gone?' I asked. 'Will Daniel and the commune be able to stay on after that?'

'Oh, no,' laughed Margaret. 'It doesn't matter, though. We are sort of squatting at the moment. Daniel has no proper rights here at all.'

I might have guessed.

Margaret went on, 'If it was not for the abbot, I don't know where we would all be living. But we will not be here much longer.'

'Where will you be?' I asked.

'We will have gone on,' she said.

'But where, dear? You must have plans, you know. How many children are there here, did you say? You have to think of them.'

'There are eleven altogether,' she said. Then corrected, 'No, sorry, eight. Eight children.'

'You can't suddenly find yourselves without a home, with all of them,' I said strictly. Goodness, I had thought Verity and M'buta were casual, but really this takes the biscuit, if I have got the expression right.

'We have plans. Of course we have,' Margaret said cheerily.

Really these hippy people are too feckless for words. When I get home, I thought, I will ring the social services and tell them about this place. Explain that this is not a suitable environment for children and that they should be found somewhere else to live as soon as possible. As well as being cold, damp and uncomfortable, I felt sure it was infested with pests. I had definitely heard the sound of something scrabbling in the night. And worst of all, the only lessons the children seem to be getting were religious ones of a dubious nature from an untrained teacher. I was amazed that the people of the commune had managed, so far, to get away with such illegal behaviour.

'And what do you do if one of the children gets ill?' All those little fevers and coughs and tummy aches that children get and this place seemed so far from any health centre. 'I hope you have some form of decent transport.'

'We don't have anything like that,' she said, still cheerful. 'We only have our own two feet.'

'My God, this is atrocious,' I cried. 'Far from anywhere, no phone, no car and eight children to look after.'

'You don't have to worry about us, Ladyma. We are in the hands of God and Daniel is guiding us.'

I did not say it, but I thought to myself, the fellow is even encouraging his followers to break the law and make illegal liquor. Not much of a holy guide about that. I wondered what they did with it. Sold it no doubt, but where and how, considering they had no transport and were so far from anywhere. Presumably their product must be collected by some middle man. I am always game for a little experimentation in the alcoholic direction and wondered what it tasted like and if I would get a chance to try some. But I did not like to press Margaret any more on the subject of bootlegging, fearing that her nervous reaction to my questioning had made her reveal something that she shouldn't have. She was a nice girl. I didn't want to get her into trouble.

CHAPTER 10

WE CAME AT LAST INTO THE REFECTORY, a room as battered, cold and miserable as all the rest of them. Already seated were the members of the commune, all, even the children wearing silly white nighties. And breakfast? I had paid a hundred and thirty pounds for this weekend and we were served a hideous and tepid gruel of lentils and rice. The children were there, all sitting together at one table. Margaret had been right. They were very good. Not one child spoke for the entire course of the meal and they ate the tasteless food in a quiet and orderly way and without any of the fuss normally associated with the young. For some of these children looked as though they were only four or five years old. Naomi's age.

I was seated next to M'buta and as soon as I had settled into the hard tin chair they had allotted me I let my feelings be known to her, my voice ringing out in an otherwise silent room so that every head was turned to look at me. There was hostility in their expressions.

'We keep silence during meals,' she whispered frantically. The other fools glared at her. The only sound in that refectory hall was the chomping of teeth, the horrid sound of swallowing and the clatter of cutlery. God, did I wish I was back home. God, was I glad I had brought my little hip flask, for even though they brewed here, there had so far been no signs of the product being served to the inhabitants.

After the meal was over, M'buta said that we must now prepare ourselves both physically and spiritually for the arrival of Daniel daSilva.

'I shall have a word with him as soon as he appears,' I hissed to M'buta. 'One hundred and thirty pounds indeed!'

'Don't you dare, Ladyma, or I'll go away and leave you here alone.'

I knew she wouldn't really, but all the same it was a threat I could not risk having it carried out, M'buta being my last link with the outside world and my only chance of leaving here till Monday. I saw I should have to fake a fit or heart attack or something, to succeed in that if she was not here. Nothing else would work. Saying I did not like it would do no good at all. M'buta was my only transport for I had learnt that the nearest train station was about twenty miles away. I was trapped. You can see the stage I had reached. Already I felt like an imprisoned person, who would have to escape secretly.

I was helped up several corridors and flights of stairs by a pair of red faced middle aged women, who handled me as roughly as if I had been a piece of furniture and paid no attention to my furious complaints. I had not seen them before and realised these must be Daniel's two trusted ones. I don't think they were in the refectory for breakfast.

M'buta whispered, 'They are Daniel's first followers and are responsible for security here.'

'Considering the state of the place and the absence of possessions, I should not have thought there was much need for security,' I whispered stiffly.

After a most unpleasant episode, during which the women nearly let me tumble to my death through a rotting gaping floor, we reached a small doorway outside which stood a couple of dozen pairs of shoes. I waited while M'buta and Margaret began removing theirs and adding them to the rest.

'Remove your shoes,' the red faced women commanded me and one of them rattled my elbow as though I was a naughty child.

'I certainly shall not,' I said. 'I shall catch my death of cold without them. Also I am not accustomed to padding about in my stockinged feet.'

The woman stood in front of the door, arms folded, and waited.

'Do it,' said M'buta sternly. 'Otherwise I shall abandon you.' She must have seen my earlier panic when she made her threat.

'That's blackmail,' I said bitterly, but was forced to do as she asked. I followed her inside the room, my feet encountering the floor with the sensation of frostbite.

Inside were about forty chairs. The women began leading me to the back most row.

'I need to sit near the speaker, due to my loss of hearing,' I said, trying to head for a front row seat but the woman rudely pulled at my arm and told me, 'You must sit at the back. Only Daniel's pure ones are allowed to sit near him.'

I felt furious but once again was forced to do as they asked and sit with Margaret and M'buta at the back.

The rest of the row was taken up by five people from outside. They had all arrived either on foot or bike. I had not seen anyone come in a car. My heart sank, for the idea had come to me of asking one of them to take me back in their car.

Now the only way of leaving this place today would be sitting on the back of a bike.

Presuming that these must be the lame and suffering people who had come to be cured by Daniel, I pointed out to M'buta, later, that they had looked extremely healthy. She said they must be people who Daniel had already cured of their physical troubles and have now returned to be healed of spiritual ones.

'To me it seems more likely that they are passers-by or hikers who have dropped in out of curiosity,' I observed.

'Daniel is famous. People come from far and wide to beg his help,' said M'buta.

We were forced to sit in this room for an hour, during which time bowls of cold water, in which floated some sort of evergreen leaves were carried round by commune members. We were told we must wash our faces and our feet in this water. I considered protesting, but saw instantly that such a course could be worse than useless, so I managed the sort of emergency wipe one does when travelling on a train with only a thermos flask for water.

When that was done, further perfumed water was handed round for everyone to wash their mouths. Can you imagine? I had to sit there, barefoot, trapped, in a freezing room filled with a crowd of gargling strangers and perform the same act myself, nearly risking the humiliation of losing my dentures into the bowl.

'Let's hope I have a miraculous cure after this insulting farce,' I hissed to M'buta, when I had managed to recapture my teeth.

'Hush,' she whispered back. 'Now you must spend half an hour silently cleaning your mind, Ladyma.'

And that was it for the next thirty minutes. Me, in great discomfort about these ill clad unhealthy looking hippies and healthy hikers, with our eyes shut, concentrating on thoughts of peace. Even I was forced to keep my eyes shut, ridiculous though I must have looked. Once I opened them for a moment and took a peek and see if any of the cyclists or hikers had shut their eyes and in spite of my disability, title and age, one of the red faced women who was hovering near gave me a slap on the cheek. Can you imagine, she struck me. I decided to take legal action for physical assault the moment I got out of here.

At last one of the dreadful females announced, 'He is coming. Quieten your breathing.' You would have thought she was talking about God, from the awe in her voice.

'Please promise to behave properly, Ladyma,' begged M'buta. 'He won't help us find Naomi if you are rude.' When I did not answer, she pressed, 'Please. For all our sakes. For my sake.'

For her sake, I thought angrily. She needed to be punished for having tricked me into getting into a situation of such miserable discomfort.

She began to shake my arm, and whisper, 'Promise? Promise,' as a ripple of anticipation ran through the room.

Then the man entered.

Everyone waited. It seemed as if they had all stopped breathing.

I could not see him very well because of my bad sight, but I guessed he was quite young. He wore a garment like a loose white robe, was short and slender and had blonde hair.

He sat, closed his eyes and sat perfectly still. The people stayed still too. M'buta closed her eyes again. Many others did as well. I was determined not to capitulate to this hysterical nonsense and kept my own firmly open. Let those dreadful women hit me in front of this young fellow and no matter what M'buta said, I'd let him know what I thought.

After a long time Daniel daSilva slowly opened his eyes and said, 'I am ready.'

I had no trouble hearing him. Had he done a miracle on me? I decided that, although I had been seated at the back – so as not to pollute the fellow with my smell, can you imagine – the room was small and his voice clear.

'Today I shall tell you about Paradise,' said Daniel daSilva. He spoke with a slight shortening to the vowels and a purring to the 'r's that betrayed his Indian childhood.

'Ah,' murmured the assembled people with a sort of mutual happy gasp. A smile consists of nothing more than a stretching of the lips yet all the same you can hear it. Especially when more than thirty people are doing it at once.

He stared round the room then looking at me, said, 'I see we have a newcomer.'

M'buta touched my hand lightly, as though claiming a small triumph.

'Come to me,' Daniel said.

'Go on,' said M'buta, giving me a little nudge. 'Daniel is calling you.'

I firmly kept my seat. I was an old disabled person and he was a young fellow and also a foreigner. He should come to me.

'Go to Daniel, go to Daniel,' the people around me began to chant. 'Go to Daniel, go to Daniel.'

Really, I thought, in spite of my state of health, age and class, they are about to mob me if I don't do what they demand. Also the jailers had risen from their front row seats and were making their way towards me. With M'buta still shoving at me and the people behind me taking me by the arms I managed to rise.

'Quickly,' said Daniel daSilva.

I paused and gave him the most haughty stare I could muster. I could not see his reaction.

'Go,' said the people round me. They were sounding aggressive now. The jailers had reached my side.

Once again, seeing I had no other option, I began, resentfully and supported by Margaret and M'buta, to shuffle over the bumpy floor on my zimmer frame. The jailers followed us menacingly.

A huge and delighted silence fell upon the audience. They leant watching, filled with expectation. How humiliating it all was.

The two women let go of me when I reached Daniel.

'Why are you hobbling like that?' he asked.

'When you are my age and have been through what I have, you will be hobbling too,' I responded sharply. A groan of horror rose from the assembly. The jailers bristled and looked inquiringly at Daniel.

Margaret whispered furiously, 'You must speak respectfully to Daniel, Ladyma.'

M'buta whispered reproachfully, 'You promised, Ladyma,' then closed her eyes and lowered her head as though with shame.

People behind us began angrily whispering reproaches to her for having brought me. Well, I didn't care. I felt well and truly tricked and did not mind who knew it. The jailer-like females grasped my arms. I tried to shake them off, but they were much too strong for me. One said, 'Shall I remove her, Lord?'

Lord! Can you imagine. Now, unless I can get my face right up close, everything looks to me as though it's smeared with a little yellow fog, but now I could see the healer better. Twenty years old maybe and all these people were grovelling to him.

Daniel shook his head. 'Leave her. She is here because I have invited her.'

'Excuse me,' I said. 'I paid one hundred and thirty pounds for this weekend and consider that I have been thoroughly badly treated. No one invited me. I was tricked into coming here by her.' I pointed an accusing finger at M'buta.

By now most of the congregation had lowered their heads and closed their eyes like M'buta, as though the spectacle of me standing up to this youth was unendurable to them.

Daniel leant forward and touched me briskly on first one eyelid, then the other. He did it so fast that I was unable to stop him. As his finger made contact with my skin, a feeling like the sting of electricity flashed through my head and, as if a blind had been pulled up, crispness rushed into my sight. The fog became exchanged for sharp outlines. Where before there had been yellow, there was now blue. His face came into perfect focus and I saw that his mouth was small. His hair was dark blonde and though it looked very thick, it was brushed tightly against his narrow head, so that it resembled a heavy cap or wig. His ears were tiny and were pressed tight against his skull, giving him the look of a wild animal, constantly tense with listening. His eyes glowed out of sockets that were so dark as to be almost black. So dark that you might suspect he had smeared them with black mascara, or had suffered from a life time of insomnia. The pupils were as sharp as purple pinpricks.

He stared into my face for a long moment, giving me the unpleasant impression that I was being hypnotised. There was no expression in his face at all, there was not even the hint of a smile in his eyes.

'You must become perfect first,' he said, as though in answer to a question I had not asked. He gave the jailer women a nod, said, 'There, you can take her back,' again making me feel like a piece of furniture and this time one that was no longer required. And as I was being shuffled back to my seat, he addressed the congregation saying, 'You must embrace that which you hate.' I had an unpleasant feeling that he was referring to myself. 'You must do things which are abhorrent to you and abandon things which you love and in exchange, purity, power and glory will be yours for eternity. And the name of that eternity is Paradise. And how do we achieve that? Through the offering of the pure sacrifice.'

I would have liked to ask him if giving up whisky for a day or two would be enough to open the Paradise door, but had had enough smacks and slaps from those two dreadful women to dare take the risk of sounding flippant.

'Had anyone got a question?' asked Daniel daSilva.

'Ask him what kind of sacrifice a person who has committed suicide would need, so as to escape hell,' I whispered to M'buta.

This time there was no rattle of discontent from those around me. I suppose that after my unacceptable outburst earlier, they considered it a blessing that I was now talking in a whisper.

'Darling Ladyma, stop thinking about hell all the time,' M'buta whispered back.

'You have told us we must give up alcohol, nicotine, drugs and delicious food? Is that enough?' asked someone.

'No,' said Daniel. 'You must give up all the sensual pleasures.'

'Sex, you mean?'

'The pleasure of sex,' said Daniel.

'But then there would be no children,' said one of the women cyclists.

He nodded. 'It is your duty to procreate children but you must find a way of doing this without pleasure.'

I remembered the pleasure I had taken in making love with Jack. Of course there was no problem for me with sex now, enjoy or not enjoy. I had no one to do it with and anyway, look at me. Even if Jack was still here, I doubt that my poor wrecked old body would be up to it. Though right up till Jack and I were in our middle seventies, we still almost as good as when we had been young, though not so frequent. It had been every day when we first met, of course. Then, in our middle seventies, the Alzheimer's struck and that was that.

I had often wondered why young men gave sperm to fertility clinics when making love to a woman seemed so much nicer, but I thought now that some of the donors could have been religious people who wanted to become fathers without getting pleasure from the sex. I wondered if I should tell Daniel daSilva about the Bereton Clinic where not only would he be able to create children without pleasure, but would also be paid for his donation. Considering how much he had charged, and how little I had received in exchange, he was clearly keen on money.

A red faced and thickset middle-aged man rose and coming onto the dais, murmured some words into Daniel's ear.

Daniel reacted with a cross shaking of his head, and his face went stern. 'No, Norman. I told you already. Absolutely not. We don't need it. '

Norman seemed about to disregard this and turned to face the audience as though about to speak.

Daniel rose too.

'Thank you, Norman. I will explain,' he said. His tone was cold. To the assembly he said, 'Norman wants me to ask for a donation of money and will not listen to me when I tell him we have no further need.'

'You idiot,' Norman blurted out, looking embarrassed and angry. And then to the crowd, 'We cannot run this movement without funds. You look like sensible people. Persuade Daniel that he, and the rest of us, need to eat.'

'We do not need food.' Daniel raised an arm, pointed sternly. 'Take your seat again.' And when the man continued to hesitate, he roared, 'Go.'

'Only fools trust God to rain manna from Heaven.' He shouted something about exposing everything.

Ignoring this, Daniel turned to the congregation. 'What do you think?'

What I thought, but did not dare say aloud under the circumstance, was that I had paid a hundred and thirty pounds for a prison cell and breakfast of tasteless gruel, that Daniel must have already made a large profit and that I had no intention of donating more. But no one else seemed to be seeing it my way. All these people around me, including M'buta, began rootling wildly in bags and pockets and pulling out money. 'No, please take it, Daniel. We want you to have it.' People were writing cheques, probably for large sums. I sat with my handbag firmly on my lap, but then I felt a light blow graze my elbow.

'You have not donated,' said one of the red faced women.

'He said he did not want it.' I was even starting to be a little timorous.

'Donate,' demanded the woman in a snarly tone.

With gigantic reluctance I pulled out a five-pound note. The woman whisked it from my hand in a moment.

By now Norman was rushing round gathering money up as fast as he could. Notes, tens and fifties even, swiftly unfurled themselves, Daniel, shrinking back a little, as though he did not wish to be associated with such sordid things, said, 'You are a fool. We are soon to gain that which is infinitely more useful and precious than money but if it is your wish, give. We will not spend this, though. Every penny will go to charity.'

I would have suggested, strongly, that the money, at least till Monday when M'buta was taking me home, be spent on some decent food and better bedding. By now I could even have accepted one of those duvet things. But I was reluctantly forced to stay silent, due to the menacing presence of the security women. Roll on, Monday, I thought and vowed that as soon as I got home I would be in touch with my lawyer.

Norman clasped his hand protectively over the pile of money and scowled.

CHAPTER 11

It was the next morning. Sunday. One more terrible night. One more ghastly breakfast. I took a deep swig of whisky, although I don't normally drink at breakfast. But this was an emergency. I needed it to keep off the cold. I was coming to the end of my bottle but tomorrow we would be home so I did not have to be careful any more.

'I don't know what you are grumbling about,' M'buta said when I met her after breakfast. 'You came here to be healed and you said that he had cured your cataract.' We were sitting on a bench outside in the weedy garden. Even with only a feeble winter sunshine, it seemed marginally warmer than indoors.

'I could have had that done on the NHS for nothing. It was only a question of a bit more waiting. Done like this it's cost me. You had implied that I would be walking again, just like before my operation, after seeing your Daniel person.' I waved an angry zimmer frame at her and said, 'Well? Do you see any sign of that?' I lifted my right foot with my hands and wiggled my foot about. 'Well, can you see any improvement there?'

'Isn't it moving a bit more freely than yesterday?' she said hopefully.

'No,' I stormed. 'After two terrible nights on a bed of stone, it's worse.'

'Well, you can't expect miracles to happen in a moment,' she said.

'M'buta, my understanding of miracles is that if you get cured on the NHS, you wait. If you are to be cured by a miracle it happens instantly.'

'Some do, and some don't,' she said firmly. 'And anyway, look at the way you behaved. So rude and disrespectful. No wonder he didn't cure you. You need to be a bit more grateful and polite to be granted a thing like that.' Then, getting up, 'Come on, Ladyma. Today is the thing we have really come for. Today he is going to find Naomi and even you must agree that that can't be done on the NHS, no matter how long you wait.'

Although I would not have admitted it to M'buta, in fact I had been impressed with the way my eyes had so suddenly cleared when Daniel touched them and so felt secretly hopeful that the fellow might really pull off the conjuring trick of finding Naomi.

Last night Naomi had spoken to my mind and it was because of that, that I had not kicked up more of a fuss about the bedding. I had been asleep but conscious. That's what it felt like, though it's a difficult state to describe. It was as though I knew I was asleep. The same sort of state I had experienced when I met Jack during my operation.

Naomi had spoken in a tiny sleepy little voice, as though she had not properly woken up and so softly that that I had to strain to hear her. Several times I said, 'Speak up, Naomi. I can't hear you,' but I don't think she could hear me at all.

'We are going to do blood precious together, Grandma and he says you will see Grandpa. And it's not riding.' I remembered Verity saying she had put money on a horse called 'Precious' in the Grand National, but that it probably wouldn't win because it was not a full-blooded thoroughbred. Ah, I thought. Another reason for Naomi's confusion.

'Who is we?' I asked her.

'He's going to give us blood precious and then I will be with you again,' she murmured. She might have fallen asleep then, but a few minutes later I heard her say, 'It won't exactly be like home, but it will be even better.'

'What will?' I had asked.

'Where I am going.' Was she hearing me or was this a coincidence?

'Where are you going, darling?' I tried to think as loudly and clearly as I could, though having never had any experience of loud thinking before, it was a bit hard to pull off. 'This is Grandma speaking,' I added, like a fighter pilot contacting base.

'I think it's a sort of no place. But we will like it.'

'Who is 'we'?' I asked again. My heart was racing with excitement.

'Uhm ... He's got a name but I've forgotten it.' She heard me. She heard me.

'Ask him,' I urged, thrilled by now.

I heard her voice murmuring, then she said, 'He can't remember either.'

'Where are you?' I asked. 'How shall I find you?'

I could hear her make a little gusty sigh. Then she said,'In a room.'

I was dreaming, of course I was. I knew I was dreaming, but you can't imagine how real this conversation felt. For the rest of the night I did not hear her voice, no matter how hard I tried, but all the same the dream had had made me thoughtful as well as hopeful. I vowed that today I would behave really well, not give any trouble at all, do all the purifying things asked of me, treat the little guru with cringing respect, and who knows, he might do another miracle and find my granddaughter.

And then, on Monday, we would be going home.

Oh, lovely home, with my hot water bottle, *Jonathan Creek* on the telly and a nice cocoa at bed time. And a whole unopened bottle of Scotch in the cupboard. I would treat myself to a mug full to celebrate, the moment I got in. I could not wait. But then I thought, if I don't find Naomi, I won't be able to enjoy home at all.

M'buta seemed impressed with my new perfect behaviour as we sat once again in the icy room, waiting for Daniel. Margaret, joyously grateful, kept patting my knee and saying, 'Thank you, Ladyma. Thank you. You are a really good lady.' Ah, if only she knew what a stink I planned to make the moment I got back. Unless, of course, the fellow found Naomi. I would forgive him everything if he did that.

'You ask the question about Naomi, M'buta,' I whispered. 'You have a better way with him than me.'

If we had been anywhere else, she would have put her arm round me and given me a hug. We were in a situation where such behaviour was not appropriate though. Anyway she knows how I dislike sentimentality. She has even apologised for kissing me that first night.

'Think no more about it,' I had told her. 'But don't let such a thing happen again.'

Today a quite different group of people had come. Presumably people searching for lost offspring. They all arrived on foot. Still no cars, though by now I had given up thoughts of escape.

Margaret told me that Daniel did not allow petrol vehicles to come within smelling distance of the commune. 'They have to park their cars on the main road,' she explained. Now I understood why, after our arrival and dropping me at the commune, M'buta had vanished off down the road again in her car. Presumably M'buta had not explained this in case I got angry, as well I might. 'It is only under the most unusual circumstances, like when someone comes who is disabled like yourself, that Daniel allows a car to come near. In fact we were all rather surprised when he said that M'buta could bring you. There have been other times when a person unable to walk has simply been told they could not come,' Margaret told me. 'Their only hope then is to be cured spiritually at a distance. Daniel does that sometimes, you know.'

'I'm pretty sure he's legally obliged to provide facilities for disabled people if he is open to the public,' I had told her snappishly.

'Daniel only obeys the law of God,' she said serenely.

'Fortunate that he is well versed in it,' I said tartly. 'Because God's laws seem to depend on which religion you follow and I am unclear about which faith he adheres to.'

She smiled and did not answer.

However, today I was behaving perfectly and keeping my feelings to myself.

There were several haggard looking mothers and a worn out father, splattered with mud like those who had come yesterday. They all perked up eagerly when Daniel entered, as though he was the only hope they had of finding their children and that he was certain to do it.

When the time to ask questions came, a young woman said she was looking for her lost lover. She was followed by a young man with the same problem. Daniel gave them both the same advice. To find someone else if human love was all they desired, but that there were more important and greater things to wish for. I would have been annoyed if I had been them, but they each seemed to find his suggestion helpful, and even satisfying. I would later discover why. They had fallen in love with each other on the spot and went away from the meeting hand in hand.

To one mother Daniel said, 'Look in your heart. Your child is buried there,' and to another, 'Stand firm.' It turned out that these children were not actually lost in the way that Naomi was. They had turned rebellious or were behaving badly. There was one family who really had lost a child. Their fourteen year old son had rushed out of the house a week before and they had not seen him since.

Daniel sighed heavily and said, as though the story bored him, 'He is at a station. You will find him there.'

'Which station?' The faces of the parents had become lit up with hope.

Daniel turned and exchanged some quick whispers with the man called Norman, then said, 'Kings Cross.'

The parents rose and you thought for a moment that they would burst out clapping or hugging or something. They started waving their arms and crying, 'Thank you, Daniel. Thank you, Daniel.'

'Sit down,' he told them impatiently.

I was filled with wonder at their gullibility. Why not wait till they found their kid on Kings Cross Station, before giving vein to all this gratitude and joy. I could imagine them dashing there this very day, finding no son and telling each other, 'He must have been here earlier. We must have just missed him.'

When M'buta's turn came and she asked about Naomi, he was silent for a short time, then said briefly, 'You will know on Tuesday.'

I felt extremely annoyed. After all this hope and expectation, that is what we got.

'Ask him where?' I hissed at M'buta.

'Where shall we find our child, Daniel?' she asked timidly.

If he answers, 'inside your heart' or something, I will kill him, I thought. He said, 'The grandmother will know.'

The meeting ended at last.

Another evening, another night. I would grit my teeth and struggle through the last dreadful hours. Only fourteen at the very most, for I was determined to force M'buta to leave at the very earliest opportunity. Six in the morning if it could be managed.

We could have breakfast in a nice hotel on the way back. Thank God I had eaten my last gruel meal.

'We will find her on Tuesday, we will find her on Tuesday, after we get back,' poor M'buta kept saying over and over. She is well and truly hypnotised. And who knows, we might. Even I felt a bit better now. Tuesday. Who knows ... Was I succumbing? Maybe, but it was better than the anxiety I had suffered from before coming here.

That night I slept right through and did not hear Naomi. I woke next morning feeling quite regretful. It was nearly seven. Heavens, I had impressed on M'buta the absolute necessity of us leaving at six. Why the hell hadn't she woken me? Had she overslept as well? I called for Margaret. Due to the shape and height of the bed, I could only descend from it with help. She came at last, looking flustered.

'Tell M'buta I wish to leave at once,' I said. 'She can skip all her morning ablutions for once since I need to get away urgently.'

Margaret kept breathing rather fast, with her mouth held a little open.

'Go on,' I told her. 'The faster you go the quicker you will be relieved of my aggravating company.'

'You must go down to breakfast now,' she said in a funny little piping trembly voice. 'That's the rule.'

'Didn't you hear me?' I roared. 'I do not want breakfast. I want to GO.' I pointed a stern finger at the door. 'Tell her to go and get the car at once and that I shall be waiting for her in the hall. Come on, help me down.'

But still she stood here doing that silly breathing.

'What?' A little chill of apprehension had started to sweep through me.

'She's gone,' said Margaret in a whimpery voice.

Well, how shall I describe that day? That idiotic pimply Margaret person hung around for a while making hopeful noises about dandelion tea till I managed to hurl her out with a few shouts and well aimed whacks of my walking stick which, luckily, M'buta the treacherous had left with me, in case I went anywhere too narrow for the zimmer frame.

Apparently Daniel had ordered M'buta to go and leave me here. Had told M'buta that if she did not do it, I would not be united with Naomi again.

I did not believe it and suspected that the whole thing had been a plot. I was hampering her and Verity in their hunt for Naomi. They had enough to cope with and worry about without having to fear I would kill myself, alone in my flat. I could see now that they must have not only found the pills in their sweet packets, but also felt the risk even greater because of my guilt about losing Naomi. They had tricked me 'for my own good' into staying in a 'home' where not only would I be looked after, but M'buta must have felt would, in the long run, cheer me and soothe my soul as hers was when she was in the presence of Daniel.

I would have to think of something. 'Jack, Jack, what do I do now?' It was the sort of thing I would have asked if he had been there and he would have had some kind of solution, always. Well, till he came down with Alzheimer's.

The last time I asked him, when we were in a tight situation, 'What do we do now?' he had started up again about Mansion polish and his black shoes. My last words to him had been angry ones and that was why it was so urgent that I found him again. So that I could say one last loving thing.

I have tried to make my mind stop coming back to this about ten thousand times, but as with a sore patch on the skin, or a tooth that hurts if you wobble it, my thoughts keep returning to it.

To stop Jack's memory from fading so fast, the doctor had suggested that I take him to places he had known in the past. I chose the banking department in Harrods where, when he was a little boy he had gone with his mother while she cashed a cheque. He had often told me how he had sat on one of the green leather armchairs, huge and tight, with the leather sticking to the backs of his bare knees. His feet had been far from the floor at first, but as the years went by and he grew taller there came a day when they reached it and he had told his mother, 'I am a grownup now.'

On Jack's last day, I had to hold Jack's hand as we approached the place because otherwise he tended to wander away and get lost. He looked as handsome as ever in his sports jacket, grey flannels and the lemon yellow lambs-wool sweater I had given him for Christmas. His moustache was trim because I had arranged for the barber to come round to our house. His tie was straight because I had tied it for him before we left home. To anyone looking at him, he was a tall, healthy and well turned out old man. If I did not talk to him, it felt almost like being with the old Jack again.

The chairs were gone. The banking department was gone as well.

I told him, 'That's where the green chairs used to be.'

'My Ducker shoes are black, not green,' he said. He would have sounded quite lucid to anyone who was listening and did not know. 'And I've run out of black Mansion polish.'

'That is the ten thousandth time you have said that,' I told him. 'And ten thousand times I have told you there's lots more in the tin and it was not called Mansion, either.'

Already I knew that the outing had been useless and there was no point in going on.

I took him to the lifts and we waited there for one to come.

He said, 'When you see Arabella, my wife, please tell her I need some black Mansion polish.'

I pressed my lips together to stop anything cross getting out.

A lift arrived. Although it was computer operated now, they had made it look the same, with its folding iron grill and interior mirror. As we stepped in I began to feel hopeful because I thought I saw a little spark of memory light his eyes.

But as the lift started moving he said, 'Mother, could you get me some black Mansion polish because my shoes have got to be done before I go to school?'

I said nothing. What was there to say?

I hate lifts. Always have. I was only using it now because it was so immensely complicated getting this pathetic new Jack up and down the stairs. When I was little, and we had stood waiting for the pre-computer clanking lift to arrive, my mother told me a story.

'A little girl, just your age, had a dream that she saw the guard leaning from a train and, holding up two fingers, say, "room for two more". Later the train crashed and all the passengers were killed. Next day the little girl and her mother were waiting for the Harrods lift. When it came, the operator opened the door, held up two fingers and said, "Room for two more". He looked exactly like the train guard in the girl's dream. The mother was going to get in, but the girl wouldn't let her. The lift went without them and it crashed and everyone was killed. Don't look so sour, Arabella. It's only a story.' My mother was always trying to train me out of taking things so seriously.

There was no operator the day Jack and I got into the Harrods lift. There was room for about six more, but there was only us two in it.

The lift stopped suddenly between floors.

'It's stopped,' I said.

'What time do we get there? I'm tired,' Jack said.

Then the lights went out. Just the two of us in the dark.

'Don't do that.' His voice sounded cross. I couldn't see his expression. I had begun to tremble.

'What do we do now, Jack?' I whispered.

And in the dark I felt his hand come and meet mine. He held my hand in the dark lift. He had not done that for a year. He said, 'Don't be frightened, Arabella. I am here.' He had not remembered I was Arabella for a year. I held his hand and clung on tightly. Clung on because Jack had come back again. Clung on because I did not want to lose him a second time. Clung on because at last he had remembered he was here and because he knew who I was.

I began to ask him, over and over, 'What shall we do now, Jack? What shall we do now?'

Then he wrung his hand from mine and said in that new tetchy tone that he had used ever since the illness started but that had vanished a moment ago, 'Switch on the light so I can find the black Mansion polish, Mother.' And I realised that the old Jack was gone again, and that I was alone in a dark, stopped lift with a person who was dead inside. And the fear that had held off till then took hold of me. I told him that it was all his fault that we were trapped together in this lift that would not go. Four steel walls without a door or window. No one knowing we were here. Lost creatures for whom time had stopped already. Dying creatures sealed off from the world of the living.

And all the time I was raging at him, he did not say anything. And when the lights came on and the lift began to move again, he was leaning against the wall and still not saying anything. And when at last it reached a floor with a little bump, he fell sideways and slithered to the ground. And tumbled slowly half-way out when the doors opened. It was too late to take him to hospital.

So you can see why it's so important for me to find him, wherever he is, and explain that I am afraid of being trapped in a small space. Tell him that I did not mean the things I'd said, tell him something I should have said when he was alive but thought was too sentimental. Jack, Oh Jack.

CHAPTER 12

AT INTERVALS THROUGHOUT THAT AWFUL MONDAY in the commune, after I had been abandoned by M'buta, I would have called a taxi if I could have worked the mobile phone. God, how I wished I had paid attention when my daughter tried to teach me how to operate the thing.

And once again it got lodged in my mind that they had planned to abandon me all the time. Verity and M'buta had become worn out with looking after me and preventing me from committing suicide. They were so full of worry about Naomi and so wearied by the hunt for her, that when an opportunity had arisen for abandoning me, they had taken it. Presumably they had made some deal with the commune to keep me on. Although I had been ripped off with this ghastly weekend, it was clearly really a very cheap place to live. Probably they did not even think they were doing anything wrong. Perhaps they even thought that, since I was seeking death anyway, a sort of living death in this place would be the next best thing and good for me too. Maybe they even felt that living here would cure me of wanting to die. I had never told them why I wanted it so much so how could they understand? M'buta had this crazed passion for Daniel daSilva and most likely imagined that my soul would be helped by staying here, near to him.

Knowing M'buta, she probably believed Daniel daSilva utterly when he said that Naomi would be found on Tuesday and had gone to collect her. Had she forgotten that he had also said that the grandmother would be there? But then a stab of worry overtook me. Was there another grandmother? Everyone has two. Naomi's donor father must have had a mother who would be Naomi's other grandmother. Did M'buta know about this person? Yes, that was the answer. She must have gone to the Bereton Clinic and because of the exceptional circumstances and also because it was a place where rules did not seem to be particularly adhered to, they had told her how to find the father's side to Naomi's family. I had learnt from Chrissy, that when a woman chose a father for her baby, the man's sperm was put in a phial with the mother's name and address on it. 'So as to avoid error,' Chrissy said. Apparently the Bereton did not take secrecy seriously at all if even Chrissy knew who both father and mother were and where the mother lived.

A shock of jealousy overwhelmed the worry feeling and hostility rose in me for this other woman who had so far not remembered a single of Naomi's four birthdays and had never given her a Christmas present, but who would, on Tuesday, be stealing Naomi's love while I was imprisoned here. I had lost Naomi. The other grandmother would find her. After something like that happening, I would never have the same place again in Naomi's heart. The bitterest thing about all this was that it was all going to happen on a Tuesday, the day of the week on which I had planned to be united with Jack.

I could see that I had brought my present unpleasant situation on myself by not trying to see things from M'buta and Verity's point of view, though I could not excuse them and would never forgive them for what they had done to me. I should feel guilty, but instead felt absolutely furious and determined to escape before Tuesday and be the one to find my little granddaughter, get to her before that other vile woman. The loving grandmother would beat the neglectful one to it. I would find a way. I had to.

When, after we arrived, M'buta discovered I had brought the phone, she had been horrified. 'I didn't know you'd brought it. They are absolutely forbidden in the commune.'

At the time I had told her, 'You take it if you want. I can't use it anyway. It's perfectly useless to me.'

But she had shrunk away from the machine as though it was a poisonous rattlesnake. She had waved her hands in front of her face, as though warding off an instrument of Satan. 'Keep it in your case, Ladyma, right at the bottom. Don't touch it again till you are five miles away from the commune.'

The phone still lay where M'buta had insisted I hid it, under everything and behind the little tear in the lining.

'You are being ridiculous,' I had said at the time.

'They might look inside your case,' she said.

'Just like home, then,' I said bitterly and was satisfied to see her face go red.

I would have liked to lock the door of my cell, but of course, no lock here.

I went to the door and looked out. No one in the passage. I am getting as timid as M'buta, I thought. But if they do take it away from me, then I am really done for. There will be no way at all for me to escape.

No one there.

I went back in, softly closing the door after me, then took the phone out of its hiding place. Verity had said. 'First you have to switch it on.' A button somewhere for that. Which? The thing looked more like a mini typewriter, with incomprehensible words on a large number of keys, not one saying 'on/off'. I began to stab at buttons. When Verity had done this, the phone had turned luminous, but now it seemed as dead as a door knob. I was doing my tenth set of hopeless stabs when I heard footsteps outside. Hastily I thrust the phone under my bottom as the door knob of my room began surreptitiously to turn. I held my breath and waited, as the door slowly opened. One of the red faced women stood there. She seemed at first flustered, then surprised at seeing me here. 'Why aren't you down at breakfast?' she demanded. In her hand she had a tray on which there was a mug of something, dandelion tea no doubt, and a bowl of that dreadful gruel. 'You are supposed to be down there by now. Where is Margaret? Why is she not with you?'

'I told her to go away. I told her I was not going down for breakfast.'

The woman's expression darkened. 'I shall deal sternly with her for having allowed you to remain here. Here is your robe.' She flung a white calico garment in my direction. 'This is what you must wear from now on, when in the presence of the Lord. Please put it on.'

The garment, a hideous thing made of raw calico, was the sort of thing I used to dress Verity in when she was little and acting the part of an angel in the Nativity play.

'I don't think I will, if you don't mind,' I told her politely, trying to hand the garment back. 'It is really not my style at all.'

She stared at me with an outraged frown. 'Put it on at once,' she said, 'I shall tell Margaret to come and get you in five minutes.'

Furious, humiliated and frantic as I was, I realised that this was an occasion where expressing rage or being stubborn would get me nowhere. This was a time for meekness. I picked up the garment, being careful not to let my bum come off the hidden phone. I examined the garment, which looked like a crude flour sack. I tried again. 'I'm afraid it's not quite my size. I think I'll just stick to my normal clothes, but it's very kind of you all the same.'

'Put it on and don't waste time,' she said angrily. And when I did not move, 'Go on. Let me see you do it.'

'I will, I promise, as soon as you are gone,' I said and went on sitting. The phone was making my bottom ache by now.

But still she stood, arms crossed, waiting. 'Come on, do it now,' she said. 'Get up. Get going. What are you sitting there for? Are you trying to hide something?'

'No, no,' I assured her. 'Of course not. What have I got to hide? But I can't dress with you there.'

'When you live here, you have to abandon all the trappings of the world and shedding false modesty is one of the first things you have to learn. The robe is necessary because today you are going to get your new name.'

'New name?' Hastily I changed my aggressive tone to the meek one. 'New name ?'

'A pure name. A name not soiled by worldly things. Daniel says that Arabella is a name for a loose woman.'

I tried to hide my huffing sound of indignation, but I don't think I managed. She stared at me with a ferocious glare, before, at last, stomping out of the room, saying first, 'Hurry. We must not keep Daniel waiting.' Thank goodness she left at last and I could relieve my bum of the phone. Fury swept over me with the force of a hurricane as the vile creature's footsteps began to recede along the corridor. I peeped out of the door to make sure she was out of earshot before giving vent to them. Then, balancing on my zimmer frame as best I could, I went about the room with my stick, shouting in my fury, beating anything I could reach. The room being so sparsely furnished, and those furnishings being of such a rock hard and impoverished quality, I was unable to wreak any visible damage on anything, so the episode was unsatisfactory. For a moment I was inclined to beat out the window glass, but I thought better of that at once. A bitter wind was blowing outside and the room was icy enough already.

I took out my whisky flask but quickly put it back again. Only a few sips left, I realised. I had expected to be home today, so had been too lavish in my sipping. I did not dare drink more, for who knows when I should be able to replenish my flask.

Finally, still panting I managed to pull my clothes on. Then I put the mobile phone inside the bra section of my M&S all-in-one-corset. This time I decided to keep the phone about my person for I could tell that there were people here who were likely to rootle among my things when I left the room. The moment I learnt how to use it, I would dial 999 and tell them that I was being held against my will. And when the police got here I would tell them that I suspected children were being held in unsuitable conditions and that the matter should be investigated. The thought of being able to pay these dreadful people back for all their slaps and insults gave me a little satisfaction. A new name, indeed. Arabella sounding like the name of a loose woman. After alerting the police, I would order an Indian takeaway and a bottle of wine. My mouth watered at the thought. And then I would hitch a lift in the takeaway van to save me the expense of a taxi.

But there was no time to experiment any more with the phone now. With a grim sigh I pulled on the ghastly garment. There was one good thing about it. It was so loose and baggy that it hid the phone tucked into my corset.

I opened the door and stood in the corridor and as I waited for Margaret I heard a sound coming from a room further down the corridor. The room where Margaret had told me the abbot lived. I had forgotten all about him till now and realised that I hadn't seen him at all since I had been here. The sound was a sobbing kind of groan. The voice of someone ill or in trouble. The red faced woman appeared suddenly out of the room, empty tray in hand, and saw me.

'Wait inside. Margaret will come,' she said tersely.

Later, in the refectory, I asked Margaret, 'Tell me about the abbot. Why do we never see him?'

'He is a hundred years old like I said,' she told me briefly, as though this was the only explanation needed.

It did not seem like an answer, but I was going in for meekness at the moment. Just wait till I get out of here, I thought.

She said suddenly, after looking at my face, 'Don't be sad, Ladyma. Today is the preparation day.'

'Preparation for what?' I asked.

'Departure,' she said.

Her words made me feel hopeful. Hadn't she told me on my first day that it did not matter that the abbey was in a mess and the children not properly catered for, because they would soon move on?

'For the next stage,' she added. Her face was shining with excitement. 'Tomorrow we will see Daniel in his glory.'

My heart sank again. This was not what I had thought of as moving on. But meekness, Arabella. Remember meekness. And I shan't even be Arabella for long, judging from what that dreadful woman had said. But I certainly did not plan to be here by tomorrow. I needed to be home again and find Naomi. I mean, that was so dense about these people. They went in for glorifying Daniel and maintaining that every single word he said was God's gospel truth, yet here they were putting me, who was supposed by his own statement to be the Naomi finder, in a position where I was unable to do it. Unless of course he had meant the other grandmother.

I entered the refectory looking a real freak in my ridiculous white robe and there found that everyone else was wearing one too and very foolish they all looked, as though they were still in their nighties.

Breakfast was, as you may imagine, as dreadful as ever, but by now after three days of it, my stomach was so hollow that I even ate it with some gratitude, though I made sure I put on a wry expression for Margaret's benefit as I swallowed. Then to the room for the wretched cleaning process and to await the demi god.

'Double god,' corrected Margaret gently. The people here have no sense of irony and also never take offence. You can say anything. Unless it's to him. Then they lose their rag.

At first all seemed much as before apart from the fact that this time the children, also clothed in these silly pretentious sack-like garments, sat in a row.

Daniel entered at last, wearing a loose white robe, though you could see from the subtle shine of it that his was not made of the cheapest material, but was probably a rather costly silk. A silken cloth covered the chair put out for him as well.

One had to admit that, with his yellow hair, golden skin and tiny features, he looked rather splendid. Even I let out a tiny gasp of admiration, luckily unheard under the moans of awe emitted by his followers. This man looked so very similar to the depictions of Jesus in classical art. Of course we all know that Jesus, being from the Middle East, would have really been dark skinned with black hair and eyes. But in the end it is how we think things are, rather than how they used to be, that becomes the fact.

Daniel was quite different today. Gone was the slightly withdrawn and stern speaker of Saturday and Sunday. He spoke with a wild passion that seemed to cause the people of the commune to lose all their inhibitions. Then something so crazy came over me, that later I suspected they might have put drugs in the food. Ludicrously I found myself caught up in the excitement. It is very difficult to explain what happened in those moments except to say that when all around you are being thrilled and noisy, it makes you start to feel like that too.

'I am God, God, God,' shouted Daniel. 'You are God, God, God.' And horrifyingly, I realised that my own throat was shouting it with the others. We all echoed the word, 'We are God, God, God.' I even felt a little godlike. I really can't imagine how such a thing could have happened.

After that he began to speak. The gist of his talk was that we were now moving into a new stage in which the world and all its filth and evil were to be left behind while we went on into a place of golden glory.

Then Daniel tore off his white robe and stood there naked and his body was beautiful. And he said, 'This is my sacrifice. This is what I have given, what will you give?' And he turned round so that we could see his naked back. And it was scored with terrible wounds. Great gouges of ripped away flesh. 'The whip burnt away my own temptations and my sins till now I am as pure as a newborn child, and today I have used the whip to burn your sins away,' he said.

People were screaming now. Horror and awe, love and dismay all mingled together in their cries. Margaret began to cry with her mouth open and tears running unchecked down her face. The children in the front row were sobbing too. Blood was still running from the wounds, as though the injury was recent. Then I saw a couple of wounds that looked as though they had been inflicted earlier. Two dark scabs that sealed a deep rip in the flesh, which looked more like bullet wounds that those from a whiplash.

'I have shed my own blood precious for all of you,' he shouted. He shook his head and corrected, 'My blood precious.'

It was in that moment that the prickling of suspicious wonder began to rise. There was only one other person in the world that I knew of who used that phrase. The thought I had just had was so outrageous that I could hardly dare entertain it. Especially in this heated atmosphere of hysteria. If the people here knew what I was wondering, they would probably tear me to pieces, for I was thinking heresy.

Was it possible? Could it be possible? Keep calm, I thought. Don't let anything show in your face. I must be imagining. One little slip of the tongue. A mere coincidence.

And the man who had been spying on Freddy had been shot twice by Jeremy. Those half healed wounds on the body of Daniel daSilva looked like bullet wounds.

Now just imagine this, I thought to myself. Just suppose we had here a virtuous young religious leader who wanted children for some reason, but wished to keep his body pure by eschewing sex. Using a fertility clinic and producing a child by AI would seem to be an option.

I had stopped shouting abruptly and I suppose my thoughts might be showing up on my face for suddenly Margaret turned and looked at me inquiringly. 'What? You look troubled.'

'I am in awe,' I told her hastily.

She smiled in relief. 'He takes people like that.'

It took only moments for me to start laughing at myself for my ridiculous notion. Because of the stress of losing Naomi, my mind was ready to seize upon anything that might give hope and because I was stuck here and unable to continue with my hunt for the child outside in the world, I was trying to carry it on inside instead. I went through all the suspicions I had had ever since she vanished, and realised that there must have been a dozen of them.

'Now you are smiling,' called Margaret over the clamour. All the rest of them were roaring away as lustily as ever.

'Only someone who has lost a child can know what I am going through,' I said.

'Don't be sad about that, Ladyma. Daniel said you would find her tomorrow and he is never wrong about anything.'

I nodded. But then considered, suppose I was right. Suppose Daniel was Naomi's father and that he had got her and that that was how he could say with such certainty that he knew when she would be found. He had longed for her so much that, in spite of his holy mission, he had been unable to resist kidnapping her, but now that he saw how sad he had made me and M'buta, he was feeling sorry and had decided to give her back again to us. But this, sensible though it seemed, made M'buta's act of doing a bunk rather odd. Especially if Daniel had told her to go. You would have thought he would have wanted her here, for the moment when she could be reunited with her child. But then, I thought, perhaps this pure holy person, disapproving of lesbian relationships, has removed his child from what he considered was an immoral environment.

But if Daniel has Naomi, where is she? So far I had never paid much attention to the rank of silent docile children, but now found myself searching among the backs of their heads in case my granddaughter was among them. I mean, I knew perfectly well really that she was not. I could not have missed her for a minute, even from a back view, even from a distance. And the miracle of sight so recently bestowed on me, made it less likely than ever that I had not seen her.

'We have a naming here,' shouted Daniel over the clamour of voices. An instant silence fell. Everyone turned to look at me. 'From now on this woman shall be called Stella.'

Stella. Can you imagine. Now, I'm sure there are some really nice Stellas around but I happen to think that Stella is one of the ugliest names in the world. Bag ladies are called 'Stella'. I'm sure they are. I mean, who would want to be called 'Stella'?

They seemed to like it, though. A little burst of whispered applause followed Daniel's pronouncement.

'I am very sorry, but I don't like it at all,' I said firmly, forgetting for a moment the need for meekness.

Completely ignoring my protest, as though I had not spoken, he said, 'Of course the star of this woman is a dying one, but there is still a little spark in it. And it is this last spark that she is going to take with her on the next stage.'

'Ah,' murmured the congregation, as though they had been asked to admire a cuddly baby animal.

'Although in this life she was beset with impurity, vanity, alcohol, sex and immoral longings, because of the god in me, she is being purged. I have forgiven. She will rise again as clean and glowing as all of you.'

'Ah.' The cuddly animal was doing something sweet and cute, though what the hell the man was talking about I could not imagine. But there he stood, talking nonsense, naked, thin, beautiful, streaked with blood, not shivering at all in spite of the cold. I, in my silly robe, had stopped shivering too, I realised. I had become quite warm in fact. Around me they were all starting to pull their robes off, now.

'Come on, Stella, free yourself from your second last shackle,' cried Margaret, hurling her robe to the floor. 'After this you will have only your corrupt human body to lose.'

They were all naked by now. Even the children were without clothes.

They began to dance slowly and solemnly at first, to perform a stately minuet, and then, without music and no other rhythm but feet and voices, the tempo increased till all around me these naked people were whirling, leaping, screaming with wide open mouths. I joined them. Can you imagine? I hadn't done anything like this in the whole of my life before.

'Stop,' shouted Daniel and everyone stopped as though struck with a magic spell. I fell panting into a chair as the others collapsed around me. They are like puppets, I thought. It is as if he had hypnotised them. Or me, the sudden startled thought came. Had I really been leaping up and down with the rest of them? Had I really left my zimmer frame behind and gone hopping and skipping without it? I could remember doing it, and my legs had seemed perfectly normal. They had felt just like when I was young. I decided that Daniel must have performed another of his healing miracles on me. Gingerly I lifted a leg and tested it out. It moved when I asked it to. I tried the other one and that was obedient too. I had not imagined it. I had been dancing.

I became filled with a flush of glorious gratitude and because it must have been Daniel who was responsible for this new walking me, he became in a moment the most truthful and beautiful person in the world. In that miracle moment, I would have done anything he asked. Did these people do anything he asked? Yes, was the answer. I wondered how far they would go. Would they commit murder if he told them to? I decided it was likely.

'Tomorrow is Tuesday and we will have our last feast before moving on,' he said, before going out.

'Oh, glory, glory,' cried the congregation. 'Glory, glory, glory,' they kept shouting as Daniel's footsteps died away down the corridor.

As soon as he had left the room, it became cold again, as though Daniel's body had been generating the heat. I remembered how, on that first day Margaret had said that the electricity for the lights came from Daniel. Perhaps she had not been joking. Now that he was gone I started shivering all over.

'Come, I'll take you back to your room so you can get some more clothes on,' said Margaret. 'You are not as used to this place as we all are and you don't want to get ill before tomorrow's feast.'

She made no comment nor expressed any surprise when I rose from my seat and walked unaided at her side. I wanted to shout and scream, to laugh and jump as we had all been doing minutes earlier.

'Feast?' I said and felt even more cheered up. I could really do with a feast after three days of tepid gruel. Even the kind of dreadful vegetarian food that these people most likely served would be welcome. I asked hopefully, 'You have a decent cook then?' I had never seen any signs of food being delivered and wondered how they were going to do it. It did not seem to be the sort of organisation that kept stocks of frozen food, or anything like that. A chill idea crossed my mind that they would be reaping the winter countryside for weeds to cook.

Back in my room, Margaret carrying the zimmer frame, I was still on my own two feet. Oh, the bliss of getting back into my clothes again. What a freak I must have looked, dancing round the room in that calico nightie. But now my legs had been returned to me, I did not even mind that. At least I had kept a little dignity, though, I thought. For a moment I had been seized with the temptation to remove my clothes like the rest of them. At least I had not given in to that. But all the same, thank God there were no mirrors in this place.

Now, in spite of my good vest and jersey, the cold in my little cell-like room felt unendurable, so as soon as Margaret was out of range, I pulled my flask out and sucked at the last drops left. All gone. By now I should have been back home with a full bottle. Damn and hell and blast M'buta. How could she have done this to me? I shook and shook the flask, but inside was as dry as a desert. I had no way of getting more whisky till I got out of here. If I managed to use that phone, I thought, I would order a crate of whisky to be delivered here and blow the cost. That would show them. Then I'd get the lorry the drinks had come in to take me home. I took the phone out and began tinkering with its little buttons again. Suddenly it became luminous. My heart leapt up with joy. One step toward salvation. But after that, nothing more. I tried every combination of keys I could think of but none brought me nearer to being able to dial 999, let alone Bottoms Up. I heard people coming along past my room and I hastily put the phone back into my corset.

CHAPTER 13

I SAT THERE FOR A WHILE, at a loss now, cold and bored. I tried to write my diary, but there seemed nothing sensible to say. How could I describe the ludicrous dance that I had performed so recently? Filled with the need to test my legs again, to see if it was really true, to enjoy every moment of the walking miracle before it faded, I decided to venture out and see if I could find some Holy Dew. According to Margaret, this was a strong alcoholic drink made from the roots of dandelions, that the monks of this monastery had been brewing since the very start of their order and the sale of which had been the source of their income. Margaret told me that though the people of the commune had kept discovering and destroying hidden stashes of this liquor ever since they came here, they still kept finding more.

'Destroying?' I said. 'But I understood you were selling it.'

'No, no.' She shook her head. 'How could you think of a thing like that? Daniel is very against alcohol.'

'But I understood you have a secret still in the cellars,' I persisted.

Obviously I had misunderstood her earlier. She assured me this was not so.

All the same, hoping I might come upon secret stashes, I decided to creep out and do a bit of exploring. I opened the door and peeped out, making sure that no one saw me. What freedom I felt now that I had the use of my legs back. But how quickly I had become paranoid and secretive. Three days with Daniel's two security women were enough to sap the courage of the most courageous person. Who cares if I got lost, I thought, as I set softly off along the corridor, if the reward was a bottle of Holy Dew. I couldn't quite tiptoe, my feet were not supple enough for that, but I went pretty quietly all the same.

As I passed the abbot's door the idea came to me that he might be able to tip me off about some of the Holy Dew hidden places. I knocked softly and there came the murmured sound of an old man's voice. 'Come in.'

I opened the door and stepped inside.

The room was very dark, with tattered curtains pulled across the small window. At first there seemed to be no one here and I thought I must have imagined the invitation to enter, then as my eyes got used to the dim light, I saw that a tiny and very ancient man was lying on the bed. He looked as thin, crisp and fragile as a fallen leaf.

Margaret had told me that even twenty years ago there had been eighty monks living in this monastery, but that over the years one by one they had died from old age and no new monks had joined because young men do not get religious vocations any more, so that now this old abbot was the only monk left. The monastery was his responsibility and it was he who had agreed to allow Daniel and his commune to settle there, in exchange for their helping to maintain the place. Every day, she said, Daniel would visit the father abbot, take instructions from him and inform him about the things going on in his monastery.

'He is old, but his brain is working perfectly,' she said. 'Because this place belongs to him, Daniel tells him – everything.' She paused before saying everything.

The old man struggled into a sitting position and said in a tiny creaking voice, 'Good day. I do not think we have met before.' The pink skin of his scalp shone through his thin white hair. He looked so old, it made me feel quite young.

'I am—' I began, then could go no further. I had so many names that I felt almost in a muddle about what I was called. Feeling that a little polite conversation should be engaged upon before opening up the topic of Holy Dew, I said, 'May I sit down?' and when he nodded, I pulled up a tin folding chair to the bedside.

'This is a beautiful place,' I said. 'It must be sad for you to see it in such a dilapidated state.'

He nodded. 'Daniel said he was going to turn this monastery into the stairway to Paradise.'

'He hasn't got very far,' I said.

The abbot fell silent for so long, that I wondered if he had fallen asleep. Then he asked suddenly, 'Are you one of them?'

'Who?'

'Why have I not seen you? I thought I knew everyone of the commune.'

I swallowed back a choke of indignation as the question reminded me, all over again, of why I was here. 'I came with my daughter-in-law for a week-end and she went off, deserting me.'

The abbot sighed. 'Won't your son be coming to get you soon?'

'I do not have a son,' I said. I could see him looking questioningly, but Verity's marital arrangements were too complicated for explanation. And also this man was a holy abbot. Perhaps he would find lesbianism shocking. 'So I thought I would make the best of it by looking round the monastery.'

'I wish you could have seen it in the old days,' he said. 'I feel disgraced now, by the state it's in, but what can I do? Daniel and his people have been here for more than a year and still have not started on the work.'

'How did you meet him?' I asked.

'He came one day, arriving on foot, when there was only me and Father Gregory left. Father has gone to his Heavenly peace now. Daniel told me he was a recent convert to the Catholic faith and wished to bring his followers to live in a holy environment. In exchange, he said, they would take care of this place and help to restore it. At the time Gregory and I both thought he was a gift from God.'

'Is Daniel a Catholic? You would not guess it from his teaching.'

'For the first six months, he and his followers were very devout. They did not start on any physical work, but they attended mass daily and seemed like good people. They were very quiet and did not smoke or drink. Even the children would sit through the whole of a church service without making a sound.'

'It must have been pleasant to have such people here,' I said.

'You are right. At first Gregory and I felt pleased, even though all the commune members ever did was sit around like zombies or dig up dandelions.'

The mention of digging up dandelions filled my mouth with the saliva of longing, but I felt it was not yet the right moment to mention the Holy Dew. 'Could you not have told them that either they must do the work, or leave?' I said.

'I have said it several times but they are still here and still nothing gets done. Lately when I try to talk to Daniel about it, he only says, "We will not be here much longer." '

'What will you do when they have gone?' I asked.

He let out a tiny sound like a groan. 'He says he is taking me with him.'

Was this abbot a prisoner like myself? Should I tell him about the mobile phone, and that as soon as I could work it, I would be ringing the police and asking for rescue? In fact perhaps he knew how to work a mobile phone. But after another look at him, I decided this was unlikely.

The need for rescue, though, had lost some of its urgency since my legs had started working again. Perhaps, I thought, by tomorrow I might even have the strength to do some walking. The nearest station was much too far, but there was a road a mile away. I had a ludicrous vision of myself standing on this road, hitchhiking as I and Jack had done together when I was a girl. We had hitched all over Europe when we were in our twenties. There had been times when we had been turned down by car after car, till at last we had to resort to the couple's hitching trick. Jack hid while I thumbed a car driven by a lone man, pretending to be alone. When the car stopped, Jack would emerge and get in too, for then it would be too late for the man to refuse us. You never see people hitching nowadays. I am told that that is because the hitch-hikers turned dangerous and began to attack the drivers who gave them lifts. Well, they certainly would not see me, an eighty year old woman on a stick, as a threat. I began to feel quite excited at the idea.

'It was the sewing that was the first sign that we had a problem.' The abbot was murmuring in a soft high pitched voice, as though talking to himself. 'For several days I had seen the people of the commune stitching lengths of white cloth and one morning my peace of mind was shattered when rising from prayer, I looked out of my window and was shocked to see the courtyard filled with naked men, women and children. They were standing round a great bonfire and throwing their clothes into it.' The abbot shuddered. 'I began to tremble at the unique sight of so many women's naked bodies and felt glad that there were no young monks in the community any more, to be corrupted by such a sight. Father Gregory was so far gone that if naked women appeared before him in his cell, he would not have noticed, but I could see all too well and feared there was about to be an episode of debauchery on the monastery premises. And after their clothes were burnt, they put on these white shifts.'

'So your fears of an orgy were unfounded?'

'There were other things, though. There were the sermons. I am an old man and Father was already out of his senses. I began to feel very tired, so Daniel asked if I would like him to preach the sermon. I should not have agreed to it, I see now. But at the time it seemed an answer to a prayer. It became a custom. I would sit and have a little nap while he talked. Then one day I woke suddenly to hear him telling the congregation that he was God. I got to my feet at once and told him to step down from the pulpit. I said I did not want him to take the sermon any longer. The congregation, which consisted mainly of his followers, all stared at me with indignation. Daniel paid no attention to me at all, but went on speaking as though I was not there. That evening I told him for the first time that I could not allow him and his people to live in the monastery any longer and that they must all be gone by the end of the week.'

'Then?'

'That night Father Gregory died.' The abbot gave a shudder and said something in a whisper. I leant closer to hear. 'What did you say?'

'Was murdered,' muttered the abbot.

'Murdered? Who by?'

In spite of what Margaret had said, this old man must be wandering in his senses. Jack had gone through a phase like that too. I touched the abbot on the hand, so as to comfort him. 'I'm sure he was not murdered, Father Abbot. You said he was a very old man and suffering from dementia.'

The abbot bowed his head for a little while, then pulling himself together went on, 'When I went to perform the funeral, Daniel daSilva was wearing my vestments. I ordered him to return them to me and leave my chapel, but once again he paid no attention. He performed the funeral service himself, as though he, not I, was the priest.' Burying his head in his hands, the abbot let out a long sad sound, that was like a sob. 'After that, Daniel daSilva said Mass instead of me each morning, as though he was a consecrated priest. I refused to attend and I told those dreadful women, Hope and Grace, when they came to fetch me, that what Daniel daSilva was doing was a sacrilege.'

'Hope and Grace? Daniel's security women?'

He nodded. 'I told them that Daniel will end up in hell if he continues this. And all of you will end up in hell for attending these masses.' He turned his head and stared out of his window, like a prisoner looking through the bars of his cell. 'Shortly after this Daniel daSilva told me that he had ceased to be a Catholic and was now something else instead. He did not bother to explain to me what his new mission was and I did not care to find out. The naked people round the bonfire were innocent as children compared to the events that happened subsequently.'

'What kind of things?' I asked.

The old man shrugged. 'Once the idea even came to me that these people were worshipping Satan.'

'Oh, dear,' I cried. 'Surely not.'

'Dancing in the nude. Animal sacrifice. I heard the sound of screaming.'

I felt like laughing now. This poor old man. 'Father Abbot, I assure you, you don't have to worry and that nothing like that is going on. It was bad and wrong of them to break the promise of repairing the monastery and also sad that they have left the church, but all the same this Daniel has certain powers. I was unable to walk unaided when I arrived here on Friday and look at me now.' I stood up and did a little hop, which was almost like a prance.

The abbot averted his eye, as though in distaste and said, 'Daniel has offered me eternal life. I told him that it is not his to bestow and that the only one who can give such a thing is God the Father and Jesus Christ his son.'

'Quite so, quite so,' I said hastily, realising that in my enthusiasm I had been insensitive.

'Now Daniel daSilva says that tomorrow they will all be leaving and my complaints will become irrelevant,' said the abbot. 'He says that after that the monastery will be purged of disrepair by God himself. He says that in spite of my having rejected his offer, he is going to provide me with eternal life all the same. He said that he has already created immortal life from his own body. I do not want the kind of immortality that Daniel daSilva offers me, Madam. I want God's kind.'

'You wouldn't, by any chance, happen to know where one might find a few looked over bottles of Holy Dew?' I asked.

He stared at me, as though getting his brain connected onto the question was a bit of a problem. At last he said in the voice of one who has never heard the name, 'Holy Dew?'

'Holy Dew,' I said and sat calmly waiting.

'Ah,' breathed the abbot, in a tone that made me feel I had said something that pleased him. 'Here, my dear madam.' And like a conjuror reaching in a hat for a rabbit he pushed his arm under his mattress and retrieved a squat bottle that was half full of a rich crimson liqueur. Reached again and out came a glass. 'One of us will have to sip from the bottle, I am afraid,' he said.

'Don't worry about that, my dear abbot,' I said. 'There are times in life when the small conventions must be laid aside.'

'In that case, since you are the lady, you must be the one to avail yourself of the glass,' he said. 'I assure you that though I shall sip, my lips will not make contact with the bottle neck.'

By this time my deprivation had lasted so long, that the touch of another person's lips did not unduly worry me. 'Thank you,' I said, taking the proffered glassful.

Oh joy, Oh joy. What a lovely old man this abbot was.

Though I was used to neat whisky, this liquor was so strong it seemed to scald my tongue. Goodness, how wonderful it was. It hit my stomach like a lick of flame. Warmth gushed through me as though my body had been set on fire.

'How do you find our brew, madam?' asked the abbot.

'Superb,' I said, when I could at last manage to speak. 'I have never tasted anything so wonderful in my life.'

So the two of us sat on the iron hard bed and drank Holy Dew.

'This was my only escape,' he said. 'The moment these people are gone I shall take out our product and put it on the market. Though there never was enough for doing anything to help with renovating this lovely building, we have enough stored hidden away down there to furnish me with a living for the rest of my life and provide me with the opportunity to say enough masses to compensate for the heretical ones performed by Daniel daSilva.'

'At least they will all be gone by tomorrow,' I said. 'Do you know how to work a mobile phone, Father Abbot?' I had drunk enough Holy Dew by now to have forgotten that the question would certainly be pointless.

'What is a mobile phone?' he asked.

I sighed. The way things were going, it looked as though not only I, but the abbot too, would have to travel with the commune to the station, for I could not see, in spite of his confidence in the hidden Holy Dew, that he could be left here on his own. But these people had no transport, though surely they could not intend to walk all the way to the station with so many children and there were too many of them to hitchhike.

They were so besotted and impractical, I thought, that anything was possible.

'Please take the rest of this bottle.' said the abbot.

'What about you?'

'I have more.'

CHAPTER 14

ODDLY I SLEPT QUITE WELL THAT NIGHT in spite of the hardness and the cold. Presumably having my legs back had improved the circulation of my whole system. Or the abbot's gift, which I had now transferred to my whisky flask.

Next morning I asked Margaret when they were going to start getting ready for the feast, after which, I presumed, would we be setting off for the station. But she only said vaguely and with irritating saintly smile of hers, 'Just you wait, Ladyma. It is going to be something really beautiful. Everything you have wanted will come to you.'

'Look, if you are planning to bring Naomi back to me today, then please just tell me when she will be coming and where she is now. I have been worn out with worry about her for weeks and I am not in the mood for happy surprises.'

'It's not like that, Stella. Daniel's beautiful promises are always fulfilled in the end but us of the commune have learnt to wait and be patient. Just wait and see. If he says she will come, then she will.'

'He promised the abbot that he and his followers would repair the monastery, and they have not done it,' I said. I knew as soon as I had spoken that it had been a mistake to let out that I had seen the abbot.

'You shouldn't talk to the abbot,' Margaret said and there was a note of alarm in her voice.

To change the subject, I said hastily, 'But what about this feast we have all been hearing of. I must say, Margaret, after three days here a bit of decent food would be very welcome.'

She caught my hands, looked into my face and, her expression brimming with joyful ecstasy, said, 'Ladyma, you will eat the holiest and most nourishing food today.'

'I don't care about holy and nourishing at the moment,' I said. 'A plate of egg and chips from a transport café would seem like manna from heaven at this moment.'

'That is exactly what you will be having at our feast, Stella. Manna from heaven. You have understood absolutely.'

If it had not been for the wonderful curing of my legs, which a whole night later still worked, the frustration of these cotton woolly answers would have made me cross and I would have made a fuss. As it was, I had no option but to follow Margaret's advice. In one day they were going to have a feast and then leave the place where they had lived for more than a year, yet I could see no signs of food being cooked nor preparations being made for departure. Even by midday, no sign of any food even arriving. Lunch was the same tasteless gruel as ever, with the same dandelion tea to wash it down.

That day went along like the previous three. Daniel talking incomprehensibly about Hell, Heaven, sacrifice and purity. Daniel emerging theatrically, at intervals, wearing his silly white shift. I managed twice, in the course of the day, to sneak into the abbot's room and share a snifter with him. The taste of Holy Dew on my lips helped to sustain me through the chill and boredom of the rest of the day's events. It was a real

Paradise-door-opening substance. My God, those monks knew how to brew.

Since the hideous episode was so nearly over, I tried coming down in the afternoon wearing my own warm and comfy clothes, but was roughly commanded back by the terrible female tyrants. You might ask why I came down at all. Those same tyrants were the answer to that question.

Still no sign of packing, cooking or ingredients arriving but some people in the grounds picking things from outside. Oh, my God.

But during the course of the day, the commune members began to be in an increasing state of excitement. There was a frisson in the air. You would think it was they, not me, who were popping in to see the abbot now and again.

Since the abbot's room was no worse than mine, I would happily have stayed in his and not gone back to mine all day, but he had impressed upon me the terrific importance of not letting the terrible tyrants discover I was with him.

'Grace and Hope are watching all the time and must not see us, or they will confiscate my little hoard.'

He seemed truly afraid, and since I had had a little taste of what they were capable of, being women perfectly prepared to slap a disabled octogenarian and that one biff from them would probably slay the fragile old man, I was very careful. But on this day, more than all those preceding it, the people of the commune seemed totally taken up with other things and hardly noticed what I did or where I went. You couldn't get into the battered bathrooms because they were permanently occupied by mothers scrubbing their docile children. I was constantly encountering people brushing their own or their children's hair, or wildly rinsing their white shifts apparently in the hope that they would be dry by the feast in the evening. But in spite of all this hygienic activity, still no signs of any cooking or packing.

I found Margaret in a bathroom, holding the protruding pink ear of a little boy in her fingers and massaging it with soap. Since both the bathroom and the water were freezing cold, the child was shivering.

When she saw me, she said, 'You must start cleansing yourself so that by tonight you are absolutely pure.'

'I am always absolutely pure, my dear girl,' I told her frowningly. 'I have already told you that. And that child will catch pneumonia unless you get something warm onto him quickly.' But it was clear I was going to get nothing sensible from her.

I tried the abbot. I was starting to think that, in spite of his hundred years and the Holy Dew, he was the only person left in this place with any common sense. Even I, over the past few days, had once or twice slipped into gullibility. How could I possibly have imagined, for instance, that I had been the subject of two miracles. What on earth had led me to believe that a young religious fanatic had cured me of my sight problem and my walking one, as though he was Jesus? For I saw now that I must have imagined that brief return of perfect sight. It must have been a trick of my brain. And as for my walking, the doctor had told me to expect improvement to be only gradual. He had not said there would not be any. What had happened to me had been perfectly natural, and had had nothing to do with the healer at all. It had merely been more sudden than the doctor had predicted.

The abbot and I were seated side by side on his stone bed.

For the first time he had allowed me to see where he kept his stock of Holy Dew.

'When the flagstone is back in place, not even the sharpest eyed person could tell it is removable,' he said. He brushed a little dust into the crack and went on, 'And the best thing is that they all believe I am too frail to lift even a cup of dandelion tea. But look at this, madam.' He pulled back the sleeve of his habit to reveal tiny biceps. 'I keep myself as fit as I can, in spite of them,' he whispered. 'I do exercises every day.'

He whirled his thin arms gently round to demonstrate.

'Hopefully we will be getting something better than dandelion tea with this feast tonight.' I spoke with more optimism than I really felt.

A small sound outside made us both turn our heads.

'Ssh,' he said. 'She might be listening. She often does.' But nothing more happened. It must only have been someone passing.

'What day of the week is it?' he asked.

'Tuesday,' I told him. A stab of regret touched me because now so many Tuesdays had gone by and I still hadn't managed to reach Jack.

'Are you the lady who wanted to die on a Tuesday?' he asked.

I stared at him, shocked. 'How do you know about that?'

'Every day Daniel comes to me to tell me what is happening in the abbey. One of the things he told me was that Madam M'buta has a friend who wants to die and enter Paradise.'

I felt a great surge of anger rush over me. How dare M'buta discuss my private life with strangers? Once again, because I was old, I had had my liberty and my privacy stolen 'for my own good' as though I was a delinquent toddler. But I only said, 'I'm glad that he keeps you informed.'

'At first I was reassured by this, thinking it meant that he continues to acknowledge me as the proprietor of this place, but now I see he is only paying lips service to his duty to me. He tells me what's happening, he hears my complaints and then leaves to do exactly as he pleases. He pays me no attention at all.' The old man rambled on, 'When Daniel first came to me he told me that his only desire was to enter Paradise. He asked me what sacrifice would be needed to get him there and if his own life be sufficient.'

'SSh,' I said. 'Listen. I do think someone is out there … '

The abbot crisped with fear. We both listened for a while and after that lowered our voices even more and talked to each other in almost inaudible whispers.

'So what did you tell him?' I hissed.

'I said that rather than die for God, he should live a holy life and provide God with pure and innocent offerings during his life time.' He looked at me with an expression of alarm. 'Why do I see that expression of horror on your face, Madam?'

'Nothing, nothing,' I said, but a terrible little icy thought had touched my heart.

The abbot went on, 'At first I thought he agreed with me, but gradually as time passed I saw a change come in his thinking. He began to believe the besotted fools of this commune, who think that he is divine. He began to talk of finding the key to power on earth that is obtained through Heaven.'

'How did he think he would get this?'

'He said that because he is a perfect and miraculous creature, anything that comes from his body will be miraculous and perfect too. The fools here retain the cuttings of his hair and finger nails, you know. Little bits of Daniel are reverenced like the relics of a holy saint. He told me he was going to offer the cosmos living things, created from parts of his own pure and divine body in exchange for immortality and absolute power.'

The irrational terrible fear went on growing in me. I had, by now become increasingly sure that Daniel was Naomi, Freddy and Melanie's father. All three looked like Daniel. I realised Daniel must have been the intruder who had tried to kidnap her that night, as I now felt sure he was the man who had been lurking round the home of Jeremy Delane. And the person who had posed as Melanie's uncle. He had been watching and monitoring the three children since they were born, keeping them pure for the moment he needed them, like a farmer waiting for his crop to ripen. He fiercely disapproved of makeup and on the evening of the intruder, Naomi had been putting on my lipstick so he had tried to kidnap her. Daniel daSilva, the father of these three children, had bred them for sacrifice. He had killed the little girl called Melanie and was now planning to trade his two remaining children to purchase himself power and immortality.

'He plans to kill,' said the abbot, as though echoing my thoughts. 'He has already killed Father Gregory.'

Even before the thought was properly formulated in my mind, I had begun pulling the mobile phone from inside my corset. I had managed to get the thing to light up yesterday. I tried to calm myself enough to do it again, and, oh, wonderful, miraculous, the keys all started glowing and some incomprehensible instructions appeared on the tiny screen. Think, Arabella, make you brain start working. A button called calls. Telephone calls, that must mean. I pressed it and at once a list of numbers appeared. There was M'buta's, there was Verity's. But there was no time for that now. I dialled 999.

'Police, ambulance or fire?' a voice asked briskly.

'Police. Quick, it's urgent.'

'What is the address?' asked the voice.

I never had time to even start the answer. The door burst open and Hope rushed in, reached over and snatched the phone from my hand, shouting furiously.

'You were told not to bring this instrument of Satan, this object of blasphemy into this pure place. I have been listening outside the door all this time and just waiting for you to make a mistake.'

The abbot cringed.

Hope went over to the tiny window and opening it and letting in a blast of even icier air, hurled my precious phone, the link between me and the world, the only thing that might have saved Naomi, into the scrub land below.

'You bitch,' I yelled. 'How dare you. When I get home I shall take legal action against you.' I do not normally use bad language and in fact have a great respect and fondness for female dogs, but on this occasion my frantic anxiety got the better of me.

Ignoring this, she said coldly, 'Be ready in the meeting room in one hour where we will prepare for the feast. And you too, Father Abbot. Everyone must be there.'

After she had gone out, I ran to the window and looked out.

It was dusk. I could see the shadows of bats emerging. Somewhere, down there among the tangled weeds, was my only hope. Then, as I stared sadly out into the blue evening light, I heard a little sound somewhere below. It was the aggravating sound of a mobile phone ringing. Mine. That vile sound, that always made me so irritated when I went on the bus to London, but now sounded like the sweetest sound in the world. It must be the police ringing back, I thought, as, without waiting to explain to the abbot, I rushed out and made for the stairs.

Thank God, my legs were working rather well. I could not hear the phone ringing once I was away from the open window, but I had carefully marked the place in my mind, so that when I got outside I would be able to find it. Inside, as I went along corridors, I passed hurrying people with white cloths, streams of fresh ivy, baskets of garden leaves. Everywhere there was the smell of soap and the sound of scrubbing. In one room behind a closed door I heard the voices of Margaret and another woman.

The woman said, 'I am told that Daniel will fill the glasses from the chalice, but only the holy children will drink from it. The rest of us are getting ordinary glasses.'

Her tone was sad.

'It doesn't matter,' came the voice of Margaret. 'Because after tonight all of us shall drink from golden chalices.'

Get there before it stops ringing, I kept telling myself. I could not believe I was really doing this, hurrying, nearly running, as I had not done since Jack died. That was when the hurry went out of me. That was when there ceased to be anything for me to hurry for. My last chance, my only chance, must get there before someone else hears it. By now, if it had not been for the flurry of preparing everywhere, someone would have seen and stopped me by now. But this time I stepped out of a side door, without being seen at all.

I stood listening. No sound. Damn my dreadful deafness. Pity I hadn't got Daniel to do a miracle on my ears. All the same, I made my way softly through the docks and nettles, trying to get exactly to the place from which I had thought the sound was coming. Over there, by the bent old alder tree that I had seen when I looked from the window. Yes, there it was. Silent now. They have given up. They have decided that, since no one answered, the problem, whatever it was, has gone away. Then, as I was starting hopelessly to hunt among the weeds, suddenly I heard the little darling ring sound start again. Over there. I had got the place a little wrong. It had been on the other side of the alder tree. Praying that the phone had not fallen into the great mass of tangled bramble bush nearby, I started making my way towards the sound. Still ringing. Still ringing. I was going to make it.

Then I heard the front door open and the voices of people approaching. Grace and Hope. They carried baskets.

Praying they would not hear the phone, I concealed myself as best I could in the shadow of the house and held my breath.

For a while I watched them furtively. I began to feel safe as they turned left, and began to walk the other way towards a great yew tree, where they bent down and started picking something from the ground. Yew berries? I hoped not but perhaps these people were so ignorant they did not know that yew berries were deadly poison. Then one of them straightened and stood listening.

'Do you hear that, Hope? Her phone.'

'Oh, silly of me to throw it out of the window without switching it off,' said Grace.

The two of them went crunching through the undergrowth like a pair of hippos. It didn't take them long to find the phone. It was still ringing as Hope grabbed it and held it to her ear. 'No, it's alright,' I heard her say. 'It was a false alarm. Oh, she's an old lady who is staying here. She is a little, you know, mentally disturbed. She suffers from anxiety attacks … yes, alright, thank you, officer.'

'Make sure you switch it off, before it rings again,' said Grace. 'Better take it up with you in case someone else finds it.'

'Daniel doesn't allow it,' said Hope.

'Nothing matters now. All the rules can be abandoned. You can keep it in the meeting room. We won't be going there again.'

Hope put the phone in her pocket.

I could have cried.

I had to stand there for ages while the two of them went back to the yew tree, and starting gathering again.

As I watched from my hiding place, a horrifying realisation came to me. I started trembling and had to make a gigantic effort to keep silent. For I had understood what was going to happen at the feast. I understood what the sacred food would be and why nothing was being cooked. And realised the need to find Naomi was urgent. I did not know what I would do after I had found her.

I stole back inside.

There were several flights of dark stairs down the cellar rooms. Which one to take? I had no time to dither. I went half way down one, then came up again and tried another. I knew, by now though, that this was not going to work. I did not have time. I might not find her till it was too late. I might get lost down there, even, while dreadful things were happening above. And after all, Naomi might not be in the cellars at all. That had only been a guess from Margaret's nervousness when I talked about the still. This building had so many rooms that she might be in any of them and I would not know.

I came back up again. The people of the commune were in such a state of suppressed excitement by now that they might inadvertently give me a clue to the hiding place of Naomi and the other two children.

I went back to the room in which I had earlier heard Margaret and another woman talking. They were still there, engaged in polishing glasses. I knew I must be careful not betray my sense of urgency but perhaps I would be able to learn something from them.

Margaret looked up and seemed alarmed at the sight of me. 'What are you doing here, Stella? You should be resting and making preparations for the evening.'

'I feel restless and would like to help you,' I said. 'I am a very good polisher so let me take over and do that one.' In reached to take the glass from her hand.

Margaret looked worried, but the other one, an older woman called Rebecca smiled.

'Here.' She handed me a tea towel.

'Are you sure?' said Margaret. 'Won't Grace mind?'

'The time for secrecy and silence is over,' said Becky. 'We are coming into the time of Paradise and all of us should be allowed to participate in the preparations for an offering in which Stella is so involved.'

'Thank you, Becky,' I said, allowed a warm gush of gratitude to infuse my tone. I took a glass and went to work. 'It is a wonderful privilege to be part of this beautiful ceremony.' I held the glass up to the light. The shattered icy room and cobwebbed windows were reflected in its surface. The two thin women with their pasty faces and inferior clothes were smiling in its glowing bulge. 'Can you tell me something about the ceremony? I would like to be totally prepared for it. I would like to play my part. For I think I have understood the marvellous thing that is about to happen.' I had mastered commune speak by now.

Both women smiled and flushed with pleasure. 'I am so glad, Stella, that you are now thinking in the same way as us. For a while we all feared that, in spite of Daniel telling us that you wished to move on to Paradise like the rest of us, that you were hostile in your heart.'

'Oh, no,' I cried. 'How could you think it? My only wish is to be back with my husband, Jack, again.'

'That is what Daniel told us,' said Margaret. 'But when you first came here, we began to think, well, not that Daniel was wrong, because he cannot be that. But perhaps that we had misunderstood what he was saying.'

'My eyes are open. My heart is with all of you. My longing to move on is greater than ever now that I have Daniel to lead me and the pure children to show the way.'

Margaret looked startled.

'Daniel has told me,' I said.

'Has told you?' Both women spoke together in identical astonished tones.

I touched the place where my heart was supposed to be. 'He spoke in here. He told me how privileged I was to be the grandmother of the divine child of a divine father.'

Margaret smiled. She looked both relieved and impressed. She said, 'At first we feared that the children had been so tainted by the world, that their souls would never be cleansed. Daily Daniel would work with them to exorcise Satan. One child was totally corrupted and nothing could be done with her, so Daniel had to send her away, but Daniel's strong treatments have conquered the Satan in the other two and they are ready to open the gates of Paradise for us.'

'What happened to the sent away child?' I asked. My heart was beating rapidly.

Margaret shook her head. 'He said that the child had gone away with her true father, and this was Satan.'

I suppressed a shudder.

Margaret was talking on. 'The other two children would have been lost too if it had not been for Daniel. Day and night he struggled with Satan, until he saved them.'

'How does Satan manifest himself in the children?' I asked carefully.

'By distorting holiness,' said Margaret. 'The spirit of holiness creates strange powers in children but sometimes the evil one manages to seize these and use them for his own ends. Thus you might have a child, say, who is able to communicate with its mind, to send its thoughts to another person. But then the evil one gets control of this ability, in the way that you might get interference with a radio reception. Then the child manages to send false messages.' She looked at me closely. Did she know about my hearing Naomi's voice in the night?

'And I suppose the children of Daniel would be endowed with more and stronger special powers than most.'

'Definitely,' said Margaret. 'Though, due to their over exposure to the vileness of the world, some of these powers were corrupted. A child whose power should have been to charm holy humans, charmed animals and pests instead. One that should be able to shower holy bliss upon her soul, creates vile money instead.'

'And where are these last two children? The pure ones? Have you ever seen them?

Margaret shook her head.

Becky said, 'None of us has. They are too precious to even meet us of the commune. They are kept separate so that there is no risk of their becoming contaminated even by us who have been so careful to retain our purity. Daniel told us that they will only come to us when we, having made ourselves as perfectly pure as we are able, are ready for the next most beautiful journey. Which will be tonight.' She became busy with her polishing again. 'You will be happy from now on, Ladyma. You will be with your Jack this time tomorrow.'

I sighed. A lethargy stole over me and I began to feel very tired. What could I have been thinking of, to imagine I could outwit Daniel daSilva and save my grandchild and Freddy from a whole commune of his crazed and gullible followers? Why not just give in? After all, was this not what I had wanted? I could almost hear Jack calling me, 'Come on, Arabella. What are you dithering for? This is the first Tuesday when you really have the opportunity to come to me. What difference will it make? Why does it matter how it happens?' Oh, how I did long to see him.

Naomi would die too, but could one say that her next life will be any worse than this one? It might even be better. Naomi's life in this world might not be happy at all, for all I knew. She might be treated badly by a husband, or be unable to have children, or become ill with some incurable and painful illness. She might suffer loss and grief and bereavement. Why not exchange one faulty life for another perfect one? The next stage, whatever it was like, would be different to that.

I will look after you, Naomi, wherever you are, I said with my mind. But then I thought that when you are four, you don't want to be dead and cared for by your grandmother. And that her life might not be a sad one. If she died when she was four, she might miss a whole lifetime of love and happiness. That what you need when you are four, is to be alive and take your chances.

Playing for time, hoping for more information, I reached up for the only thing left that had not yet been polished, a beautiful chalice of the sort that contains the host at Mass. Unlike the glasses, which were crude and cheap, this chalice looked very ancient and as though it was made of solid gold. It reminded me of something the abbot had told me earlier, when we had been drinking Holy Dew together. That Daniel had plundered the monastery chapel and taken the medieval chalice from it. But as I reached out for it, Becky snatched my hand away, saying in alarm, 'Don't touch that. It is sacred.'

'I'm sorry,' I said hastily, withdrawing my hand. I mustn't offend in any way. Naomi's life depended on my compliance.

CHAPTER 15

I LEFT AT LAST FEELING THAT, though I had learnt something, it was not enough. I still did not know where the children were hidden. But I must try what I could. There was not much time left and there was only me. I was the only person in the world who could save Naomi's life now.

Margaret had told me that the ceremony would start at ten. It was now – I looked at my watch – eight. Two hours for me to think up something without anyone here having the smallest idea that I was not ecstatic at was to come.

I headed for my room so that I could think in privacy, but as I passed the abbot's door on an impulse I knocked and entered that instead. He might be able to think of something.

He was sitting up and gave me his gentle calm smile. He looked very clean and spruce. Apparently people had been with him, preparing him for the evening ceremony.

'I think they are going to kill my granddaughter,' I told him. 'I think that Daniel daSilva has bred her to be a sacrifice.'

'Ah, yes, I have been told of these poor children,' he murmured. 'So you are the grandmother he spoke about, are you? What do you want me to tell you?'

'How to save her. You know these people. What can I do?'

He shook his head. 'Nothing,' he said.

'A four year old child is about to be murdered, and you say that nothing can be done?'

He pressed the tips of his fingers together and said, 'Your grandchild is too young to have seriously sinned so I am sure her soul will go to heaven. Because of that her death will not be a tragedy.'

'Suppose you did not think like that, but thought that such a death was terrible, and should not happen, then what?' I knew already I was wasting what little time I had with talking to him. He was too old and weak, and his brain had become slow. My doubts became confirmed when he said suddenly, 'Holy Dew.'

'No thank you, Father Abbot. I have more pressing things to do at the moment than drink with you,' I said.

'Holy Dew might save her.'

'How?'

'It is the same colour and consistency as the draft they gave Father Gregory.'

'Father Gregory?'

'When Daniel came here, Father Gregory and I were the only monks left. Father became very depressed when one by one our fellow monks died and no young ones came to take their place. He began to say he wanted to die too and join the rest of our community in Heaven. I even began to feel afraid that he would commit suicide, which, as you know, is a mortal sin.'

'Yes, I know,' I said.

'I persuaded him not to do this, but to wait till the Lord was ready to take him but although he agreed, he continued to be sad. Then Daniel and his people came to live here and Father Gregory's spirits improved. He began to say over and over, 'My prayers have been answered. A miracle has been bestowed on me.'

'He must have felt that after all young people were becoming monks again.'

The abbot nodded. 'I suppose so, even though there were now women and children among them. At the time I thought that perhaps Father Gregory, who I think by this time was a little wandering in his wits, was too far gone to notice them. He began to say he wanted to offer a sacrifice to thank God for answering his prayers and sending these young strong people to the monastery. I tried to persuade him that his saintly life was all that God wanted, but he would not listen to me. He listened instead to Daniel, who told him that God wanted the sacrifice of a pure and perfect person.'

'But surely this is not in line with the teaching of the Catholic church.'

'It is certainly not,' said the abbot. 'I suppose by then, though we did not realise it, Daniel was already slipping away from the church.'

'So Father Gregory offered to be Daniel's sacrifice?'

The abbot nodded. 'Though at the time I did not realise it and imagined that the idea of sacrifice was a symbolic one, in the way that the communion wine is turned into the blood of Christ. My objection at that stage was that Daniel was tampering with the ritual and tradition of the church, nothing more at first.'

'What about Father Gregory? Surely, since you were the abbot, he had to obey you.'

'It was as though, by now, Father had become lost to the spirit of God, and instead was in the thrall of Satan.'

'So they gave Father Gregory a cup of poisons to drink?'

'How did you know that?' He gave me an interested glance. 'But you are right. That is what I think happened. First Daniel performed this distortion of the Mass, as usual wearing my vestments. When he held out the chalice for Father Gregory to drink I remonstrated, telling him that this was a sacred thing and the receptacle for the blood of Christ, but you have seen Daniel daSilva. Even then, before he became a heretic, he was totally headstrong and did not bow to the authority of the church. Anyway, there was Father Gregory standing before the altar, wearing that ridiculous white gown. All those silly commune people did some shouting and chanting, then Daniel held out the golden chalice for Father to drink from. I did not know that what he was offering to Father was poison. It was so similar in texture and colour that I thought it was Holy Dew. Daniel said, 'Drink this in my name and this day you shall be with my father in Heaven.' Father Gregory drank the contents, then crashed down dead on the steps of the altar.'

'It must have been terrible for you. And what happened to his body?'

'There was no great problem there,' said the abbot. 'Father Gregory had been ill for a long time. He had had several small strokes. There was no reason for anyone to suspect anything but that he had had yet another stroke, which had finished him off. The doctor arrived after a couple of days. You see how we are situated, so far out and without either communication or transport. By the time he arrived, Daniel had already made arrangements for the funeral. The doctor merely signed a certificate to say that Father Gregory had died from a cerebral haemorrhage. A massive stroke, in fact.'

'Yes. I can see how it must have been.'

'I tried to speak privately with the doctor, to tell him that Father had been poisoned, but Daniel managed to persuade him that I was old, my mind muddled and that grief from my fellow priest's death had unhinged me. The doctor prescribed me a sedative, and departed. Father was buried and that was the end of that.'

'Didn't you tell anyone in the church?'

The abbot nodded. 'Next day I tried to contact the bishop but by this time Hope and Grace had moved in. They put a stop to all communication with the outside world. And that is how it has been ever since.'

'Couldn't you have sent a message through people who come to hear Daniel speaking?'

The abbot shook his head. 'You have seen how close they keep me.'

'And did you know about the children?'

The abbot nodded. 'Daniel told me that he had now created a better purer sacrifice than Father Gregory. This time, he said, it was ones he had created from his own body and they would be immortal and therefore so powerful that they would create a path for all the rest of us to enter Paradise. I know now that he must have been talking about his children.'

'Do you know where the children are? Can you tell me how to find them?'

The abbot shook his head. 'I have never seen them, though I heard them screaming when Daniel cast their devils out.' He was silent for a moment, then said, 'There were three at first, but Daniel failed to drive the devil out of one. I shiver when I think what happened to that poor little girl. I hope she was not your granddaughter, Madam.'

I shook my head. 'She was called Melanie.' I was trembling all over. I must pull myself together. I could not afford to go to pieces now.

'The other two children are doomed as well unless you find a way to substitute Holy Dew for the poison drink,' said the abbot.

'How do I do that?' I was feeling wild with worry. 'That sounds like an impossible thing. These people are watching all the time. They would not even let me touch the chalice when I tried to clean it.'

'You have seen the crazy way these people behave when they are filled with what Daniel calls "the Holy Spirit". Even Daniel starts leaping madly and screaming. Take advantage of that.'

What else was there for me to do but follow his advice and try to trick them with the Holy Dew? There seemed no other option. I must try this and if I failed, at least I would have done my best. 'It is a good idea, Father Abbot. I would be grateful for a bottle of Holy Dew for the substitution,' I told him.

'You must leave quickly,' said the abbot, handing me a bottle. 'People will soon be coming to take me down for the ceremony.'

I slipped out, the bottle now thrust under my corset where the mobile phone had been and realised I was only just in time. I could hear approaching voices and footsteps on the stairs.

But as I set off for my own room, despair set in again. The scheme was laughable. I would be stopped in a moment.

'Try it,' the abbot had said. 'Remember God is on your side.'

I still felt very doubtful, though. The plan was pathetic, but I could think of no better one.

Half an hour later Grace appeared with a tray of small cups filled with some sort of strange smelling drink. She was smiling, an act I had not known her face muscles were capable of.

'Drink this,' she said, handing me one. 'It will soothe you before the ceremony.' She stood for a moment watching and I took a token sip. I have a little problem with my bladder and did not want to risk taking in fluids just before being involved in an event, which, knowing the commune, might take some hours and during which I would not be able to get to the loo.

'Drink it quick,' she said. 'I have a lot of other people to give it to.' The smile had faded so utterly that I might have imagined it. Her words alerted me, though. I took another pretending sip, gave her a beaming smile of ecstasy, said, 'Absolutely delicious, Grace. I will have to drink it slowly if you don't mind. I have reached an age where speedy swallowing is not possible.'

It was very delicious, I must say. The first decent thing they had given me to eat or drink since being here.

'Mind you finish every drop,' she ordered me sternly, before hurrying off.

As soon as she was gone, I opened the window a bit, and, regretfully, poured the rest of the drugged drink out.

They came to take me to the ceremony at last.

Then there came the first blow.

I had imagined, even after the things the abbot had told me about the sacrifice of Father Gregory, that this evening was to take place in the refectory. I had imagined the commune members leaping and cavorting round the room, as had happened the previous day. While this was going on, I had planned to quickly tilt away the poison and replace it with Holy Dew. Even doing that had seemed so difficult and unlikely that it was nearly impossible. But once I was ensconced in a pew, rising from it, making my way past the others seated or kneeling there and then secretly managing to exchange Holy Dew for the poison drink, would be completely impossible.

Margaret had taken my arm and was helping me along as though I was still the disabled disorientated old person of four days ago. Leaning and bent, I tottered against her. The worse I seemed, the less suspicious they would be.

'I would like to help with the preparations before we go in,' I said, trying one last chance. Perhaps I could do the substitution before they took the poison to the chapel.

'What preparations?' she said a little impatiently. Then, 'Come along, Stella, do. Nearly everyone else is there already.'

'Filling the chalice – It would be such a great honour.' I hoped the abbot had remembered his promise to bring a bottle of Holy Dew as well so that we had enough.

Margaret looked shocked at my suggestion. 'Oh, you can't do that,' she cried. 'This is a sacred ritual, Stella. Only Daniel and his chosen ones are allowed to touch the Heavenly Ambrosia.'

I had no option but to allow myself to be led into a pew. Inside the chapel, on another occasion my soul would have been uplifted by the way the sunlight melted softly through the stained glass windows and the gnarled, dark pews shone with three hundred years of the hands and bodies of praying monks.

Now all I saw was the image of Christ in dying agony and felt anger because this sort of thing was what had created Daniel daSilva. It was because of such a concept that all these people were about to die.

There was no chance of saving anyone now. All the people of the commune were doomed, including Naomi and Freddy. Though there was nothing I could do, I was unable to let go of my last tiny crumb of hope.

I asked Margaret humbly, 'Just this one time, may I sit at the front, because of my lack of sight and hearing?'

After a whispered word with Hope, I was escorted there.

I took my seat stiffly and tried to stifle the shaking of my hands and the rapidity of my breathing. The abbot, looking no more disabled than I was pretending to be, was seated at my side. He too, I knew, had somewhere hidden on him a bottle of Holy Dew. I was careful not to meet his eye. I was at the front and only the abbot sat between me and the aisle. Perhaps I might get a chance after all, to save these people.

I was going to get no help from any of them, I could see. Even the children's faces were blank. Only Grace and Hope had retained normal signs of life in their features. The rest of them looked drugged.

To calm myself, I tried to breath in the smell of ancient incense, old cold stone and three hundred years of beeswax, but the sweet strong smell that was on the breaths of those around me was stronger. It even nearly drowned the smell of cheap soap from them. I was glad I had not drunk the nice little drink that Grace had offered me. I could see that the abbot had drunk his, however, for he had fallen asleep already.

The bottle of Holy Dew nudged uselessly against my ancient breasts, like a hidden revolver. Hope and Grace were moving among the congregation pushing people into place, threatening them into silence and against their hips I saw the outline of a bulge. With a shock of disgust and amazement I realised that they, unlike me, really did carry revolvers.

Hope and Grace went out and after a while Hope returned carrying glasses and laid them in a line on the altar rail.

Daniel entered, wearing the vestments of a consecrated priest and carrying the golden chalice. The people gasped with awe. He placed the chalice on the altar rail. The chapel became filled with a bitter smell. I saw a little shiver of apprehension cross Margaret's face, which she swiftly suppressed. You could see why Grace and Hope might be needing guns in spite of the drugs.

'This will be brief,' said Daniel daSilva. 'I will not talk to you long, because I know you are impatient to meet my father, in Heaven.'

'Ah, ah,' breathed the people of the commune.

There fell an expectant silence. Daniel stood waiting. After a while there came the soft sound of footsteps and Naomi and Freddy, dressed in white, ivy round their heads, came in with Grace, Daniel's children, the commune's key to Paradise.

In that moment I felt like doing something I had never done before. I wanted to jump up and hug my grandchild. I forced myself to stay in my seat and make no sound.

The children walked slowly and carefully like well trained dogs. Naomi looked up, her eyes met mine. I saw an excited flicker in them as she made me a tiny kiss mouth. It came and went in a moment. No one could have seen, who wasn't a grandmother who knew her ways. I felt thankful that she was here, alive and had not been drugged. But then I remembered the golden chalice on the altar.

The children stood waiting, with the expressions of early saints on their faces. They had clearly been well trained in painted wooden holiness.

'Hail, holy ones,' chanted the people of the commune.

The two children pulled back their mouths into artificial simulations of smiles.

Then, just as I was working out ways of pouring out the poison and refilling the chalice with Holy Dew, Hope came in carrying a jug in which, from the colour and the smell, was poison.

Hope began to fill the lined up glasses with a little of the liquid from the jug.

When all were filled, Daniel said, 'You may come to collect your glass now but do not drink until I say you may.'

The people began going up to the altar rail and taking their glasses from the hands of Daniel daSilva. The moment of death had nearly arrived.

As each commune member took his or her glass, the holy children placed their hands upon the recipient's heads.

I went up, took my share and Naomi laid her little hand upon my hair and her finger gave a tiny signalling tickle into my scalp.

When all had received their glasses and been blessed by the holy children, they returned to their seats and sat holding their glasses and waiting.

Daniel did not take a glass. Presumably he planned to share the drink in the chalice with the holy children. In that case, in the unlikely event of my managing to do my substitution, all would be lost. He would recognise my trick as soon as he tasted the Holy Dew. Oh, how I was tricking myself. How could I possibly manage the substitution anyway? But I kept on with my silly hoping, because otherwise I would have been unable to bear it.

The abbot held his glass with a trembling hand. A little of the scarlet juice slopped over and stained the white cloth of his knee. The man on the other side of us put out his own hand and steadied that of the abbot. There was a terrific quiet in the church. Everyone was waiting. Even the commune children, always silent, seemed to become more so.

One of the mothers, who sat with her arm round the shoulders of her two small daughters, gave a sudden shudder as though she was waking up from some bad dream. Hope's fingers clasped around the hidden revolver. There was no escape. No one was going to be saved from this.

'The sacred moment is upon us,' said Daniel daSilva. 'The holy children will lead the way.' He went over to the altar, took up the chalice and coming down with it, held it to the lips of Freddy Delane. 'I offer you eternal bliss. Drink my little son,' said Daniel daSilva.

The boy's lips pursed as he prepared to sip and I was about to scramble to my feet in a last futile effort to stop him, when there came the unbelievable sound of a car engine outside. The chapel window burst into a sudden blaze from headlights.

The child flinched. Scarlet juice ran down the front of his white gown.

People turned their heads, shocked.

Daniel daSilva returned the chalice to the altar rail and told Hope, 'Go and see.'

The woman went off and after a few moments we heard the front door opening. While we all waited, there came a murmured conversation. We heard a voice say, 'Police,' and 'emergency call'. And heard Hope say, 'It is not a convenient time. We are at prayer at the moment.'

I did something then that I have not done since the day I found a rat in the kitchen and yelled to Jack to come and deal with it. I opened my mouth and screamed 'Help!' as loudly as I could. 'Help, help, help! He is killing the children!' I shrieked. I did not know I could yell so loud. 'He is going to kill all these people.'

The abbot woke with a start and said, 'Is it a fire?'

A tiny stir of discomfort ran through the congregation. At a signal from Daniel they lowered their heads.

'The Lord is coming,' I heard someone murmur, and people around began to take up the chant..

'Listen to me. Stop your silly prayers,' I shouted. 'Don't do this, you fools. Children, don't drink that stuff in your glasses. You will die if you do.'

One of the commune children let out a subdued giggle.

'Speak, children,' commanded Daniel.

A terrible fatalistic calm lay upon the congregation.

'Speak, as I have taught you, my children,' ordered Daniel again and softly Freddy and Naomi started softly chanting. They recited like parrots, 'Death is our release. Death will bring to us a joy greater than anything this life could bring us.'

Gently the abbot dropped into a little snoring slumber again.

Throughout all this Grace stood, her muscular arms folded across her breast. She was watching me with an expression that was half amused.

When the children fell silent I was about to appeal to the mothers, 'Save your children at least. At least don't let them die,' but as though Grace's patience was ended, she came over to my side and her great hand came slapping over my mouth. I writhed under her grasp, but could get no sound out.

Daniel, who had been watching with his usual celestial serenity, nodded to indicate that the matter was at an end. He had allowed my silly little show of defiance, I had been given a chance to understand the determination of these people to not only die themselves, but also kill their children. Now enough was enough.

'It is all right, though,' I thought. 'The policeman must certainly have heard my scream. Even if Hope tried again the line, 'Only a poor old demented lady,' he would still insist on coming in to investigate, I felt sure. In fact at that very moment I heard her say, 'The poor old thing does not know what she's talking about half the time, officer, but the peace of our commune is helping to ease her suffering a little.'

'We will stay in holy silence for a while,' said Daniel daSilva. 'We will restore our graceful peace before continuing with the service.'

The woman who had flinched earlier had begun to look round nervously. Daniel made a signal to Grace with his eyes and going over to the woman she whispered something. The woman looked afraid but stopped peeping.

Grace continued to hold her hand over my mouth. There was no point in my shouting again, though. The front door was shut again. The policeman stayed outside. He had believed Hope's story.

The kind of hope I sought was gone.

The mood in the chapel had altered, though. There was a slight tension among the congregation, where previously there had only been placid acceptance.

Try to come in. Come and question us, I inwardly begged of the policeman. Insist on coming in. But already I could hear the sound of footsteps outside, people retreating. Sadly and despairingly I waited for the sound the police car engine to start up again to signal they had left and our last chance gone. But Hope did not come back, and the sound of the engine did not come. The car was still out there and after some moments there came a man's voice presumably talking on a mobile phone.

Daniel raised his hand, to keep us silent.

'There have been allegations concerning the people who live here, ' I heard the man say to Hope.

'What kind of allegations? '

'That there are people living in this house who are being kept here against their will,' he said.

'There are no such people,' said Hope.

'All the same I need to meet the occupants of this building.'

'Now?' There was outrage in her tone. 'This is not a good time. They are participating in a sacred ceremony.'

'I am very sorry, Madam, but these are my instructions,' said the policeman.

'We are at prayer, Officer. We should not be disturbed.'

Please please, let them insist on coming in.

'It will only take a short time,' the policeman said.

We are saved, I thought.

'Could you not come a little later, when our prayers are complete?' Hope persisted.

'Please stand aside, madam, and allow me to enter,' said the policeman sternly.

A great delicious relief surged through me. In a minute the policemen will come into the chapel. They will see the kidnapped children and recognise them. My prayer was being answered.

Daniel had the same thought. He gestured to the two holy children and said to Grace, 'Take these away quickly.' At last she removed her hand from my mouth.

Now we could hear heavy footsteps approaching. The police were outside the chapel door. Hope said, 'The chapel is a sacred place, officer. Please enter as silently as you can.'

Oh, quickly come in here and save Naomi, my mind was screaming.

Grace and the children had reached the sacristy door. Come in now, before they are lost to us, before they are hidden down there in their secret cellar room, I prayed.

But by the time the policeman, accompanied by a female constable, had come in, followed by Hope, the children were gone.

Daniel's expression took on a look of warmth and love and he approached them, his hands outstretched. 'Welcome, officers,' he said. 'How may I help you?'

The policeman gazed at the bowed heads and seemed a little bewildered, as though he was not quite sure what to do next. The policewoman stood at the door, waiting for instructions.

'I am sorry to disturb you, Sir,' said the policeman at last. 'But I need to ask some questions of the people here,' and then more loudly, to the congregation, 'Is there anyone here who has a complaint to make?'

People looked up, out of their hands and smiled blissfully at him.

'Is there anyone who is present not out of their own choice?'

'Here is happiness. Here is Paradise,' came the gentle murmur.

'Pay no attention to them,' I wanted to shout. 'They have been brainwashed, can't you see?' But now that Naomi had become a secret hostage, I did not dare in case making a fuss increased her danger.

The policeman nodded, apparently satisfied. The policewoman wrote a few words in her notebook.

Then the policeman asked, 'Who is the lady who made an emergency call from here earlier?' I forgot, for a moment, the danger Naomi was in and getting to my feet I began to scramble out of the pew shouting, 'It's me. It's me. You must put a stop to this, officer.' I stumbled along the pew, grabbing the wrist of the abbot as I passed him. 'Father Abbot, tell the policeman, go on tell him what is happening here,' I gasped as I tugged at the old man's hand.

The abbot, who had by now blinked into wakefulness, told the policeman wearily, 'All these people are planning to kill themselves and their children.' He added. 'And I doubt if you are going to be able to do anything about it, my dear man.'

I began shaking with desperation. 'Of course he will be able to do something,' I cried wildly. 'Can't you see this is a policeman, Father Abbot?' Leaving go of the abbot's hand, I wriggled the rest of the way out into the aisle and told the policeman,

'They've got the kidnapped children hidden in this building. The ones in the news.' I was almost screaming.

Hope shook her head sadly in an, 'I told you the poor lady was out of her senses,' way. Around me I had the feeling of people were smiling inside their folded palms as at a little child who was behaving badly.

Daniel made a gentle signal to the congregation and they all, including the children, bowed their heads in an attitude of prayer. I caught one or two of the children peeping interestedly through their fingers.

The policeman looked doubtful for a moment. Then, while he was pondering, suddenly his mobile phone rang. He listened for a moment, said, 'Mr daSilva ? … right … right … I'll find out.' He turned to Hope. 'I understand there is a Mr daSilva living here.'

Hope bowed her head towards Daniel.

'I would like you to come with me to the station to answer a few questions, Mr daSilva,' said the policeman.

'Officer, we are at present engaged in a holy service. Is there no way you can question me here? You may ask me whatever you wish.' Daniel spoke serenely.

'We have had a report of a stolen car and have had information that you were the driver.' When Daniel looked blank, the policeman looked at his notes then said, 'The car belonged to a Mr Philip Bereton.'

'Ah,' said Daniel. 'He lent it to me. He was in New York on business and told me I could use his car since I do not have one of my own.'

A faint frisson of surprise seemed to ripple through the congregation. I supposed this must be because Daniel's hostility to petrol driven vehicles was well known.

The policeman looked at the notes again, then continued, 'And that, on the fourteenth of September you were in this car, outside the home of Mr Jeremy Delane.' Daniel said nothing.

'May I take your silence as confirmation, sir?'

'I was waiting for you to give me the address. I could not answer your question till you told me where this person lived.'

The policeman read out the address.

'Yes, that is correct,' said Daniel.

'This gentleman has made a statement asserting that you were spying on his child.'

Daniel laughed. It was a very cool laugh, as though he did not really think anything was funny.

The policeman went on, 'And since this child has been subsequently kidnapped, we are investigating every avenue.'

'The child is here. Hidden in this very building,' I shouted.

'I will be taking your statement in a minute, Madam,' said the policeman, giving me a quick sympathetic glance. 'In the meantime I would like to hear Mr daSilva's answers.'

'Of course,' said Daniel. 'But I am sorry to say that Mr Delane is an unbalanced person, and perhaps his words should not be taken too literally.'

'Can you explain yourself, sir?' said the policeman.

'He launched an unprovoked attack on me.'

There came another gasp of sleepy astonishment from the congregation.

'Please continue.'

'I was driving along a lane when a man came running out of his house and took a shot at me. A lunatic like that should not be allowed to go free round the countryside.' He paused and raised his arms to show the scar. He still wore the silken gold embroidered vestments of the abbot. He said, 'Look at me, officer. I am a man of God. I have a congregation who love, know and follow me. Do I look like the sort of person who drives round the countryside, peeping at children?'

The policeman pressed his lips together. Here was a young and beautiful man, with a holy face. You could not imagine him doing anything impure.

There came the sound of a snore from the abbot. The police officer looked at him and smiled.

The eyes of the woman who had flinched and hugged her daughters were now filled with love and peace again. I guessed that the contrast between the policeman with his coarse red complexion and loud voice, and the pure features and gentle tones of her leader had reignited her faith.

The policeman's phone rang. After listening he turned to Daniel and said, 'It has also been reported that there are persons here with unregistered firearms.'

'Norman,' I heard someone near me whisper.

Daniel said nothing.

'It will be necessary for us to make a search,' said the policeman.

'Look where you like,' Daniel calmly.

'Please will everyone rise and come to the front.' The policeman nodded in the direction of the altar.

There was a gentle, dreamy and reluctant shuffling as the people began to stream from their pews and gather before the altar rail on which stood the golden chalice.

Good, good, I thought. At any moment they will find the guns on Grace and Hope, and once those two dreadful women are disarmed, we will all be out of danger.

The police started to move among them, checking and questioning each person slowly and rather shyly, as though they did not like to have to stamp around so grossly in a holy place among such religious looking people. The members of the commune were so obviously people who did not carry guns. I began to feel increasingly discouraged because Grace and Hope were being given plenty of time to hide theirs.

All around me, the commune members were searched. It came to Daniel's turn. He offered himself like a holy sacrifice. A smile was on his face as he raised his arms for the policeman. He had his back to me. The rest of the congregation were standing round him as though on guard, as though determined to prevent a sacrilege.

A glass got knocked over and a trickle of liquid, scarlet as blood came pooling out. The policewoman picked the glass up, sniffed it, grimaced and looked inquiringly at Daniel.

Daniel said, 'It is a drink sacred to our ritual and made from various local ingredients.'

The policewoman said, 'It smells dreadful.'

'We use it for purification,' said Daniel.

It was Hope's turn now. They are going to find it, I thought. All will be well in a moment.

Nothing. Well it was to be expected.

Grace next. The policewoman began to run her hands down Grace's body. 'Please continue to face me, Madam,' the young woman ordered when, on the searching hands reaching her bra, Grace tried to turn away.

The policewoman's fingers found the gun.

'Kindly remove it, Madam,' she said.

We are saved, I thought. Waves of relief flooded through me. Thank you, Jack. Oh. Thank you.

The policeman took the gun, examined it, then said, 'I shall have to ask you to accompany me to the station, madam.'

'Certainly,' she said. She did not seem unduly concerned.

'May I take it that you are finished with the rest of us now so that we may resume our service?' asked Daniel.

The policeman shook his head. 'I am very sorry sir, but these are very serious allegations, I will have to ask you to accompany us to the station to file a formal statement, also.' And to me, 'And you, madam, please.'

'I shall do as you ask, officer,' said Daniel calmly. 'Pause in your prayers, my people.' Gently the praying people began to stir and to raise their heads. Softly came the sound of glasses placed upon the flagstone floor. And then turning to Hope, who stood at his side, Daniel told her, 'Please take over, Hope. Please deal with things.'

'Yes, my Lord,' said Hope and pulling up her skirt she reached into her bloomers and took out a second revolver. Before the policeman had time to react or understand, she had pulled the trigger. The shot made no sound.

The policewoman looked up from what she was writing, gave a little scream and came running towards the fallen policeman. Grace shot her half way down the aisle.

There was a short quiet, during which all the people gazed at the fallen figures with blank expressions.

'Shall we continue with the ceremony now, Lord?' asked Hope after a long moment.

Daniel shook his head, and gesturing to the dead bodies on the aisle, said, 'These are impure souls and must be removed before we can go on. The heavenly chariot will refuse all of us, if these venal bodies lie among us.'

'Come on, get up and carry these people away,' said Grace. 'Did you not hear what Daniel said?'

People slowly rose, moving like sleep walkers and began to drag the bodies towards the door. A trail of blood got slithered down the aisle.

Hope gave a gesture in my direction and said to Daniel, 'And what about this one who has now proved herself so unworthy?'

When he was thoughtful for a moment and said nothing, she took out her revolver and aimed it at my breast. My goodness, you can imagine what my feelings were. Here was the opportunity I had been waiting for. Jack would still be glowing and at the pull of a trigger, I would join him. But if I died now, Freddy and Naomi would be truly doomed. I had lost all hope of saving the rest who now sat with their poison doses at their feet, but a tiny chance remained of saving the holy children.

Daniel was still standing there, looking at me with a thoughtful expression. He closed his eyes as though asking some higher force for advice. At last he said, 'There is no time. Soon the police will be sending reinforcements. We must hastily continue with the ceremony before it is too late.'

Hope reluctantly pushed her pistol back into her pocket. Grace took hers from the dead policeman's hand.

The hope that police reinforcements would arrive before it was too late rushed through me.

'We must act very fast,' said Daniel.

Grace returned with the two holy children.

'Jack, help me, oh help me,' I begged. And as though in answer, the dead policeman's mobile phone began to ring.

The shock disturbed the congregation in a way that the shooting of the police had failed to do. Or perhaps the effects of the drug had started to wear off, and their awareness was returning. People began to rush at the body, and rather wildly start hunting through its pockets. Others put their hands to their ears, as though to block out the sound of Satan. The ringing of a mobile phone seemed to perturb them more than the prospect of death. But then, of course, they had been trained to welcome death.

Just as someone managed to find the phone and get it out, that of the policewoman started ringing too and there came much scrabbling over her body. Obviously they had not been trained to anticipate such an event as this. Daniel, obviously hurried by the prospect of a police back-up arriving, was busy too, trying to orchestrate an orderly search and body removal.

It took me a moment to tilt the chalice with my elbow. The spilt fluid mingled unnoticed with that of the fallen glass.

Only Naomi saw. She opened her mouth as though to speak. In my mind I begged, her to keep silent. She closed her mouth again.

People were searching fumbling for the phones, trying to turn them off, while others were still tugging and pulling at the bodies, trying to get them out of the chapel before starting the ceremony. The aisle was pooled with blood.

'Clean this impure blood, quickly, quickly,' said Daniel.

People began running and returned with mops and buckets.

In that moment of commotion, pouring a drink faster than I had ever done in my life, I managed to whisk the contents of my flask of Holy Dew into the chalice.

The phones were silenced and the bodies at last outside. The last trace of blood removed. The people began to calm down and reassemble.

The abbot woke and shouted, 'Are we there?'

I hoped that the disruption had made Daniel change his mind or the people of the commune come to their senses. Perhaps now they would refuse to go through with their dreadful plan.

But then Daniel went up into the pulpit. He turned and looking at me, raised his arms as a priest does when he bestows a blessing and said, 'I forgive you, Stella. You are absolved of your sin. Tell Ladyma she is forgiven.' The whole congregation began to chanted it together, 'I forgive you, I forgive you, I forgive you.'

'Now,' said Daniel, 'You must cast aside the shackles of impurity. The things of the flesh and the flesh of your bodies must be laid aside so that the world, and the universe, and the whole of the cosmos can become peopled by the obedient, submissive and immortal cells of my own godhead. I shall now offer the cosmos the perfect sacrifice of my own children, who, though they have come from impure vessels, had been cleansed by me and have now become worthy.'

The implication that Verity was impure made me feel very cross, though of course, due to the trickiness of the situation, I said nothing.

'And because this lovely sacrifice will have been accepted and the price paid, when your foul human bodies are laid down, the chariot will descend to waft your souls into Paradise,' Daniel daSilva said. 'And I myself will be vouchsafed immortality.'

The congregation leant back, calm and relaxed. The abbot fell asleep again and began to slide sideways in his chair till his head was resting on my lap. The man on the other side propped him up again.

After that Daniel made us kneel, heads bowed, silent, for several minutes, then the glasses were put back on the altar rail and a little was taken from each of the others to replace the liquid from the spilt one.

When it was done, Daniel leant down and reverentially lifted the golden chalice. He paused and looked into it. My heart seemed to stop beating. He gazed at the contents for what seemed like ages. He is going to sniff it. He will realise that the bitter smell is lacking. Naomi is done for. A small frown even briefly crossed his forehead. But then, perhaps because of the smell coming from the spilt fluid deceived him, his face relaxed and he carried the chalice over to the altar and placed it there. My heart began to beat again.

Turning to the congregation he cried, 'Heaven awaits you. Everything you have ever wished to own or be will soon be available to you, my beautiful ones.'

Expressions of heavenly bliss shone in the faces of the congregation.

They brought the two holy children back at last and stood them once again before the altar.

'The moment has come,' cried Daniel, coming down with the chalice, offered it to Naomi instead of Freddy this time. 'Drink,' he ordered.

She took a swig, reeled with shock and came up gagging and choking. Daniel, looking satisfied, offered it to Freddy. The congregation watched with bated breath. 'Drink deep my children,' cried Daniel daSilva. 'Drink more. Drink more. Tell the cosmos that you are the children of one who is divine. Tell the Cosmos that your father has earned immortality.'

The children choked and gagged and swallowed and the congregation watched them with a mixture of awe and fascination.

Turning to the congregation, Daniel said, 'It is done, the way is prepared, the great sacrifice has been given. Now, like letting birds fly free from cages, you may release your souls. A feast is awaiting you in Heaven.'

The two children were toppling and staggering a bit. How well I know the effects of Holy Dew. He is going to notice, I thought with terror. He will know. Freddy hiccupped. But Daniel seemed unsuspicious. Perhaps the symptoms of alcohol are the same as that of poisoning.

Mothers began holding the glasses to their babies, then sipping themselves. All round the chapel children were coughing and spluttering. It was unbearable but nothing in the whole world would stop them now. A man took a deep swig, then grabbed his throat and let out a strangled cry of agony. People began crying out, 'Praise Holy Daniel. We offer ourselves to the cosmos so that you may be made immortal,' then drank.

Daniel turned to look at the holy children. Though they were coughing, they were still upright. A tiny worried look crossed his face, as though this was not quite what he had expected. Worry almost made my own heart stop working altogether.

He held the chalice out to them again. There was still doubt in his expression.

Grace and Hope were moving among the pews now, their revolvers out, threatening those who had suddenly lost courage. At the sight of them and of their weapons, people began to swallow speedily.

They kept passing me and watching with particular care. I had had a difficult job, trickling out from our glasses the deadly mixture of myself and the abbot. My knees were soaked with scarlet poison, it had run into my knickers but before it was too late, I had emptied our glasses of every drop and refilled them with Holy Dew.

Each time the women hovered near me, I would take a hasty and apparently terrified gulp at my glass, and, temporarily satisfied, they would pass on. It was imperative I stayed alive for, in the unlikely event of the children surviving after all this, who would take care of them afterwards otherwise?

The abbot, rather drunk by now, kept falling asleep and each time they saw him one of the terrible women would slap his cheek to wake him. In the end the Holy Dew, on top of his earlier drugged drink, sent him into such a deep slumber that even when they slapped hard, he did not stir. Looking satisfied, as if assured the poison had taken effect, they passed on, leaving him alone. I started arranging myself into a deathly sort of slump.

Daniel put down the chalice. Satisfaction had replaced his expression of doubt.

He moved down into the body of the chapel and walked among the dying commune members, murmuring words of love to them, wishing them happiness and peace on the lovely journey that lay ahead.

But something was going wrong with the dying process.

Children started screaming as the agony of death began to bite. Mothers, sobbing, clutched their dying toddlers against their breasts and fell dead on top of them.

Presumably Daniel had expected these people to die serenely and with joy. He cannot have expected screaming, agony and vomiting. People began leaping up and running, scarlet vomit pouring out. Two rushed up to the altar and began grabbing at the vases of flowers, apparently trying to drink the water there.

The two holy children stood, rocking a little now, their faces distorted by drunken squints. They gazed blankly and uncomprehendingly at the horrific scene. They were like people watching a complicated cartoon film that they did not properly understand.

There came a sudden scream. A woman lay, bleeding, by the door. Her two little daughters, who had been running, stopped and stared at their mother's fallen body. Two more shots rang out and the girls fell too. Grace blew into the barrel of her revolver, shoved it back into her pocket and then turned to Daniel, a look of questioning inquiry on her face.

He, however, was noticing none of this. He had returned to the altar and was gazing at the two, still standing, holy children, with awe on his face. He began murmuring something that I could not hear through the turmoil of people dying.

Grace and Hope stared at each other across a huddle of dying people. They must have witnessed the gentle death of Father Gregory and imagined that young fit people would leave their bodies as gracefully.

Hope said, 'They are all done, my Lord.'

Daniel said, 'Good.' His tone was indifferent.

Grace whispered something to Daniel that I could not hear. He snapped back, impatiently and still staring at the children, 'Yes. Now drink it. Drink it.'

Grace nodded to Hope. The two women picked up their glasses and looked hopefully at Daniel. He seemed to have forgotten them. His attention was somewhere quite else.

'We will meet again in Paradise,' said Hope.

'Drink it,' said Daniel without looking round.

I heard the sound of Grace and Hope swallowing and it should have been a hopeful one. But Daniel had drunk nothing, I realised. He was still left. The danger was as great as ever.

I tried to maintain my corpselike slump but it was hard to stay still, I was so crisp with apprehension.

In a moment, even when Grace and Hope were dead, I would still be faced with Daniel. I, an eighty year old woman, disabled, deaf, and partly blind, trying to protect two children from a healthy young murderer. After all, my efforts had failed and we were done for. Naomi gave a drunken burp. Freddy tittered softly.

As Grace and Hope crashed to the floor, Hope's revolver spun clattering from her pocket and came slithering across the flag stones to land near my foot. I stared at it, imagining myself picking it up, aiming it at Daniel, even pulling the trigger and killing him. I, who had had such enormous difficulty in working a mobile phone, seriously planned for a moment picking up a revolver and shooting Daniel daSilva.

Daniel seemed to have fallen into a trance as though the holy children had transfixed him.

'Even this evening,' he said. 'I had doubts. I was not sure if immortality was possible. But now I know because the children of my body have drunk the poison and are still alive. You, my children, have shown me the way.'

I touched the revolver with my toe.

He saw the movement and slowly turned to look at me. I made my hand do the sort of twitch I had seen a corpse do in a TV horror film. He gazed at me suspiciously.

I felt like someone in a nightmare, with the instrument of escape at my feet and my body unable to respond. I had gone so far in rescuing the children and at my side was the final solution to the crisis, the one way of saving them and I could not do it. I just could not. I kept trying to tell myself, remember how it is done in thriller films. You just pick the thing, poke it in the direction of the person you want to kill and pull the trigger. I couldn't. The children are going to die, I thought, because I am unable to take the only course of action open to me.

Daniel now turned his gaze back to the topply children. He took up the chalice and peered into its interior. And on his face was an expression of awe, not suspicion.

I was starting to feel very stiff from maintaining my posture of death for such a long period and feared that at any moment the abbot might wake. Any movement from me or him and the children would be done for.

And as I had the thought he did indeed start stirring. If I had not become completely rigid already, I would have become even more so from fear.

Freddy's squeaky little voice piped up suddenly at that moment.

'When's the chariot coming, Daniel?'

Daniel stared up at the roof, as though expecting something to come from there.

Naomi gave Freddy a nudge. 'You've got to call him Lord you silly. Otherwise Grace will smack you.'

'Lord. When's the chariot coming, Lord?' amended Freddy. He added, 'And she's still asleep, silly.'

Jack, help us, I was crying in my mind. If you exist at all, do something now.

I was not going to be able to keep up this corpse position a moment longer. I knew too that in a moment the abbot would wake completely.

It might or might not have been due to Jack's intervention, but at the very moment of the abbot's snore starting to resume, Daniel daSilva threw himself down before the altar and began declaiming in a voice so loud that any other sounds were drowned by it, 'Here is my offering to you, oh God. I have done all that You asked of me. I have created children out of my own body as a sacrifice for You. I have watched them from the moment of their birth and preserved them from impurity. When the special powers of charm and the fulfilment of desires became corrupted in these children, I removed them from the base people they lived among and retrained them in this holy place. I have kept my own body perfectly pure by conceiving them without sexual pleasure. I have created a retinue of inferior souls as a gift for You, and who You now see lain before You.' Still prostrate, he gestured with his hand behind his back, pointing out to a watching God the sprawl of corpses littering the chapel. 'You told me that if I gave you these things, in exchange you would send a shining chariot to carry my living body into Heaven, where I would live alive and immortal for the rest of time. From where I would gain total power over the cosmos. My children have drunk the poison chalice and still live. You have made them immortal and for that I thank you. But you have promised more. Where is this chariot? Where? Where?' He was screaming now. He began to beat his head his head against the floor then he leapt up, gesturing wildly into the air. He is completely mad, I thought, and hoped that Naomi had not inherited this gene.

He became silent after a while and stood waiting restlessly like a person impatient for a delayed train. Then, turning upon the children he burst out, 'How shall I make myself immortal like you? Where have I failed?'

When they remained silent, he rose and stepping among the corpses, went towards the door. There he stopped and looked back.

'This is a God who does not keep promises,' he said. 'I go now to seek another, more reliable deity. When I find it, my immortal children, I shall return.' He went out. The two children stood staring after him. We heard his footsteps fading away down the corridors. The great front door made a grinding sound as he went out.

'I don't think the chariot's coming, Freddy,' said Naomi.

'It's got to come,' cried Freddy, emphasising the word 'got.' 'Daniel said it would, so it's got to.'

'Lord,' corrected Naomi.

'Lord, I mean. Lord said it would … '

By this time I was managing to get my stiff body moving again. As I wriggled numb limbs back into movement, I could hear Daniel's footsteps scrunching over the driveway now. Had he done a miracle on my hearing? Otherwise how could I be hearing all this so well?

'Look, my grandma's got immortal too,' said Naomi joyfully and rushing over she flung herself into my tingling arms.

'Grace will hit you if you do that,' said Freddy disapprovingly.

'She's asleep,' said Naomi.

'She might wake up at any moment and suddenly get immortal like your granny, though.' Freddy paused to burp. Then, 'Naomi, why did they all go to sleep anyway?'

'Too much blood precious,' said Naomi cheerily and reached out for the golden chalice.

'Oh, no you don't,' I cried, snatching the chalice back from her.

'But I want some more,' cried Naomi. 'I like blood precious, Grandma.'

'Certainly not,' I said sternly. 'I totally disapprove of children drinking.'

Keeping a firm grip on the chalice, I took a deep swig from the chalice while Naomi watched enviously. The abbot had sat up by now, so I passed the chalice for him to take a sip as well.

'I suppose all we have to now is sit and wait till the police backup arrives,' I said. I did not much like the idea of sitting here, in this chapel surrounded by corpses but supposed that they would not be very long.

'I'm hungry,' said Naomi.

'So am I,' said Freddy.

'Well, there doesn't seem to be much in the way of food around this place,' I told them gloomily.

'Why don't you ring for a takeaway,' suggested Naomi.

'Mmm, scrummy,' said Freddy, hugging his tummy.

This seemed like a good idea. But an instant later I realised how hopeless it would be. First, even though I discovered the place where Grace had put my mobile phone, I still had only learnt how to ring the police on it. Secondly I had no money to pay for the food, even suppose I could have got through to a restaurant. Thirdly, the police would probably arrive before the food did.

Then another idea came to me. 'If only I knew where my mobile phone was, we could ring the police and ask them to bring us a takeaway,' I said.

'Why don't you use the policeman's phone?' suggested Freddy, pointing to where the commune members had thrown it. Before I could respond, he raced over and seized it.

'I have no idea how to work that thing,' I told him despondently.

Freddy was sitting on the ground, by now, tinkering with keys. In a moment he had the phone unlocked and the machine lit up. His little fingers whisked over the keys.

I stared, awed. 'How do you know how to do it?' I asked.

'It's a mobile phone, Grandma. Everyone knows how to use a mobile phone.'

'Police,' Freddy said into the phone. 'Then, after a moment, 'I would like to order a takeaway meal for four ... '

I snatched the phone from him and explained to a bewildered officer our present predicament. I added, 'And since the two young children and we two old ones have not eaten anything for many hours, we would be most grateful if the police would bring us some nourishment.'

'Madam, have you been drinking?' asked the officer.

'Of course I've been drinking,' I shouted at him. 'All four of us have been drinking, and if we hadn't we'd all be dead by now.'

www.transita.co.uk

transita

To find out more about Sara Banerji and other Transita authors and their books, visit the website for:

- News of author events and forthcoming titles
- Exclusive features and interviews with authors
- Free extras from the books
- Special offers and discounts
- The lively Transita chat group